whisper

Phoebe Kitanidis

whisper

WITHDRAWN

BALZER + BRAY

AN IMPRINT OF HARPERCOLLINS*PUBLISHERS*

Balzer + Bray is an imprint of HarperCollins Publishers.

Whisper
www.harperteen.com

Library of Congress Cataloging-in-Publication Data
Kitanidis, Phoebe.
Whisper / Phoebe Kitanidis. — 1st ed.
p. cm.
Summary: Although fifteen-year-old Joy, who uses her mind-
reading ability to grant wishes for people, and her older sister
Jessica, who uses the same ability to bring misery into the lives of
others, do not get along, Joy tries to find and protect Jessica when
she goes missing.
ISBN 978-0-06-179925-9
[1. Psychic ability—Fiction. 2. Sisters—Fiction. 3. Missing
children—Fiction.] I. Title.
PZ7.K67123Wh 2010   2009024223
[Fic]—dc22   CIP
                                                   AC

Typography by Andrea Vandergrift
10 11 12 13 14 CG/RRDB 10 9 8 7 6 5 4 3 2 1
❖
First Edition

For my best friend and mad, long-standing crush,
Robert Brydon

1

My sister showed me how to Hear a Whisper when I was three. "All you have to do," she said, "is touch somebody else, and if you don't Hear one right away, just hold on." She'd grab my wrist, encircling it with her bigger hand, and I'd listen to the Whispers, desire stacked up on desire: *I want to discover new planets. . . . Hope I'll kiss a boy someday. . . . Wish I could fly over the Grand Canyon like a hawk.* Even at six, Jessica was full of bold wishes and longings.

Now, at seventeen, her mind was often silent as a shadow . . . and while I could Hear most people's Whispers from across the room, she was the only person who could sneak up on me.

"Last-minute primping before the apocalypse?"

I spun away from the bathroom mirror, sliding in my socked feet, dropping my half-finished braids. "What's up, Icka?" My palms were already turning to ice at the sight of her dreadlocked silhouette slouching in the doorway, slim arms folded across her EVOLVE TO VEGAN hoodie. Now I was trapped, a helpless victim of whatever conversational attack she was in the mood for. Frantically I Listened in, hoping to pick up even the softest Whisper from her. Psychic radio silence. Would it be her classic Humanity Is Evil rant, her tailored-to-me You're a Mainstream Sheep rant, or something worse?

"I brought you a birthday present." Hall light glinted off the half dozen metal rings in her weary face. "Sort of."

"Uh, thanks?" I glanced at her open, empty hands. Black-polished nails bitten down to the quick, raw red fingertips. The idea of her anxiously biting her own skin made me feel a twinge of pity. Living with her was tough enough, but I couldn't imagine what it must be like actually *being* her. I should be nicer. Try harder. "What kind of present?"

"Information." She shrugged. "Call it a warning."

Goose bumps prickled my arms under the sleeves of my flannel pj's, and a familiar throbbing sang out in my temples. Another tension headache . . . and no wonder. Was my own sister threatening me? Mom and Dad had promised nothing bad would happen this year. They'd keep a close eye on her, keep her away from my party. . . .

"Whoa, Joy. Forget about your birthday already—what

are you, five?" Damn it, how come it seemed like she always Heard me when I could almost never Hear her? "Wake up, you've got real, serious problems now," she went on, pointing to the bottle of Tylenol on the sink next to our toothbrush holder. "I know why you're getting all those headaches lately."

"Huh?" I stopped tugging at the loose strands of hair. What was she playing at now? True, ever since high school started, a month ago, I'd had a few pounding tension headaches. (Like the one looming now.) But that was all they were—not some medical mystery. "Those are from stress," I said. "Dr. Brooks said I need some more downtime is all." Which I was totally planning to schedule . . . one of these days.

"Please." Icka rolled her eyes. "That's such a cop-out. It just means Brooks couldn't find anything wrong with you. Medically," she added, "because what's wrong with you isn't medical. It's the curse you and Mom call a superpower!"

I sighed. So we were back on *that* debate. Didn't take long. "Hearing is a gift," I said automatically. "I really like being able to help people." Understatement. I didn't know who I'd *be* without my Hearing.

"That's the spirit, honey!" Icka sang in a breathy falsetto that in no way resembled our mother's voice. She clasped her hands together and fluttered her lashes. "Girls—let's make this world a brighter, happier place!"

Because that's such a horrible crime? I felt like saying. Wanting to make the world better? Sometimes I'd have given anything just to understand what planet Icka was coming from, whether she even believed half the things she said, whether she cared about anything other than driving me crazy.

She had to be Whispering *something*, didn't she?

I stood still, waiting for her words to flow into my mind, but of course none did.

"The pain's only going to get worse if you ignore it." Her bloodshot blue eyes met mine in the mirror. "Believe me, I know."

Thank you, Ms. Gloom and Doom. "Come on, it's just a headache." Not that I'd ever admit this to her, but the pain *was* getting worse. A tender spot pulsed at the crown of my head, as if someone were prodding it with a skewer. Please go away, stress. Go away, Icka.

I turned away from her, yanked open a sink drawer, and pulled out a mass of rubber hair bands. "If Hearing had anything to do with it," I said, "don't you think Mom would know?"

"Joy-Joy." Icka's voice was soft as she pressed her palms against the doorframe's sides and leaned toward me. "Isn't fifteen a little old to get all your info prechewed by Mom?"

That stung. "I think for myself."

"Right, you just happen to be a carbon copy of her." She pinched the bridge of her nose as if I were giving *her* a headache. "I swear, you are so scarily naïve. Part of me wonders if there's even any point trying to talk to you about . . . well, your Hearing problem."

4

I swallowed. Hearing problem? Okay, what was that supposed to mean? That I was going Whisper-deaf, like Aunt Jane had? All because of a few stupid headaches? I concentrated on tying off my braids. Ignoring Icka's relentless gaze and the pebbles suddenly lodged in the pit of my stomach. I didn't want to give her any ins, any idea that I cared. But she must have Heard my curiosity, because her permascowl flipped up into a smirk.

"You know, maybe I should have waited." Her tone went all smug suddenly. "Let you try to work this one out all by yourself. Until you have to come crawling back to me for help. You'd be the one begging me to be friends again . . ." She cringed.

I wish I hadn't said that part.

Aha! Finally, a Whisper—the first I'd picked off her in weeks. *And* she'd given away her game: Icka was just trying to trick me into getting close to her again. Scaring me, to make me think I desperately needed her. As if she could turn back the clock and change me back into the little girl who'd idolized her big sister. Of course she had no valuable insights—she never did—just the usual lies and conspiracy theories. Anger covered the pity I'd felt earlier. She'd played on my greatest fear. Losing my Hearing. Turning into Aunt Jane. All alone. A recluse. Why did I keep giving Icka the benefit of the doubt, when all she did was lash out at anyone in target range? The only way to be safe was to stay away from her. "I should go help Mom in the kitchen," I said.

"Listen to me." Icka blocked the door.

I hesitated. In some ways, nothing had changed in all these years. It didn't seem to matter that I was five inches taller than her, that I was stronger, or happier, or had made more friends in a month of high school than she had in three years. All that mattered was that she wouldn't let mere social custom (like, say, not blocking a door when someone wanted to leave a room) stop her. She'd always find a way to get to me.

"Listen," she said again. "You are so screwed, beyond your wildest nightmares. I'm *worried* for you."

I shook my head, as if to stop her words from taking hold. Don't believe her. She's just trying to scare you, to get you to need her again.

"I thought this day would never come, but the signs are all there. You're not losing your Hearing, dummy. You're gaining more of it. More than you ever wanted, and I bet it's more than you can take."

I took a chance and pushed past her.

"Fine, go plug yourself back into the mother ship!" she screamed after me. "But get ready. You're about to turn into me."

From the bottom of the stairs I could see the glow of the kitchen light, and by the time I reached the front hallway I could even feel the oven's warmth and smell cinnamon sugar, orange, and vanilla in the air.

Mom stood by the sink, looking a little like a fairy in her old blue satin robe, dark blond hair falling in gentle waves to her shoulders. Her left hand held open a book, *Creative Cupcakes for Any Occasion,* while her right was busy wiping down the already spotless white countertop. "Cute braids!" she said, and stifled a yawn—it was, after all, midnight. "So, are we all cam-ready for tomorrow?"

"Almost . . . I still have some tidying."

"Your friends think they're surprising you," she reminded me, letting the cookbook snap closed. "Your room doesn't have to be squeaky-clean."

"You mean like *that?*" I indicated the immaculate counter she was scrubbing.

"Fair enough." Mom grinned. "I'm afraid we both inherited Granny Rowan's perfectionism."

Carbon copies. The phrase just popped into my head.

Mom stopped wiping and regarded me over her reading glasses. "Honey, are you okay?"

I hesitated. "Yeah. Well, no." There was no point in lying to a Hearer that you were okay when you weren't. "I was talking to Icka upstairs."

"Oh." Mom blinked and examined the sponge up close, a tiny furrow forming on her brow. I knew what she was going to Whisper before I Heard it: *I wish you girls talked to each other more often.*

I squirmed. Whispers about me—or worse, addressed to me directly—were hard to ignore. It's not like I had some cosmic responsibility to make desires come true. I just hated the thought of letting people down. I mean, imagine you had to know about it every single time you failed someone.

I must have looked pretty lost, because Mom flipped the switch on the electric kettle. "You look like you could use a hot cup of tea."

"Maybe . . . with some milk and honey?" I knew I sounded like a little kid, but as much as I hated to admit it, Icka's "warning" had shaken me up. "My Hearing—it's not going to . . . I don't know, change or something, is it?"

"Change?" She sounded puzzled. "Your Hearing finished growing when you were in elementary school, just like Jessica's." Mom was the only person who still called my sister by her full first name.

"But what about after that?" I reached into the cupboard and pulled out twin pale blue Laura Ashley mugs. "Did Ick—Jessica mature *more* than me, somehow? Did she have a growth spurt and get to the next level or something?"

"Ah," Mom said as if understanding, then shook her head. "Your ability doesn't work that way." She pushed up her glasses to fix her gentle gaze on me. "There are no secret levels and mysterious growth spurts. There's nothing to worry about or be scared of. Your Hearing's fully matured, it's healthy and stable. And just as strong as your sister's."

I let out a breath I hadn't realized I was holding. Icka was full of it; what else was new? But one thing still bugged me. The same thing that had bugged me on and off since seventh grade, when I first noticed it. "How come it seems like she can always Hear me," I said, "but I can't always Hear her?"

"You're still worried about that, huh?" Mom smiled.

"Remember, the world is full of Whispers. Too many for any of us to catch. It'd be like trying to count every grain of sand on the beach at once. Or every star in the sky."

"True." I nodded at the familiar metaphors. They made sense, just as they always had. More sense than Icka's doomsaying anyway. I quelled the strident little voice in my head—the Icka voice—that suddenly wondered what the heck counting had to do with Hearing. And how was sand (cold, dead sand) anything like a human Whisper? Icka could overanalyze a McDonald's menu and find the cracks in its logic, but where had overthinking gotten her? Nowhere I wanted to go.

"No two Hearers pick up all the same things," Mom went on. "But if you look for the good in people, you'll almost always find it."

"Then why does she only look for the worst?" My vehemence surprised me.

Evidently it surprised Mom too, because she shot me a look. "Sometimes a person can get stuck," she said slowly. "Looking at the world through dark glasses, reading the worst into every Whisper. It's a hard way to go through life, because the more you come to expect darkness, the more you find it. From Jessica's point of view, people are out to hurt her. She's never had your knack for fitting in, she's never found a place for herself the way you always do."

"She, um, doesn't seem to try very hard though." Why was Mom always defending Icka? "It almost seems like she wants to be unpopular."

Mom winced at the word, and I felt guilty. "That's just how she protects herself, sweetie," she said. "Think how lonely she must feel. Making friends comes naturally to you, but she just doesn't know how."

Because she spends all her time locked in her room feeling superior, I thought. And talking to her is like being tortured. "I hate to say it," I said, "but I can sort of see why no one wants to be her friend, you know?"

The electric kettle trilled sharply. Mom turned it off and began pouring water into our mugs, while I rummaged for decaf Irish Breakfast tea bags, milk, and honey.

"It wasn't so long ago," she said softly, "that the two of you were best friends."

I dug two teaspoons out of the silverware drawer and stayed silent. What could I say? It sure *seemed* like long ago.

I was relieved when I heard footsteps on the back porch. The kitchen door opened and my father walked in, the full moon behind him, his arms full of brown legal folders, his U of O coffee mug balanced on top.

"Hey, gang." His drooping eyebrows seemed to perk at the sight of our steaming mugs. *I'd love a cup of coffee.*

"It's tea," Mom said, standing. "But let me fix you a pot of fresh—"

"Oh, no, Kell. Don't get up. I should hit the sack anyway." He set his folders and mug down on the kitchen table. "So what are we all talking about here?"

I glanced at Mom for help. There was no way Dad

would understand our conversation.

"Just girl stuff," she said cheerfully.

"Right, I get it." He held up his hands. "Hearing stuff."

As he passed us and headed toward the hall, his shoulders seemed to slump. He didn't say anything about my birthday being tomorrow—technically today. I wondered if he even remembered.

Poor Dad. It couldn't be easy, living with three women who could Hear your Whispers when you couldn't Hear theirs. Three women who were all part of a club you could never join. He didn't complain about it, but for a while now I'd been aware that this must be part of why Dad was so involved with his work. Law was an escape, another world with its very own language he'd mastered the way he could never master ours.

It hadn't started that way. In fact, he'd started out working so hard *for* us, putting in fourteen-hour days so Mom could afford to stay home with two small girls. Girls who cried and curled up when confronted with crowds, or even small groups of people. Their combined desires overwhelmed us back then. We Heard them as one relentless hum, an incoherent psychic rumbling that drowned out all other sound . . . nothing like the crisp Whispers that came through when we actually touched someone. Mom kept saying by the time we each started school it would be different, little more than a distraction. And anyway, in a few years our Hearing would be fully grown and strong enough to pick up clear Whispers

11

all the way down the *street*!

Mom was our family's cheerleader, speaking with the confidence of experience, as well as wisdom passed down from her mother and grandmother and all the women in the family stretching back to forever. I doubt it had ever occurred to her that one of her daughters wouldn't *want* her Hearing. Would resent the gift. And would take out her anger on the rest of us.

A kitchen timer beeped, and I jumped. Mom grabbed a pot holder I'd made back in third grade and opened the oven door to pull out a pan of steaming-hot cupcakes.

"Wow, that smells wonderful!"

"Just three more batches after this." She glanced at the microwave clock and yawned again. "Then time to do the icing. But you should go to bed."

I felt a twinge. I wanted to sleep, but the thought of her staying up till three A.M. to bake for my party made me feel horribly selfish.

"Why don't you let me help you with the rest?" I said. "Tomorrow after school."

"Oh, sweetheart, you don't have to make your own birthday cake."

"But I want to." Sometimes it was like this with Mom—each of us wanted to help the other so bad we ended up fighting over it. Still, when I compared that to the fights my friends had with their mothers, I knew how lucky I was. "It'll be more fun together."

"Well . . . okay." She smiled and kissed my cheek. "Night,

honey. You're going to have such a great day tomorrow."

"I know."

I didn't say what I knew we were both thinking: if Icka doesn't ruin it.

At my twelfth birthday party, she had replaced the treasure-hunt treasure with a cow's brain swiped from the Lincoln High science lab. We all stared, dumbfounded, as maggots crawled between its grayish pink hemispheres, and then Natasha Trimble threw up on Ada Marcus's shoes.

For my thirteenth, Icka had invited seven homeless people she'd met downtown, saying we had plenty of food and it would be wrong to waste it. Mom handled it with her usual grace, treating the homeless to a feast in our dining room while my friends and I moved our party to the pool. Until one of the men escaped Mom and tried to kiss Helena on the lips, and Mom got an angry phone call from Helena's mom.

Last year, she had spray-painted MEAT IS MURDER on every box of pepperoni pizza we'd ordered and poured fake blood from a magic-supply store over the pies themselves.

I stacked our mugs in the dishwasher and turned to leave the kitchen, trying not to think about what Icka might be planning for tomorrow.

"Joy?" Mom called me back from the doorway. "I Heard you," she said, "and I promise. This year, I'm not going to let anything ruin your birthday."

13

2

Finally the kidnappers arrived.

At the sound of excited Whispers in the hallway, I sighed and wrapped the comforter around me like a warm tortilla. Since I'd braided my hair before bed, the back of my head didn't look like a bluebird family's home; which was good, because I didn't want to look any stupider than I had to in the inevitable candids people would be snapping with their phones. I arranged each mousy lock across my pillow, popped another Altoid, and practiced my surprised look one last time.

With a rustle, my bedroom door slid open. A streak of light teased my closed eyes, but I focused on breathing slow and regular, like a person deep in sleep.

Helena Sargas crept into my darkened room first. She was Whispering, in her usual Eeyore-like tones, about a wig: *Oh, gosh, I hope this thing fits over her hair!* My heart thumped at the realization: We were now past the point where I could stop it from happening. Bree McIver, ninja quick despite her trademark high heels, was already sneaking in close behind Helena. Last was Parker Lin, my best friend, who I knew had planned the whole thing. As their feet crossed the carpet, their minds sent a harmony of Whispers tumbling into *my* mind. Snatches of thought bouncing off each other like wind chimes:

Oh, gosh, I wish we'd gotten her the gold wig instead.

Just hope they don't dress me *up on my birthday!*

Praying Aunt Cece's bell-bottoms aren't too short for her legs—

Someone flipped a switch, and light flooded the room. "HAPPY BIRTHDAY, JOY!" my friends' voices yelled in practiced unison.

I let out the scream *I'd* practiced and bolted upright, squinting as if the light hurt my eyes (which it did) and also as if I was totally confused as to why three girls were fanned around my bedside wearing expectant grins and gazing back at me.

And clicking their cell-phone cams in my direction.

When really I was thinking, So far, so good.

They'd totally bought my surprise. I'd been worrying on some level that it wouldn't be, you know, satisfying.

15

Trying to surprise someone unsurpriseable . . . but I'd fooled them. It was almost too easy. Then again, when you're a Hearer you get pretty good at feigning surprise, kind of like how most people get good at pretending they love a lame gift. Just another harmless little white lie, right? I hammed it up.

"Oh my *gawd!*" Ham, ham, ham. "What the hell are you guys doing in my room?"

That made them laugh. They laughed like evil masterminds on cartoons. Bwa-ha-ha-ha! Because even though my friends didn't know about my Hearing—no one did—they knew that any Lincoln High School student would know what they were up to by that stage.

Kidnapping was an ancient tradition at Lincoln. The concept was simple, and sort of stupid too if you thought about it too long. Ambush your best friend on her birthday; force her into a bizarre, idiotic costume; then march her off to school where everyone makes fun of her for looking bizarre and idiotic. The custom was established hundreds of years ago, or at least kids were already doing it back in the eighties when Dad was QB for the Lincoln Cougars and Mom was head of the spirit squad (still called the Cougarettes, before it got changed for being "sexist language"). Mom had been kidnapped her senior year, and she said it was one of her favorite memories from high school.

My sister called it a barbaric ritual of humiliation and said she'd never let anyone do that to her in a million years.

The really sad thing was, no one would ever *want* to do

that to her in a million years.

For better or for worse, one's chances of being strapped down and forced into an embarrassing getup were directly related to one's level of popularity. Thus, kidnapping was practically mandatory among varsity cheerleaders, soccer studs, model types, and student body presidents, but among the terminally friendless it was as rare as being fried by lightning. To be honest, as a freshman who didn't stand out in any way (except maybe my height), I'd figured I was pretty safe too.

That illusion shattered Monday at lunch, when I was nearly blinded by the sight of Gina Belle, our student body president, cruising by our group's quad bench in a lime green gaucho suit, pink cowboy boots, and rainbow clown wig. Gina was acting totally normal, though, smiling and holding her head high, and I was staring after her, trying to figure out how any human could be such a good sport, when beside me I Heard Parker Whisper: *Hey, I want to do that to Joy this Friday.*

My heart dropped right down to the wooden bench. I knew it would happen too. Parker was just one of those people; her wishes were commands. She would plan and she would execute, just like she did in her successful campaign for frosh class president. So it was settled, then. I had eighty-nine hours to look forward in dread.

It wasn't that I hated attention, exactly. I'd just rather give it than receive it, which I tried to explain to Parker once, but she just kept screwing up her forehead into tighter and tighter furrows of confusion, so I finally changed the subject. This was after we all took this stupid *Cosmo Girl* quiz "What Kind of Friend Are You?" and everyone else got Lovin' the Limelight while I got Groovin' Behind the Scenes. No one was really surprised. (Is anyone ever surprised by quiz results?)

My friends were like most people. They wanted to be special, to stand out as being the best. And I wanted that too . . . for them. As for me, though, helping people *was* what I did best, and between cookie baking for Parker's campaign, helping Mom with chores, and late-night IM chats reassuring Helena on her extra-down days, it was no wonder my report card was an endless column of Bs and the only hobby I could think to list on MySpace was "hanging with my friends." But that didn't matter, because I knew something Mom said it took most people their whole lives to learn. That making *other* people happy was more fulfilling than competing for the crown of Most Special.

If I was honest with myself, there was a second reason why I didn't long to be special. Standing out could be a curse—that much was obvious from watching Icka. Stars that shone too big and bright could implode, become black holes. Your own specialness could betray you, painting not a spotlight but a bull's-eye over what was once your face.

Still. Birthdays were the one day a year even I dared to let myself be special. Even the most average girl on Earth, I told myself, *must* score some attention on her birthday. A cake with her name written in frosting, basking in a circle of friends and gifts, everyone looking to her, singing to her, Whispering they hope she likes their present best of all . . . As Parker shook something crinkly out of a plastic bag, I reminded myself that it was okay to have other people focus on me all day.

That this would be just like the attention I'd get on any birthday . . .

"We *so* got you!" Parker held up a sparkly purple disco wig.

. . . except, well, there'd be a whole lot more of it.

"Show Joy the fab look she'll be rocking at school this morning."

On cue, Helena presented a corset-top minidress in vomit green with bubble gum polka dots. Bree held up a pair of stretchy magenta bell-bottoms with electric orange peace signs all over them. Gleefully Parker swatted my pillow with banana yellow opera gloves.

For a moment I lost my will to be a sport. For starters, Bree's Aunt Cece was clearly at least five inches shorter than me. Seemed like everyone was, these days: Mom and Jessica both stopped at five five, while Parker was five foot one and so wiry she needed an extra small in Juniors. At best, stretched over my long legs, these pants were going to be sausage tight, not flowing. And speaking of bad and wrong, the ugly dress had built-in bra cups. That meant the fabric would pucker and bag out in the places where my breasts were scheduled to be (but had not yet shown signs of arriving, or called to let me know what the hell was taking them so long).

Under those circumstances, I felt sure, not even Gina could have pulled off queenly poise.

But my friends were beaming down at me, Whispering hopefully . . . and I realized I was supposed to be reacting to the outfit. Protesting, giggling, that kind of thing. Not just sitting there petrified.

I swallowed. "No . . . no way!" I said, gaining strength from the words. "I'm not wearing that crap to school! You can't make me wear *eeeeek*—"

They fell on me like a wolf pack.

The room filled with shrieks and giggles as I struggled, flailed, ducked, and dodged. But I wasn't fighting hard enough to really get in their way. In two minutes, my blue cotton pj's were history. Scratchy material went over my head and the satiny pants slid up my calves, then stretched like a second skin over my thighs. Sigh.

The sun was rising pink and orange outside my window by the time they put the finishing touches on my makeup. I'd stopped struggling long before. Sat back and let them work on me, work *with* me, like they were all on that show *Iron Chef* and I was the secret ingredient. It was a weird feeling to be Project Joy. Weird, but not unpleasant. Bree, the head makeup artist, kept wishing she'd brought her other blush brush; Helena was hoping the wig would stay on all day. My shoulders had started to relax. It was fun, if I was honest with myself. Fun, having all eyes on me. And maybe I'd been looking forward to this birthday more than I'd realized. More than I'd let myself admit.

Maybe more than I should have.

"Okay, she looks redonkulous!" Bree pronounced with a giggle. "Our work is done."

Everyone squealed and took one of my hands or arms and guided me down the hall to the bathroom Jessica and I shared. The platform sandals they'd strapped onto my feet felt unsteady, like stilts. When I saw my reflection, I let out a gasp. A real, sincere gasp.

"Oh my god," I whispered to the mirror. "That can't be me."

I looked like a Goth hooker mime.

My face. Doll-skin white with two (uneven) coal black diamonds with tips at the center of each brow. Sloppy circles of red paint marked my cheekbones, as if drawn by a child. Exaggerated cherry pout. On my forehead in lip liner, the number 15 in Parker's high, angled writing.

I thought I would feel embarrassed, but somehow seeing my face like that made me feel fantastic. The best way to explain it is to say I felt like my face wasn't really my face anymore but some kind of scary mask, like a witch or Richard Nixon or something else you could buy at a drugstore at Halloween, and I was a kid and I was getting ready to go and collect tons of little Almond Joy and Mounds bars. The scarier my mask looked, the better.

Then I Heard Bree Whisper, *I wish I hadn't made her look sooooo bad. Hope she's not mad or anything.*

I blinked. Her wish had sort of bounced me back to

reality. I wasn't supposed to be a little kid having fun on Halloween, I was in high school, for god's sake! Any normal high school person would be embarrassed to look scary and ugly, duh. Sometimes it scared me to think what a social retard I could have been without my Hearing. In fact, back in first grade, when I still couldn't Hear without touching, I'd thought nothing of skipping off to school in red sneakers, neon lime leggings, and a pink tank top that said PRINCESS in rhinestone letters. Shudder.

"Oh my god, I look like crap!" I moaned, then grinned. "I am going to *kill* you guys."

They all laughed with relief, and I did too.

In the kitchen Mom was squeezing organic oranges. She burst into applause with juicy hands. "Beautiful job, girls! I can't wait to get photo coverage. Sit down, food's almost ready. . . ."

"Can we help with anything, Kelli?" If Parker had said that to any other adult, Bree would have tipped her head back and puckered her lips with a smacking sound. But my friends treated Mom as an honorary member of our group.

It made sense, since Mom was trained to talk to teens about their problems. She worked with runaways at the Beaverton Teen Center three days a week, ever since I'd started middle school.

She waved away Parker's offer of help and motioned for us to take our juice to the table. I sat in my usual place and immediately spotted a tiny white package on my place mat. I covered it with my napkin and hoped no one saw me.

Too late; Parker noticed everything. "What's that thing?"
I shrugged.

"Is it from your dad?"

Crap. "I don't know." In fact, I could tell it was from
Dad because the card wasn't a normal card from Hallmark
or something, but a quarter-page ripped from a legal pleading. I didn't want to open it in front of my friends because
my dad's gifts could sometimes be weird and embarrassing.
Like last year, he gave me this rusty metal jewelry box with
a dent in it. Not that I expected a diamond tiara, but you
could tell this was some old thing he'd had lying around,
or maybe found on the curb, and he'd just grabbed it and
wrapped it at the last possible second.

Sometimes it seemed like Dad gave up on us a long
time ago. Once when I was five or so, I remember Dad
ruffling my hair and silently wishing he could take Jess
and me to Disney World. I stared at him, but he moved his
hand as if from a hot stove, then coughed and went away
to go walk Scarlett, the Irish setter puppy he'd gotten us
for Christmas. That was the only time I ever heard him
Whisper about us.

Mom caught my eye and raised her eyebrows. I Heard
her inner voice:

I want to see you open it, Joy!

Sighing, I tore into the package. I don't know what
I was expecting—a bottle cap, a twig? But I felt pretty
guilty once I saw the sparkling pendant on its silver chain,
the stone a glossy honey yellow.

23

"Topaz." I ran my finger over the slippery gem. "It's my birthstone." I turned to Mom. "Did *you* pick this out?" She shook her head and smiled. Which meant he'd chosen it just for me, stab, more guilt.

Everyone crowded around to look at the sparkles.

"Warm tones are great for making hazel eyes pop," said Bree, her own green-contacts-wearing eyes wide with seriousness. She was the only person I knew who went to the library to study fashion mags.

"Really? What's good for brown eyes?" Helena leaned on her elbows and frowned. "Or are those just hopelessly boring and unpoppable?"

Parker turned to me. "It's a beautiful necklace," she said quietly. I knew she meant it because I could Hear her wishing she had one like it.

I started to feel a little bad about dissing the jewelry box last year. Maybe Dad's plan all along had been to fill it with goodies. Maybe it had belonged to his great-great-grandmother and he'd been saving it all these years for me. It would be just like him to do something like that and never bother to explain.

Mom came around with full plates, none of which looked remotely alike. She placed poached eggs and toast at Parker's elbow, yogurt and strawberries in front of ever-dieting Helena. And for me there was a stack of banana pancakes dusted with powdered sugar.

"Gosh, Mrs. Stefani, how do you always know what I'm craving?" Bree asked as she dug into her waffle.

24

"Oh, I know you girls pretty well by now." Mom winked at me. "Tuck in!" Then she glanced at the clock—seven twenty-one—and hugged everyone and said she'd see them at the party tonight.

As soon as she was gone, something really weird happened. It was like the good mood drained out of our group, like she was somehow holding us up with her cheeriness, and without her we all slumped into gloom.

That was bad. We didn't have time to be gloomy, realistically speaking. It was nearly seven thirty, and Mom was gone, and we'd been loud before with all that giggling and screaming, so we were seriously tempting fate now.

Icka was a very deep sleeper. But even she couldn't sleep forever.

If I'd been thinking "proactively"—as Parker would say—I would have stood up and hustled us out of the kitchen, backpacks on and out the door. Instead, I sank into my chair and toyed with a forkful of pancake for two minutes that we just didn't have. I blame it on my friends' Whispers. They were the upsetting kind. The kind where something's wrong and I couldn't do anything to help, and I couldn't even bring it up because I wasn't supposed to know about it in the first place.

Like Helena wishing her "bad skin" would clear up. That made me sad, because despite one tiny little blemish on her jawline, Helena's skin glowed. Its golden tone almost matched her wide-set eyes and the caramel waves that zigzagged to her hourglass waist. She reminded me of a sunbeam brought to life . . . yet her Whispers echoed her critical mother's more every day.

Then there was Parker next to me, staring off into the distance, pining after this senior guy she had a crush on, Ben Williams.

I was still pondering why that one bothered me when I heard a door slam upstairs and then angry boots clomping down the hall.

3

"You guys—let's *go!*" I shot from my chair, but in my panic forgot I was wearing the stupid platforms and bashed my kneecap under the table. Tears stung my eyes. By the time my friends glanced up from their shaking plates, Icka was blocking the kitchen doorway.

Parker and the rest sat frozen, staring. People always did that, even after they'd seen my sister a bunch of times.

Hope it's just a phase. That's what our relatives always Whispered when they saw her. Or *I wish she didn't hide how pretty she is.* And then there were the If Onlys. *If only she didn't wear shredded, baggy workmen's clothes from Goodwill. Didn't store metal in her lip, nose, and eyebrow. Didn't smoke like a barbecue*—a vegan barbecue. *Didn't boycott shampoo.* (She claimed she was "part of the no poo movement," as if sporting neglected dreads somehow qualified as a movement.) *If only she didn't coat her eyelids, raccoon-style, with black liquid liner. Didn't let her pale skin run to pasty*—no, *beyond* pasty. Next door to translucent. But Icka did do all those things, and slouching there in the doorway, she was very far from pretty. She looked like the ghost of grunge.

Beside me Helena sat nervously biting her straw, praying my sister wouldn't single her out for humiliation.

I bit my lip—my knee was still screaming—and waited for Icka to fire the first shot.

Instead, she stumbled forward, yawning, and slipped past us all without a glance, as if she really were a ghost. At her heels trailed Scarlett, dragging herself across the floor with even less enthusiasm. (The dog had an excuse; she had a bad leg.)

My friends and I managed a four-way glance of panic, but Icka just turned away from us, stretched her arm, and retrieved a sustainable, reusable glass jar of granola from her personal kitchen shelf. "Caaaarbs," she croaked in an early-morning smoker's voice. Then she paused to yawn again. I narrowed my eyes. What the hell was going on here?

Since when was Icka too sleepy to be a bitch on my birthday?

There were exactly two possibilities:

A) She was trying to drive me nutso with suspense, or,

B) She was lulling me into a false sense of security so she

could spring some evil plan at my party tonight.

Knowing my sister, B seemed a lot more likely.

With infinite slowness, Icka unscrewed the jar's lid and popped a handful of cranberry granola into her mouth—right there at the counter, without the aid of bowl, spoon, or soy milk. I saw Parker's nose wrinkle at the matted blond dreads hanging down the back of Icka's work shirt and felt embarrassed we were related. A tiny part of me couldn't help feeling sorry for Icka too. If Parker ever looked at me with such withering disgust, I'd positively shrink. Bent on her skinny forearms, my sister did look smaller—like her actual height, five five, instead of a seven-foot-tall avenging goddess.

And that's when it occurred to me that as long as she was busy chewing, my friends and I had a chance to *escape.*

"Come on." I jumped up, wobbling on my platforms. "Let's go!"

Parker nodded and dove for her purple Eddie Bauer bag. Bree stood too, and Helena rushed to follow, slamming in her chair. So far Icka hadn't turned to look at us, kept crunching her granola. My heart flip-flopped. Was it possible she was more interested in whole grains than in ruining my life?

She must have Heard that spark of hope, because she spun around. A funny little half smile like an Old West gunslinger. The drowsiness was an act. She was wired. She was just waiting for me to build up hope so she could smash it. These little mind games were what she lived for.

Her leering eyes met mine. "Joy-Joy! You finally look like what you really are. A freak."

Reflexively, I shrugged, though my hands were shaking. Icka knew how much I hated it when she said things like that, making little veiled references to our shared secret in front of my friends. Luckily, Parker already had my gray Timbuk2 bag by the strap and was coming over to help me put it on over my costume. I saw Helena scrambling into her jacket in the doorway, ready to skitter from the room.

Why oh why was Bree still standing by the table?

Then I Heard it:

I wish someone would tell loser girl to shove it.

Oh. My god.

Bree had crossed her arms, was glaring at Icka. "Why would you say that," she demanded, "to your own sister on her birthday?"

Helena and Parker widened their eyes at her, but Bree had gone to a different middle school. She had only met the rest of us a month ago. She didn't fully understand what Icka was capable of.

"If you want to be a bitch to me, fine," she went on. "I can give back as good as I get, whatever. But, oh my god, this is *Joy*! Girl couldn't be mean if she tried. My little puppy has more mean in him. You should be ashamed, seriously . . . what the hell is wrong with you?" I couldn't get over the outrage in her voice. Outrage for *me*. Part of me wished I could cover Bree's mouth—or maybe just grab her and run out of the house with her, like people carried cats

30

out of blazing buildings. But at the same time, gratitude was bubbling up inside me. Bree, who I'd only known for a month, was standing up to Icka, standing up for me. "So don't go calling Joy a freak," she finished, "when we all know you're the only freak here." I felt like bursting into applause.

"She's right." Parker gave me a sheepish look. *I wish I'd been the one to speak up.*

I gave her a small smile to let her know all was well between us. Anyone who knew Icka would know better than to engage her.

Icka stared at Bree, taking in her highlighted hair, her curve-hugging pink V-neck sweater and black pencil skirt. "No offense," she said, "but who are *you* supposed to be?"

Bree squared her broad shoulders as if ready for a fight, then she squinted, confused. "Um, what?"

"Icka, you know Bree." I didn't know where Icka was headed with this either, but I didn't like the sound of it. "She's been to our house like ten times—"

"Whatever—I don't need a full report." Icka still had Bree pinned with her gaze. "I'm just saying, don't get too comfortable. You obviously won't be in this clique long." She said all this seemingly without malice, gently even, like a doctor announcing that a healthy-looking patient had brain cancer. Then, at our collective stunned silence, she broke up snickering. "What, people? Hello, am I the only one who can see this little experiment in diversity can't

31

last? I mean, look at her . . . now look at the rest of you. Do-gooder alpha prep"—she pointed to Parker—"mousy beta prep"—Helena—"and freak posing as prep"—guess who. "Just where do you think you'll fit in, Miss *InStyle Is My Bible?*"

Bree was blinking over and over, wishing Icka would shut up. Helena flinched and stared at the wall. Parker's frown traveled from Icka to Bree, as if she were considering my sister's words despite their source.

And the terrible thing was . . . well, I didn't want to be thinking this, but Bree really *was* a little different from the rest of us. She was from Southern California. She'd gone out for cheerleading "to meet people," which sounded like something you'd say at a beauty pageant, but that was just how Bree talked. She wore emerald green contact lenses despite having perfect vision and sported a polished, almost varnished, pink mouth even in P.E. class . . . I shook my head. Bree was our friend. Icka was just baiting us, as usual, with stupid mind games, adding a drop of truth to her lies to help them slide down smoother.

"I am so sorry about her." I folded my yellow-gloved arms. "I mean, we're all different in our own ways," I added, trying not to think of my own huge, secret difference. "It hasn't stopped us from being friends, right?"

"E*xact*ly," Bree said, falling on the word like she'd been waiting to say it to the first person who spoke in her defense.

Icka moved straight to her next attack. "Kinda shocked

to see *you* here, Helena. I thought your family was all about the doing nothing on birthdays."

Helena stiffened, then glared at me. I knew what she was thinking, that I'd blabbed to Icka the story of how her mom and stepdad spaced on her birthday last year. No doubt she was picturing the two of us snickering about it together, thinking that underneath the "teasing" we were, secretly, close—BFF sisters—and that I wasn't the nice, kind person they all thought I was. I dug my nails into my palms so hard I winced, but what could I say? There was never any point with Icka. I'd repair the damage later, like always.

"Nobody talk to her." I almost didn't recognize the commanding voice as my own. "Just head for the door."

We speed-walked into the foyer, Icka chasing behind. "Wait, I forgot to tell you something!" None of us was stupid enough to turn. "A message for the Joyster," she yelled anyway. "Your boyfriend called last night." Ha! I'd never even had a boyfriend, so her ruse was pathetic. I opened the door and stepped aside so my friends could go through. Helena propelled herself down the porch steps. I wondered if she'd dare come back for tonight's party.

"Did you not hear me? I said Ben called."

I saw Parker flinch, and Bree hesitated in the doorway. My stomach dropped.

"Ben Williams, remember? Your True Love, TM?"

Parker's dark, intense eyes were fixed on my sister's blue ones. *I hope this is just what I think it is, another lie.*

33

"She's such a liar! Icka, be quiet." I turned to Parker. "I would never—"

"Joy, I know, believe me." Parker pointed a French-manicured finger at Icka's chest. "You. Are lower than pond scum." Her voice shook with anger. "Like I'm really supposed to believe Joy would steal Ben from me?"

"That's crazy," I echoed. And it was: I wasn't some kind of frenemy who'd steal my best friend's crush. Besides, though Parker was too kind to point it out, Ben with his sexy olive eyes and basketball-star coolness was far out of my league . . . he *belonged* with someone amazing, like Parker.

Icka snorted and shrugged. "Well, don't take my word for it, check it out yourself." She fished a scrap of paper from her hip pocket. "This guy called, okay? It was around nine. Joy and Mommy Dearest were off at QFC," she added, "buying flour and sugar and rich creamery butter with which to kill our guests. There." She held out the scrap so we could all see the phone number scrawled on it.

Parker turned to me in confusion. "That's Ben's number."

I felt a funny chill run through me.

Suddenly everyone outside was staring at me, not at Icka. In the silence, I felt myself blushing—blood filling my cheeks so I could feel my pulse everywhere. Was it possible that Ben had really called? I reminded myself that while Icka was a good liar, she was even better at using the truth as a weapon. Stretching it, torturing it on the rack . . . till it fit her purposes. Despite the cold October air blowing in, my face felt hot as July. I was grateful for the clownish makeup.

Not that it mattered but . . . if Ben *had* called, what would he call about? We had no classes together. The only time I talked to him was when he stopped by our group's quad bench at lunch, to flirt with Parker. Could it be he'd decided Parker was too . . . perfect, or something? Decided he liked me instead? Not that it mattered.

"He must have called to get directions to the party," I said lamely.

"I already gave him directions," Parker snapped. "When *I* invited him."

"Well, one guy out of three point three billion." Icka winked at me. "You'll meet more at Stanford."

"Shut *up,* Icka!" I turned to Parker. "I'm so sorry about her. Maybe Ben lost the invite. Or something." I was desperate to reassure her. To smooth the wrinkle out of her brow, put a smile on those set-in-stone lips. But I couldn't think of anything reassuring to say—the situation looked pretty damn suspicious! Icka had planned it that way, and she was much smarter than me. Besides, if Ben had really called, then there was nothing I could say to make Parker feel okay about it. Helena was staring as if seeing me for the first time. Bree's eyes had narrowed to poison darts of suspicion.

"Whatever, it doesn't even matter." Parker flashed me

the frosty, businesslike smile she saved for customers at her mom's nail salon.

I blinked back tears. This birthday had started so well . . . how did Icka manage to knock it all flat in minutes? It was hardly the first time she'd been nasty to my friends or spoiled our fun, yet somehow today she'd upped the stakes. She must have been plotting this for weeks, I realized, all alone up in her room, hating me for having friends when she had nothing. So she attacked my friendships. Nudging our group toward chaos. Hinting that I was disloyal. Hacking at the bonds that held us together, that held *me* together. Was her goal to make me as miserable and lonely as she was?

Icka pinched a glob of granola off her dirty shirt and popped it in her mouth. *Crunch, crunch, crunch.* She pulverized it, drawing out each grinding chew as if her teeth were crushing rocks.

"We should go before the first bell rings," Parker said, not looking at me. "I don't want to be late for math."

4

I hobbled down the sidewalk after my friends, a white rage growing inside me with each step.

I wasn't just angry at Icka—I was angry at myself. I could have prevented what had happened at breakfast, if only I'd bothered to think ahead.

It's not like this was the first time she'd tried to sabotage my friendships. She'd never been okay with my having friends, period.

In second grade, I brought home my first BFF: plump, freckled, awkward Heather Mackey. Jessica had so far failed to bring home from school anything but perfect papers, bruises from having ice plant lobbed at her at recess, and the mocking nickname Icka, which stuck like superglue. She treated poor Heather like a fire that needed to be stomped out. She stomped on Heather's feelings, then her glasses ("accidentally"). Heather Mackey never came over again.

When I won "Sweetest Smile" in the fifth-grade yearbook poll, she taunted me all summer, grinning like a baboon every time she saw me. "That's what your smile looks like," she informed me. "What's wrong with you? You might as well get a tattoo that says, 'Desperate to be liked.'" By then she herself had already given up on being liked. Two schools had expelled her that year for punching other students out of the blue—really, she confided, it was because they were "Whispering something jerky."

But the worst was a couple years ago, when Mom talked Aunt Jane into coming over for Christmas dinner, and she told us some of the old family legends passed down through her mother's mother.

I liked the one about Great-great-aunt Sadie, a spunky Old West gal. She'd used her Hearing to best every poker shark in the saloon, then gave all the money to charity.

Icka's favorite was the story of Hope and Faith, Puritan-era twins who'd supposedly opened up a psychic link one day when Faith was spinning wool and miraculously Heard her sister's voice from miles away. Hope was drowning in the river, but Faith, Listening to her sister's Whispers and even picking up mental pictures through Hope's eyes, was able to find her and save her. According to the legend, Hope lived on to become our great-times-nine grandmother.

(Or maybe it was Faith. Changed every time we heard the story.)

"That Jane." The stories made Mom shake her head and smile. "I can't believe she remembers all those old family fairy tales."

But Icka didn't see it as just a fairy tale. She couldn't get enough of the story. It stuck in her head: sisters bonded for life. This was right around the time I was starting to make more friends. People like Parker and Helena. Icka began the extremely annoying and creepy habit of calling me daily on my cell phone to ask, "Can you Hear me right now?"

"I hear your voice on the phone, if that's what you mean . . . ," I'd say, getting suspicious and worried.

"Oh, that's all?" You could just hear the disappointment in her voice. "Too bad. Because right now I'm lying across the railroad tracks." Or sitting in a grocery cart at the top of a steep hill. Or wandering through the park alone at night.

This went on until the first time I ever slept over at Parker's house. I was nervous. Parker was the most popular girl in my grade, and she liked *me*. We had a great time, though, and had finally drifted off to sleep around two A.M. . . . when my phone rang, waking Parker's older sister and her hard-working immigrant mother, talk about embarrassing. It was Icka, of course, wanting to know if I could Hear her. She'd snuck out, walked to the mall in the dark, and climbed to the second floor of a construction site. I told her to go back home immediately, said I was calling

Mom and Dad. Suddenly she yelled and the phone went dead, and I screamed. (It turned out an eraser-sized hunk of plaster fell from the ceiling and hit her on the head.)

"I am so sorry about all this," I said to the Lin family an hour later as the four of us sat around the kitchen table in our nightgowns, after 911 had dispatched police and an ambulance to her location and returned her, safe but concussed, to my parents. "I'm just really sorry . . ."

"Hey, don't apologize." Parker had put her hand on my shoulder. "It's not your fault what your psycho sister does."

She wasn't saying that now.

No one spoke, in fact, as we trudged down Rainbow Street past stucco ramblers with green and shiny lawns, driveway after driveway curving back far from the sidewalk. No one even smiled. The sandal straps chafed my ankles and I felt guilty for holding up the group with my slowness. When Icka ran past us, every single one of my friends began wishing and praying I'd hurry up, and they kept at it until we reached the quad.

At which point the second bell rang and they all scrambled for their respective first-period classrooms, wishing I hadn't made them late.

I watched them scatter, but I didn't make a move toward Ms. Phelps's language arts class. Even though it was my favorite class, there was something else I needed to do today.

I marched at turtle speed past E building, all the way down to the metal shop. Hardly any people were milling around that part of campus; there's only a couple of reasons to be down there. Two upperclassmen painting a mural paused to smirk at my outfit. Gingerly, walking pigeon-toed so I wouldn't lose my balance, I traveled past the end of the concrete and onto the leafy, muddy ground.

It was like this: Deep down I knew Icka's performance at breakfast had only been a warm-up. A month ago, when we'd planned the party, Mom had assured me she wouldn't let Icka anywhere near it. Dad would offer to take her to the movies, and if she refused, then Mom would simply ground her to the upstairs—with the threat of taking away her art supplies if she so much as put one foot on the top step before every guest was gone. At the time, I'd been shocked that Mom—whose motto was "expect the best and people rise to your expectations"—was finally admitting she expected bad behavior from her older daughter. Now it was clear that Mom still needed to adjust her expectations down. Icka was determined to wreak havoc. She'd possibly done years worth of damage in *mere moments*. Whatever she was planning for tonight, I had to stop her . . . which meant I had to find her.

And I knew just where she'd be.

Unfortunately, the idea of going there made my breakfast bounce in my stomach. Lincoln was a friendly school, and I already felt welcome anywhere on campus, even on the quad, where freshmen were supposedly banned from sitting. But the path behind the metal shop wasn't techni-cally on school property. That was its sole appeal as far as I could see, and why it was legendary at Lincoln as a stoner hangout. Dad said back in the eighties they called the Path's denizens druggies, and in the seventies it was burnouts, but the idea was the same. Freaks and losers, people who couldn't pass as normal, got pushed to the edge of campus life. You always wondered what would become of those people after high school . . . something I wondered about Icka too. Surely if you'd told Mom and Dad ten years ago their oldest would grow up to be a stoner/druggie/burnout and hang out at the Path, no doubt they'd have been disappointed. But the truth was sadder: Even *those* people wouldn't hang out with Icka.

My sister spent her breaks and lunches—and too many class periods—about a hundred feet beyond the Path, on the other side of an old dry creek bed that was closer to the woods than to school. My heart pounded just thinking of venturing out there. Was I crazy? Looking for Icka was like driving toward a hurricane. But I couldn't stand back and let her destroy my life until it sucked as much as hers. I had to try.

The stoners were congregated exactly where I knew they would be, clad in black leather and denim, smoking cloves and bidis and other weird cigarettes of a possibly less legal variety. I tried to walk quickly, but the damn shoes held me back.

"Hey, look!" A stoner girl pointed at me. "One of the trendies is defecting!" A burning joint crash-landed on the ground to vanish behind a black backpack, and a dozen mocking eyes were suddenly fixed on me, like I was the freak.

"Wow, I didn't know sheeple could venture so far from their quad pasture."

"Maybe she has a message from our popular overlords?"

"Nah, she's trolling for a homecoming date."

"Hey, cutie, I'll go if you promise to wear that dress."

A chorus of snickers. And they say popular people are the mean ones? I smiled my Gina Belle smile, straightened my shoulders, and kept walking.

"She thinks she's running for Miss Universe," a leather-jacketed girl said. More laughter.

The tallest guy in the group I recognized as being in my government class. It took me a moment, because he cut class a lot. A lot a lot. He'd always struck me as shy and odd, but not mean. I had this bizarre urge to say hi to him and prove I wasn't the snob they thought I was. But before I could I Heard him Whisper: *I hope she doesn't talk to me in front of everyone here. I don't want people to get mad.*

So much for that.

The last thing I Heard before I crossed the dry creek bed—and the stoner pack moved out of my Hearing range—was from the girl who'd made the Miss Universe crack: *I wish people like her would stay away from here and leave us alone.*

Youch. Who would have thought the denizens of the Path would be so harsh and excluding? Normally, Hearing nasty Whispers like that could cast a shadow over my whole day—even week—but I couldn't afford to nurse hurt feelings now. I had to keep going. Steeling myself for what was ahead.

Icka sat alone on the other side of the creek, sprawled on a boulder. Lit cigarette in one hand, matted white blond dreads sticking to her long, graceful neck. If not for the glint of metal in her lips and nose, the tattered men's clothes, and clunky Docs, she could have been a mermaid. Even her raccoon-painted eyes looked otherworldly. A lot of people were intimidated by my sister, even if they didn't like or respect her. Me, I wasn't fooled; her pose looked posed. She was waiting for me, just like I'd waited for my friends at five thirty A.M. Still, it infuriated me that she could Hear me and predict my actions when I could rarely pick a Whisper off her.

My wig rustled in the breeze and red and orange leaves crunched under my platforms, but Icka didn't lift her gaze till I was less than a foot away. Then her mouth curled into this smug little smirk that made me want to strangle her.

It also made me nervous. Had she Heard something from me, just now? I didn't *want* to know what my desires sounded like at this moment.

"Hey, Icka," I said, trying to keep my voice calm and even. "How's your day been so f—"

"Get to the fucking point, if you have one."

"Fine." I folded my arms across the front of my hideous

44

dress. "You were evil to my friends this morning. You can't do that again."

"Oh, Joy." Smug impatience changed to smug pity. "When you find out what those plastics have been Whispering about you, it's really going to break you."

Here we go again . . . she was so full of crap. "I don't want to fight with you, okay? But Mom says my Hearing's already done growing so—"

"Mommy says I'm all grown up," she copied in a baby voice. "You planning to bring Mom with you to college so she can keep on telling you what to think? I hope you realize it's not natural to be your mother's clone at age fifteen. You're supposed to hate the lying bitch . . . like I do."

"Do not talk about Mom like that. Ever." My heart was hammering. Poor Mom, who loved Icka so fiercely, who defended her still. Poor Mom! "You're the liar."

Icka jerked her head sideways and laughed, a high miserable sound of pain. "We're all liars, Joy-Joy!" Just like that, her voice had gone shrill and jerky, dancing toward hysteria. "Have you, by any chance, noticed that our whole family *lies. All. The. Time!*"

I stared into her bloodshot eyes and felt a chill. "Icka, are you high again?" She'd tried just about every kind of drug—she even owned a fake ID claiming she was Allison Monroe, age twenty-two—but no matter what she did, her Hearing always came back.

"Seriously, we should change our name to the Liarsons."

I couldn't help but notice she'd dodged my question. "The only one who tells the truth about anything is Aunt Jane. You should ask *her* about your headaches." She hiccoughed and it turned into a giggle. *Wish she'd go away so I could finish.*

"Finish?" Aha! A Whisper. "So you could finish doing what?"

She shrugged.

I narrowed my eyes at her army bag loaded with science-fiction paperbacks. It appeared to be propped up right next to her boulder, but my eyes zeroed in on a 7Up bottle behind it. I bent down and swiped the bottle. Icka examined her fingernails in an exaggerated display of not giving a damn. There were no bubbles in the clear liquid. I took a tiny sip and spat it out on the dirt.

"That would be vodka," Icka said unnecessarily.

"You're drunk, Icka. Jesus. At *school*."

"Oh, who gives a shit?" She grabbed for the bottle, but I held it over my head, miles out of her reach. "For god's sake." She actually sounded amused. "If you're worried about my education, I know what's in every teacher's head better than they do. Dr. Kendricks, for example, spends half his time daydreaming that he'd made it as a real scientist, and the other half wishing he could bang Ms. Phelps." I shook my head, not wanting to hear more. Not believing her. "Hey, I didn't want to know this stuff either, believe me," Icka said. "*Speaking* of Ms. Phelps, did you know she's into—"

"Stop it. Now." I held my hand up. Ms. Phelps was my

favorite teacher . . . as Icka well knew. "None of that is true," I said forcefully. "It's just like Mom said, when you think the worst of people, you Hear the worst. You read too much into everything."

"You know the real reason Mom Hears no evil?" she said. "Because her Hearing's just as crappy as her parenting. She can't Hear a word below the surface. Must be kinda nice, being so clueless."

"Mom is far from clueless." I shook my head. "It's just that there are too many Whispers in the world for anyone to pick up all—"

"Oh, good god, there you go quoting Mommy Dearest *again*." She tipped her head skyward and broke into a hyena laugh. "You're like her Mini Me. It's creepy."

"No, what's creepy is trying to poison all your sister's relationships! And if you're so jealous Mom and I are close, try being nice to her for once." I paused, breathless with anger. None of this was going how I'd wanted it to. She was pushing my buttons with that sneer, sucking me into her psychodrama vortex. I couldn't let her. I inhaled more slowly, straightened my itchy wig, planted my hands on my hips, and exhaled. "Okay, look, I just came to tell you one thing. I'm not going to let you ruin *this* birthday." It didn't sound like much, and Icka's patronizing gaze made me painfully aware of how stupid I must look trying to sound tough in my kidnap victim's getup. But I was proud of myself just for getting it out. I'd put up with so much— way too much—until now, but today I was taking a stand.

"Do you hear me?" I added. "Am I being clear? Stay away from the party . . . and my friends."

She gave a short laugh, more like a sob. "I keep telling you, you don't have friends! None of us does."

The way she said it, I wasn't sure if she just meant our family or the whole planet. Either way, she was wrong again—so wrong it made me sad for her. *No one* had friends? That's what she needed to believe? Even the stoners had each other, and it didn't take a genius to see why she wasn't welcome in their dark leather huddle, let alone on the quad. As for the future, things looked even grimmer. At least now she had teachers checking up on her, and parents to go home to. But what would happen to my sister when she turned eighteen without a friend in the world?

"Hey, hey." Icka touched a hand to the top of her head. "Don't you start a pity party for *me*, Joy-Joy. I have my problems, I admit it, but at least I don't need to pretend I'm best pals with the A-list, or should I say the A-hole list."

Any sympathy I'd felt for her vanished like smoke. "You can't go after my friendships anymore." I'd never heard my voice so certain, words tumbling out unplanned but deeply felt. "If you ever do it again, it'll be the last time I speak to you."

She snorted and waved her hand as if to shoo a gnat. "Oh, you're not actually mad at me for that. You have to admit it was funny to watch."

"It was not funny! Can't you even see that?"

"The only reason you're mad," she went on with infuriating calm, "is because just like that"—she snapped her fingers—"I proved that all your supposed friendships are bullshit. Remind me, how many seconds did it take loyal BFF Parker to turn on you?"

"She did not turn on me!" I was yelling now. "You played on her Whispers. You knew she liked Ben. Your little mind game was just stupid and cruel—not to mention a complete lie. Ben Williams would *never* call me." I held my breath.

Icka smiled at me. "You're so hoping he did, though."

"I am not!"

She shrugged. "I can Hear you."

I lowered my voice, glanced around, even though we were alone. "Maybe I wish someone as cool as Ben would call me, all right? That's not the same." I was aware of the defensive catch in my voice and the slow drunken grin spreading on her face. What was she Hearing now? "So what if I hoped!" I blurted out, hating the satisfaction in her eyes. "So what? It was just a stupid Whisper. Maybe I *am* attracted to Ben. Who wouldn't be? It's not like I'd ever let it affect my actions, so what's the big deal?"

"Oh, I get it!" She widened her eyes and pretended to twirl her hair. "It's not a big deal if you like him, it's only a big deal if Parker likes him. She gets whatever she wants, your desires don't count. Sound fair to you?"

"That is not what I said!" Suddenly I was shouting again. "And it's not true!"

"You're wishing it wasn't," she informed me with a superior grin. She jumped up from the boulder, as if Hearing me incriminate myself had given her new energy. "It means I was right, part of you already knows the ugly truth." Now she was inches from my face, vodka on her breath. "Congratulations, little sis, you're finally seeing the sad, shitty light of reality—where some of us have to live every day." Her knuckles rapped the side of my head. "Our little Joy-Joy is finally growing up!"

Something snapped in me when she tapped my head.

I knocked her hand away, hard. "I hate you." I didn't mean for those words to come out, and when they did I was amazed at how hard my voice sounded. But as I watched her take a slow puff on her cigarette, watched her smirk at having got to me, I realized I wasn't done. Not close to it. "I hate what you do to our family," I said. "I hate what you do to my friends. You act like you're so much better than all of us, when you're nothing but a mean, nasty, negative . . . bitch." I heard her snicker at my hesitation to swear, but I felt detached. This was no longer a conversation, or even a fight. I was just telling her how it was. The ugly truth. "You're not a misunderstood victim," I said. "You're just spoiled and selfish. You have a gift, a power that could make this world a better place, but all you do is make people miserable."

"Oh, grow up. Making people happier doesn't make them better." Ahh, the Humanity Is Evil rant. "People suck. Get it through your head: They're beyond saving. If

50

you want to help the rest of the planet, stop spraying chemicals on your head. Stop eating tortured animals shipped using fossil fue—"

"Shut the hell up, you self-righteous bitch." I was on a swearing roll. Icka's eyes nearly bugged out of her head. "I am so tired of feeling sorry for you, when all you do is hurt me and hurt our family and hurt my friends. It's like the only thing that makes you happy. Well, I'm sorry you can't be happy, Icka. I really am! I'm sorry you hate your gift. But I'm not going to let you drag me down too. Because I'm not like you. I'm not a freak, like you." It felt freeing to say the words, so I said them again. "I. Am not. A freak. Like you."

She groaned. "Too true, you're not a freak. You're just like everybody else, another stupid human Whispering stupid, horrible, disgusting desires. I Hear things, all the time. Things that would make you curl up in a fetal ball . . . and not just from creeps on the bus, either. It's everyone." She stared right into my eyes. "It's you too. What the hell happened to you, Joy? The things you want these days. The things you pray for . . . it makes me sick. And I don't have the luxury of shutting bad things out." She bared her teeth, reached out, swiped back the vodka bottle before I could stop her. "The only thing I can do is stay the hell away from everyone . . . even you."

I put my hands on my hips, nearly tottering forward on my four-inch platforms.

"Good, keep talking like that," I said, surprised at how

tight and angry my voice was. "You're going to get your wish—you'll end up all alone, with no one, with nothing. Hiding away from the world like Aunt Jane did. And you know what? The world will be a happier place without *you* in it." My heart was pounding as if I was about to jump off a cliff—or maybe I'd already jumped. I had tried so hard. To love my sister and be loyal to her, no matter what she said or did, the way Mom could. But we had become the people we'd become, and I had to protect myself. "Stay away from the party tonight," I heard myself say. "Stay out of my life from here on out. I'm done with you, Jess."

A strange look had come over Icka's face. Maybe it was the childhood nickname that no one had called her for so many years. Maybe it was the hardness in my tone—me, Joy, the good sister, owner of the Sweetest Smile. Stiff superiority drained from the corners of her mouth and her eyebrows seemed to sag. I was shocked to realize I didn't feel a bit sorry for the harsh things I'd just said. I was being cruel like she'd been to my friends, but they had been innocent while she completely deserved it. Even when her black-painted lower lip trembled, all I felt was a sour satisfaction.

Slowly she ground out the cigarette with her boot, then looked up. "I have to go now." Her voice sounded flat, not even angry anymore, almost like she wasn't even talking to me. And then she had her bag and her fake 7Up and she was weaving farther down the path, away from school. Into the woods. Typical. She would probably cut the rest of the day. She'd miss her calc test, Mom would get another call from Mr. Rich . . .

I leaned against the cold boulder and sighed. I'd done it. I'd finally stood up to my sister. I felt different: grown up. Strong. I also felt alone. But maybe that was part of being grown up and strong. I watched her black-and-purple shape shrinking as the eucalyptus trees around her grew taller. When she was the size of an ant, she seemed to stand still for a second, and my heart thumped. Was she marching back here to fight with me some more? Then I Heard her, as clearly as if we'd been side by side watching Cartoon Network together on the old beanbag chair: *I wish, I wish, I wish I could go back in time.* A moment later, she disappeared behind a tree.

5

Ten years, one month, and three days ago, my first day of kindergarten never really happened.

Instead, Jessica's cool small hand on my back woke me in the darkness. *I wish you'd get up now, Joy.*

"Already?" I rolled my head to one side. Two stars twinkled outside my window. "Is this a dream?" I said hopefully.

"Nope," Jess said, whispering out loud this time. "It's time for me to walk you to the school bus. Now hurry." She tossed me the hot pink overalls and short-sleeved white T-shirt Mom had gently laid over my desk chair the night before.

I must have dozed off again, because next thing I knew

Jess was shoving one of my arms through an armhole of the T-shirt, then the other. The shirt had a ribbon at the neckline. Even my sneakers, socks, and underwear were all brand-new and had lain in tissue paper for weeks, sacred, waiting for The Day.

I frowned as she snapped on my overalls. "Mom's s'posed to walk me."

"She was going to," Jess agreed, "but then she found out today's a special early day for kindergarteners and third graders, so she asked me to do it."

I took this in. Mom hadn't mentioned a special early day, but Jess was eight. She knew everything. "What about breakfast?"

"I'm bringing it with us," Jess said in my ear. "We have to be really quiet till we get to the bus stop, okay? Let's go." I wanted to ask why we had to be quiet, and what about brushing my teeth, but she didn't give me time, she just pushed me out the door. I had to keep moving forward or I'd stumble.

In the kitchen, Jess swooped down and grabbed the pink tote bag she had waiting behind the back door. As soon as the latch snapped shut behind us, she grabbed my hand and Whispered, *I want you to run!* and together we ran in the cherry- and-peach-colored dawn up the street, and down another one. When we were several blocks from home and my heart was racing, Jess breathed a huge sigh. "We made it!" She consulted her Hello Kitty digital watch. "Twelve seconds before the bus."

I felt a funny feeling in my stomach. "Jess? I thought the bus was yellow."

"Not the third-grade bus," she said, and she was a third grader so she'd know.

She took my hand, and as I followed her up the steep steps I Heard her frantically praying I wouldn't say anything in front of the driver. I didn't know why, but I stayed perfectly silent. She plunked down four whole dollars, and the driver, a lady, narrowed her eyes and asked, "Shouldn't you kids be headed for school this morning?"

"We're homeschooled, ma'am," Jess lied smoothly. "We're going to Canon Beach to meet our aunt." I tried not to show how startled I was. Why did Jess lie to the driver? I kept quiet while she led me to the back row. As soon as we sat down, Jess pulled away from me so we weren't touching.

"Why'd you tell that driver lady we were going to the beach?" I said quietly.

"Oh, that," she said, "that's just the password code to get on this school bus. It's a pretty long ride," she added. "Why don't we play I Spy?"

I knew she was trying to distract me, so I just folded my arms.

"I Spy with my little eye, something that is pink."

"My overalls!" I blurted out, engrossed despite myself. We played until the bus driver said, "End of the line!"

It was a weekday in September, so when the bus dropped us off right across from the beach, the sand was deserted.

Haystack Rock rose up ahead of us like a small mountain, reaching for the sky.

I remembered this place. Earlier that summer, Mom and Jess and I had come here at dawn to meet Aunt Jane, who was taking a one-day break from being a hermit to sell some mushrooms she'd foraged. But Aunt Jane never showed, and pretty soon the beach filled up with strangers. The drone of Whispers I couldn't understand surrounded me, and I curled into Mom's lap, covering my ears as if that would help drown out the noise. When Mom said we had to go home, Jess protested, and Mom had snapped at her to be more considerate, not so selfish. Which was what Mom said a lot to my sister back then.

At the beach Jess let out a whoop, dropped her tote bag, and ran across the sand shrieking. Then she ran back and lay down with her head resting on a perfectly round boulder. Had she lost her mind? "We did it!" she crowed. "We did it."

Worried, I peered over her. "Why are we here? Where's the school? Why'd you say we were meeting Aunt Jane?"

She turned to me. "Because we are. She's going to come and get us and take us to her forest to live with her and her pet wolf." My stomach felt like I'd swallowed a stone. "And then neither of us will ever have to go to school again."

I sank down onto the sand and started to cry. "But I *want* to go to school." Up until that moment I hadn't been so sure of this—I knew I was supposed to go, and I wanted to be good and do what Mom said, but I was also scared of school. Part of me had been wishing I wouldn't have to go after all. Now, on this white, deserted beach alone with Jess, I felt a sudden longing for all the things Mom and I had talked about: cubbies and backpacks. Sitting in a circle and raising your hand to talk. Juice in a plastic cup. "I miss Mom," I whimpered. I'd never been away from home without her. "I want Mom to come take me to school."

"Joy." She knelt down to squeeze my hand, and what I Heard confused me, a mixture of hopes and regrets bouncing off one another. "Trust me, you don't want to go to school. I couldn't stand to see you go there and be . . . be like I am. That's why we're going to go live with Aunt Jane."

Weird, how until she'd mentioned it again I'd sort of tricked myself into forgetting her scary plan. "Mom's going to worry about us."

"I doubt it. She doesn't worry about Aunt Jane being so far away." Her voice had taken on that icy shell it got when she was arguing. "You just go play. I'm going to concentrate on Whispering to Aunt Jane that I want her to come find us. Jane has the most powerful Hearing of anyone in the world!" She closed her eyes and mouthed wishes I couldn't Hear. Each time she opened them, her eyebrows drooped with disappointment that Aunt Jane had not yet appeared.

My new white school sneakers were gray with sand dust. Slowly I pulled the Velcro tab off one, then the other, took them off, and shook them out, concentrating on removing every pebble and grain of sand. I could have cried. But I wanted to be brave because I was a big kid now, ready for school. So instead I decided to pretend we were on vacation. While Jess Whispered to Aunt Jane, I played quietly in the waves.

A few minutes later, Jess dug into her tote and unwrapped peanut butter and honey sandwiches with the crusts cut off. She'd prepared them exactly the way I liked, and when I took a single bite I realized I was starving. I bolted the whole thing and promptly fell asleep. When I woke up, Jess was concentrating on my face, squinting the way she did when she was trying to memorize something so she could draw it later.

"Your eyes and your lips look just like mine," she informed me.

"They do?" I felt a swell of pride. "Maybe it's because we're sisters."

"Duh." Her eyes got that irritated, impatient look, and I knew she was done talking. She jumped to her feet. "Let's play that we're mermaids. No, twin mermaids!"

We were engrossed in a complex mer-family saga, standing in the shade of the rocks, when it happened.

Two motorcycles roared up from each side of Haystack Rock. The riders wore shiny helmets that made them appear inhuman. Identical blue uniforms. Then a squad car with the lights going and a megaphone on top. I was so startled and so scared that my heart suddenly felt huge and sore in my chest. Later we found out the bus driver had tipped them off. They said a bunch of words, probably—in retrospect—something meant to be gentle and calming to a couple of little kids; but all I heard was my own heartbeat, the jumbled buzzing noise of their Whispers, and Jess's scream.

She grabbed my hand and started to run. My shorter legs could barely keep up, but her grip was so tight I thought my hand would break off if I fell behind. One of the cops spoke through a megaphone, going on about how no one was going to hurt us and we weren't in trouble and that our parents were very worried. There was nowhere to go. We were surrounded. But we ran through the sand anyway, tripping on rocks and glass and garbage, running toward the waves and into the freezing ocean, soaking Jess's jeans and my pink overalls to the waist, and all the while her grip on me never loosened, her frantic Whisper never changed: *I wish I could save you, I have to save you. I need to save you.*

6

At first after Icka left, I stood alone by the old dry creek bed, trembling. I didn't know why I felt so cold, or even how long I stood there. It could have been one minute, or twenty. I just couldn't stop shaking, teeth chattering, head down, hugging myself. Then, without my consciously planning it, my platform-stilted legs started moving me back toward school.

I drifted into the caf, where I bought a hot chocolate I knew I wouldn't drink. Something warm to hold on to. My stiff fingers fumbled, and I dropped all my coins and had to apologize to Esperanza, the grouchy lunch lady.

Slouching on a splintery quad bench, I clutched my Dixie

cup and watched as chocolate-scented steam vanished into the air. A trio of geeky boys passed by and ogled my outfit. I tried to smile winningly, but my smile flickered and backfired, refusing to stay up at the corners.

Relax, I thought, willing my shoulders to drop. It's going to be okay now. Look for the silver lining, right? At least I finally got through to her.

But was that *true*? Or did I only believe it because I wanted to? I shook my head and sighed. I was so tired of Icka playing games with the truth, confusing me about what was real and who was right. My cell phone bulged in its special pocket on my bag's strap. I could reach for it, dial Mom's work extension, blurt out the story to her. She'd know just what to say, she'd dole out advice and help me feel better. . . .

Then, with a flash of humiliation, I remembered Icka calling me Mom's clone, her Mini Me.

Maybe I didn't need to call Mom. Icka, much as I hated to admit it, just might have a point that I relied on Mom an awful lot for a fifteen-year-old. In my defense, my Hearing brought up issues normal teens simply didn't have to worry about, and Mom was the only one who understood. Not to mention I slept down the hall from Daughter Number One, the cautionary tale of what happens when kids don't keep their parents in the loop. Still, I was reaching an age where it was embarrassing to have your mother as the first number on your speed dial. Maybe *this* was the silver lining, an opportunity to not go running to Mom for once and start relying on myself. Start trusting myself. If I was strong enough to stand up to Icka, I was strong enough to stand this pain, to comfort myself and move on.

The bell rang, and students mobbed the quad, filling it with sunny laughter, hoots and hollers, bustling movement. Voices, talking and Whispering voices, enveloped me. I leaned toward the sounds and took a tiny sip of cocoa.

The rest of the day zoomed by in a blur of cellophane-wrapped roses, hugs, and Hallmark cards.

In algebra, my study group had pitched in to get me a Starbucks gift card, and the girl I sat next to presented me with a giant kitten-shaped card.

In chem, my lab partner Quint handed me a shiny bronze box: Godiva truffles!

Our other lab partner, renn faire dork Pauline, put her head on the desk and sighed. *Wish I had my own personal Valentine's Day.*

A pang of guilt hit me as I glanced down at my growing embarrassment of birthday riches. Cards, candies, half a dozen hot pink or red single roses with baby's breath. It felt good to have people give me presents, but I hadn't stopped to think it might make someone else feel bad. I tore open the Godiva box and thrust a big milk chocolate truffle at Pauline.

"My chocolate, your chocolate."

"Seriously?" Her eyes got round. "You rock the galaxy, Joy."

"Okay, people." Dr. Kendricks loomed over us, his scowl

cutting into my warm glow. "Let's pretend we actually care about science here!"

As I whipped open my lab notebook, my mind flashed once again on Icka. What she'd said about Dr. K wishing he was a "real" scientist. It occurred to me that Icka wouldn't have had to Hear anything to guess that teaching didn't satisfy him. That was obvious to anyone. How like her to figure something out through common sense, then lie to make it seem like she could Hear things I couldn't! I shook my head, smiled to myself, and flipped to the first blank page. But a tiny part of my brain still worried: What if she really could Hear better?

Near the end of study hall, my phone vibed. I swallowed tightly when I saw it was a text from Parker: omg mr J is insane . . . pop quiz 2day!!! Btw hope ur having a good b-day! :)

My jaw muscles relaxed. She didn't even mention the Ben thing—just moved right past it.

In the lunch line, tons of guys made fun of my outfit, but in a funny or flirty way. Girls wanted to know every detail of my kidnapping. Did they blindfold me? Did I scream and fight back?

When I finally joined my friends at our usual bench, they wouldn't let me apologize for Icka.

"Oh, it's not *your* fault," Helena said, sighing, though I noticed she'd applied a thick coat of concealer and foundation since this morning.

Bree downed a slug of Metro mint water and nodded. "Your sister's . . . how to put this? The spawn of Satan."

Helena grinned, her teeth tinted purple from her açai smoothie. "Wait, does that make Joy's mom Satan?"

"No, Icka was adopted," said Parker, "from a demonic orphanage."

Everyone laughed, and I unwrapped my chicken burrito. We were back to normal.

One weird thing did happen that afternoon. Bree saved my usual seat for me in government, but *someone* had left a single white calla lily on my desk. I raised my eyebrows at Bree. She leaned halfway out of her chair and murmured, "It was that stoner idiot in back. James, or Jamie . . . whatever his name is."

"Good afternoon, citizens!" Mr. Jensen marched to the podium, and Bree snapped back to her seat. I pretended to drop my pencil so I could sneak a peek at the last row. There he was, the boy from this morning. Lanky body hunched over, eyes downcast so his brown emo bangs brushed his desk. I frowned. He hadn't even wanted me to speak to him in front of his friends at the Path, and now he was giving me a gift?

As Mr. J kicked off his daily rant about the evils of the electoral college, I Listened for Wishes. All I caught at first was Mr. J's political angst, surrounded by a torrent of psychic Prayers that there would not be a quiz. Then, from the back of the room, I Heard a soft, low voice:

I hope it makes her happy. I want her to be happy.

I blinked, stunned.

It wasn't the first time I'd Heard someone Whisper unselfishly. Though it wasn't as common as wanting, say, an iPod, some people really did want to make others happy. Others like their wives, their kids, their best friends. But this Whisper had come from a class-cutting stoner boy I hardly even knew. *Weird.*

Did he have a burning crush on me? Or was he just a super-kind person?

Either way, it troubled me that I hadn't noticed.

I twisted around, just in time to see his black backpack disappearing out the classroom door. No one else had even looked up to see him leaving. Mr. J was still talking about the electoral college, his bald dome shining with sweat. I ran my finger down the lily's waxy, bell-shaped petal. Was this—was I—the only reason he'd come to class today?

A folded note landed on my desk. Bree tugged on a strawberry blond curl and looked away. *Ew,* her note said. *Don't touch that thing. He probably stole it from the cemetery!! XO —B*

I shot her a quizzical smile as if to say, "You're kidding, right?" but she just stared back at me meaningfully.

Slowly I pulled back and studied the bloom. Then I poked at it with my pencil tip. On close examination, it did look slightly weathered. And Shadelawn Memorial Park was only a block away from campus. . . . So where would a carless underclassman pick up an unwrapped, not-quite-fresh lily?

He stole it.

From a dead person.

Bree caught my eye, and both of us burst into giggles.

Joy has to get that creepy thing off her desk! her mind Whispered.

I hesitated. As uncomfortable as I was holding a dead person's stolen flower—shudder—it *was* still a gift. His intentions had been good. But it was always hard to resist a direct plea.

I hope there's no such thing as angry ghosts, Bree Whispered. *And I hope Joy isn't keeping the death flower on her desk because she's* into *that guy. I wish she'd throw it away before it contaminates her with gross graveyard germs.*

Then again, I thought, the boy wasn't here to see me. Using a notebook page as tongs, I swept up the lily as if it were a huge bug and carried it to the wastebasket. As I dunked it in, I felt the familiar warm high from giving someone exactly what they yearned for, and grinned. But as I looked up, I saw the stoner boy loping past our classroom window outside. Crap. He'd definitely seen me toss his gift.

Then, to my surprise, he smiled.

I just want her to be happy.

Double crap. I averted my eyes, but I couldn't ignore the guilt building up in my chest. I'd only thrown away the flower to make Bree happy, but in making her happy I'd been cruel to the boy who gave it to me. And now I had been mean to two people—him and Icka—in one day. Was it possible I was on some kind of roll I couldn't stop?

A strange thought popped into my head. Could it be the costume, the goth hooker mime getup, bleeding into my personality somehow? Maybe I should go home, I thought. Scrub off this makeup mask, put on jeans, be my normal self again. But I shook my head. That was crazy, and besides there were only two and a half class periods left.

"Citizen Stefani, you are not immune from tests just because it's your birthday." Mr. J was passing out sky blue half pages to every row. He always copied our quizzes on brightly colored paper, said it gave them more "pizzazz." "Back to your seat, please."

I slunk back to my desk and uncapped a fresh pen. By the time I'd answered every question, I'd managed to shrug off the nagging worry that I was turning into someone else.

7

The wind teased my hair as Waverly Lin's gleaming white '66 Mustang zipped down Rainbow Street. Parker had folded her small body into the makeshift center seat between her sister and me, while I was jammed into the passenger seat, clutching my colorful bouquet to my chest. Backpacks and shopping bags buried my calves. The sparkly wig peeked out from a Macy's bag, rippling like some alien sea anemone.

"So, who's your date for this party?" Waverly demanded, turning her perfectly made-up face toward me. Unlike Parker, she had a heavy Korean accent, but it never stopped her from speaking her mind. In that, and their slender-boned beauty, the Lin sisters were alike. But while Parker dreamed of becoming the first Asian-American president, Waverly's sole ambition was to have fun. She went clubbing every night and answered phones by day in her old high school's main office, her prom queen photo from four years ago proudly displayed on her desk. Just one more example, I thought, of how two people could have the same genes but be from totally different planets.

"I, um, don't exactly have a date," I told Waverly with a little nervous chuckle, bracing for the shocked response I knew would come.

"What?" Waverly jerked her head back. "All those flowers and no date?"

I smiled weakly, shrugged. My pathetic love life was something I tried not to think about, let alone discuss. Guys did crush on me, sometimes—thanks to my Hearing I always *knew*—and I'd go through the motions of flirting. I'd even gone on half a dozen dates, to the movies or the mall . . . but we never really ended up *connecting*. Two flat kisses at the eighth grade semiformal summed up my romantic experience.

Parker was no help. "Maybe you'll hook up with someone tonight." She snuck a sly glance at me. "Quint Haverford's going to be there."

I made a face. Quint and I got along great in chemistry, but we had none. My Hearing told me he was not so much into girls—whether he knew it yet or not. "He's super nice," I said. "I'm just . . . not sure we have sparks."

70

"But he's always talking to you," Parker pressed. "And he's totally your type! He's smart, he's cool"—she tapped out his stellar qualities on her fingers—"he's funny, he even dresses well. . . . God, now that I think about it, he's perfect for you."

"Wow, thanks," I said, because she was complimenting me, in a way. Saying *I* was smart, *I* was cool, etc. But why was she suddenly so into the idea of Quint-plus-me?

Then I Heard her Whisper, *I want Joy to be able to double date with me and Ben!*

Oh.

My chest tightened at the sudden mental image of Parker and Ben holding hands in the front seat of his Land Rover, while I sat trapped in the backseat with funny, well-dressed Quint. A totally icky feeling . . . that was totally Icka's fault. I'd been comfortable with the reality that Ben was out of my class, till she opened her big lying yap this morning and filled me with hope. False hope, I reminded myself. And stupid hope too. Because—reality check—even if Ben *were* to lose his mind, stop liking Parker, and ask me to be his girlfriend, I could never actually date the guy. She was my best friend!

Waverly made a sharp turn into my driveway and parked next to Mom's blue Prius. I banished Ben *and* Icka from my thoughts.

"Promise you'll give Quint a chance tonight!" Parker said, a parting shot as I gathered my things and climbed out.

"You never know, sparks could fly. . . ."

"Yeah, don't be so picky, Joy," Waverly added. "Picky girls end up single."

I glanced from one Lin sister to the other. They were as different as an owl and a peacock, yet those two girls never missed an opportunity to stand by each other. To support each other. Envy rushed through my veins like caffeine, jolting every cell in my body. No, not exactly envy. It was longing. I missed the days when Jessica and I had faced (or hidden from) the world as a team. Today had made it clearer than ever—those days were never coming back.

"All right, all right, I can see I'm outnumbered." I rolled my eyes and grinned to cover my distress. "I'll flirt with Quint at the party. Who knows, maybe sparks *will* fly between us." More likely pigs would fly between us. But the sisters' approving smiles felt like warm water flowing over me.

I stumbled through the front door, my arms so loaded with packages I could barely see ahead of me. Our whole house smelled delicious. Vanilla and cinnamon wafted through the air, growing stronger with every step I took toward the kitchen. Judging from the lack of clutter and angry voices, Icka must not have gotten home yet, or else she was safely locked in her room. Good. At the breakfast bar, Mom had already assembled a battalion of vases to hold my birthday flowers. She was arranging them and nodding into the telephone receiver as I entered.

"Uh huh, yes, definitely." She looked up at me and

winked. "Right, gotta go now," she said to the caller, and hung up—way faster, I thought, than I ever got off the phone with *my* friends. "Welcome home, sweetie!" Her flour-smelling hands reached over to relieve me of an unwieldy bag and several bouquets. "Good birthday so far?"

Before I could decide whether to bring up my mega fight with Icka, the phone rang.

"*Don't* pick that up, please." Mom smiled a little tensely as it bleated a second time. "It's just your aunt Jane with more emotional processing. Now I'm sorry if this makes me a bad sister"—she dropped her voice as if the neighbors might be listening in—"but sometimes I just need a break!"

"Mom. You, a bad sister? You could never be a bad anything." I patted her soft cable-knit shoulder and shrugged away a creeping sense of guilt. If Mom thought she was a bad sister for dodging one call, what would she think when she heard I told Icka to get out of my life forever? How did Mom manage to keep giving of herself, even to the most difficult people?

"I'll call her back soon." Mom sighed. "Poor Jane."

"I know," I said.

Mom's younger sister had always been a star. Whether she was impressing teachers or acing job interviews, she knew how to use her sharp Hearing to her advantage. By age twenty-six, she was VP of sales at a high-tech firm, owned a three-million-dollar home in the hills, and was engaged to a semifamous singer. That, of course, was before.

We still don't know the exact details of what happened

and why—she doesn't talk about it much. But we do know that one day, instead of driving home to her mansion in the hills, Jane began driving north. Before she disappeared into the Olympic rain forest, she sent notarized letters to her family and friends, assuring them she was safe, healthy, and of sound mind (though of course they all doubted the last part).

For an entire decade she lived off the land as a hermit, having little contact with the outside world. Icka and I could count on one hand the times we'd met her in the flesh; she was more a legend to us than an aunt. When she had finally emerged five years ago to rejoin the human race, she looked nothing like the stylish, smiling lady from her old pictures. This Aunt Jane was lean and leathery and serious, her hair streaked with silver. But the biggest change was her Hearing. It was gone.

Instead of even trying to pick up her old life, Aunt Jane sold her house and moved into a studio apartment near Portland's Pearl Street. There she'd sit on the floor meditating, reading, or whittling innocent pieces of driftwood into what would become her bizarre "sculptures." Our family, out of concern, began visiting frequently. I wasn't proud of it, but I always tried to find an excuse to avoid going along. Sitting in a coffee shop with the new, psychically impaired Aunt Jane was painful. Losing my Hearing was an unbearable thought. Worse than having both arms hacked off. What could I say to the victim of such a tragedy? Other than "Um, yeah, school's going well, thanks."

It was Icka, who'd always looked up to Aunt Jane, who seemed to know what to say. The two of them just clicked. Aunt Jane never asked *Icka* how school was going; they talked about the environment and sexism and world politics, like two adults. Two bleak, lonely, broken adults, but still. It was probably as close to a friendship as Icka was going to get in this life, so I didn't begrudge her it.

Besides, the terrible truth was I tried very hard these days not to think about Aunt Jane. I didn't like to think of her, for the same reason I didn't want to visit her: What had happened to her absolutely terrified me.

I drummed my fingers on the counter. Moping about Hearing loss wasn't improving my mood. I needed a distraction, and maybe I could make myself useful while I was at it. I Listened to see if Mom needed my help with anything. Dishes? Mixing batter? Putting the roses in water? Just give me a task.

But Mom was silent. She just stood there gazing at the phone, as if she too couldn't get Aunt Jane out of her mind.

At last, uncertain, I grabbed the scissors and began snipping stems.

"Oh, hon!" Mom turned and waved her hand distractedly at me. "I can take care of that. Don't you want to change out of your costume?" Her eyes darted back to the phone.

I Listened again. Mom wasn't acting like herself. Was she really worried about her sister this time? "It's okay, I'll just take off the shoe— Ow!" I gasped at the sudden sharp, grating pain at the top of my head.

Mom pursed her lips. "Another headache?"

I nodded, still catching my breath.

"If you want to go lie down, I've got things covered here." As if to illustrate this, she turned away from me, bent over the oven, and pulled out a pan of golden brown cakes. "See? Last batch."

"But weren't we going to decorate those together?"

She folded her arms. "Dr. Brooks said you should rest if you have a headache."

"It doesn't hurt that bad." It kind of did, but I wanted to stay and help her in the kitchen. She'd taken the whole afternoon off work to prepare for my party. The least I could do was pitch in.

Mom must have Heard me, though.

"You help out every day, Joy," she said softly. "I hope you know how much I appreciate knowing I can always count on you." She paused and her brow creased, and for a moment I thought she was about to wish that she could count on Dad and Icka the same way. Instead she said, "Honestly, I think I overestimated the workload here," Mom said cheerfully. "You're off the hook!" She started transferring a previous batch of cupcakes from cooling rack to counter. Then she dipped a knife into a Pyrex bowl of pale pink frosting and spread it evenly, expertly, across the first cake.

"Come on, let me do a few." I ran to the sink and started soaping up my hands. But the sweet cupcake smells I normally loved were making me want to gag. My headache was getting worse. Muscle tension, that's all it was, I told myself.

Don't think about Aunt Jane or Icka's stupid warning.

"Go on, shoo!" Mom made a waving gesture with her flour-dusted hands. "I can handle a few silly cupcakes. If you don't feel like lying down," she added, "why don't you go thank your father for his lovely gift?"

"But—" That stopped me. "Dad's home already? Where is he?"

She gave me a look.

"Never mind, dumb question." Beyond eating and sleeping, Dad spent nearly all his time at home in his home office. He even had his old treadmill set up in there and would, when working on a tough case, clear his head by taking a brisk jog to nowhere. I made a face. "Well, at least let me put these flowers in a vase first."

I reached to turn the water on again, but she put her hand over the faucet.

"I can take care of that." Was that agitation in Mom's voice, or was it my imagination?

I was about to insist, but her tone stopped me. If Aunt Jane or something else had managed to upset my super-calm mother, I sure didn't want to add to her stress level.

Then it occurred to me. People who were upset almost always Whispered. They wanted things to be different from how they were; that was practically the definition of "upset." I watched Mom's knife spreading pink frosting with a surgeon's steady hand. Her eyes stayed glued to her task, as if the cupcakes were a matter of life and death, yet her mind expressed no desires. In fact, I hadn't picked up a single Whisper from her since I got home. So she *couldn't* be upset, right? She must just be tired, too tired to think.

Ow, ow, ow. My head felt like someone was probing it with a skewer. "Okay," I agreed, deflated. "I'll stop by Dad's office and then I'll go lie down."

When I was in the doorway, she called after me, "And I do *not* look tired!"

I laughed, which hurt my head enough to make me cringe. "Sorry!"

Some people might think it's weird to apologize for your thoughts, but in our house it was a normal part of life.

I let the back door swing behind me as I ran across the dewy lawn.

Dad's home office was a blue cottage in our backyard, half hidden behind Mom's apple trees. Years ago, when we first moved to Rainbow Street, Grammy and Grandpa Stefani had started Whispering that they'd like to move into the "in-law apartment" and be closer to us. I was in favor; the senior Stefanis were energetic and funny, and loved spoiling us girls with oatmeal cookies and zoo trips. But Dad wasted no time installing his cherry corner desk in the main room and spreading his collection of boring, leather-covered law tomes all over it, and Grammy and Grandpa stayed in their duplex in Salem after all, and only came to visit for birthdays and holidays. In fact, after it was finished, they never set foot in Dad's office. I think they felt hurt.

Then again, Mom and I rarely found ourselves hanging

out here either. Only Icka made a habit of spending time in Dad's space. She claimed to enjoy their lengthy debates on construction defect law, a topic that always made my brain vaporize.

No one answered my three polite knocks, so—as usual—I sighed and went in. I almost tripped over the treadmill.

Dad was at his computer, slumped statue still in his four-zillion-dollar director's chair, staring at a ceiling beam. (No doubt brooding over a defect in its construction.) "Hi, pumpkin." He gave a listless wave in my direction. He'd changed into jeans and a U of O sweatshirt, his second uniform after Armani. I caught a Whisper: *Sure would be nice to have a BMW.*

A BMW? It was all I could do not to groan at some of my dad's Whispers. Despite owning a perfectly nice Mercedes, he was forever desiring some other kind of luxury car. Why couldn't he just be happy with what we had? Or better yet, take TriMet to work, like Mom often did? I just didn't get his car obsession.

Then I remembered why I was here and lifted my hair to show off my bejeweled neck. "Dad, thank you so much for the necklace! It's gorgeous."

Finally he looked at me. A shy smile. "Oh, it's no big deal." He ducked his head and sipped from a glass of wine barely balanced on a mountain of stiff tan folders. "It's nothing."

Nothing? I blinked. How could it be nothing that he'd remembered my birthstone? That he picked out a special, beautiful present just for me?

"I'm just saying, I don't want you to feel any pressure over it," he said.

"Pressure?"

"Like if it's not your thing, if you don't actually like it, don't feel bad."

I was mystified. "But I do like it!"

It was as if he hadn't heard me. "See, my idea was to give you money," he said, shrugging helplessly. "So you could choose what *you* liked best. But your mom, she didn't think cash was a very warm gesture. What do *you* think, Joy?"

I held back a sigh. All our conversations were like this. I never knew what he wanted from me, and I couldn't even Listen in to find out. His Wishes were all about work, cases, cars, *stuff*. "I—I don't know, Dad . . . I just wanted to say thanks, that's all."

"Oh. Oh, okay. Well, good. You're very welcome." Dad cleared his throat and coughed. "So," he said. "Uh . . . how are you?"

We went through the how-are-you-fine-how-are-you script. Dad's face was reddening, just from the stress of chatting with his own flesh and blood. Though his gaze was settled on me, his thoughts were already flying back to work: how much research he hoped to get done today, how bad he wanted to win this case. I couldn't even hold his attention for ten minutes.

"Looks like you're swamped," I said, and pivoted as if to go.

But suddenly Dad leaned forward, shook his head, and

grinned. "Am I ever!" he began. "So much on the docket, Joy, October's shaping up to be even crazier than September was. I've got one deposition Tuesday in Eugene, one in Bend the next day." He leaned back in the chair and pointed his thumbs in opposite directions. "And those damn repair specs for Winchester, they're not even eight-oh-three'd yet, and it's already the seventh. . . ."

I want to get that new paralegal up to speed ASAP.

I nodded, blinking to keep my eyes from glazing over. "Uh-huh . . . ?"

It never failed. My brain spaced whenever Dad spouted legalese, no matter how hard I fought to stay on track. Instead of asking smart questions like Icka would, I caught myself wondering if Ben would wear his ripped jeans to the party, or maybe those tight black ones Parker secretly thought of as "the butt pants." Then I reminded myself it didn't matter; there was no point in thinking about Ben that way. But turning off the thoughts was harder now that Icka's big mouth had made everything complicated.

" . . . and then there's the Tisdale building." Dad was winding down. "Opposing counsel's already harassing me with a whole redwood tree's worth of memos, I swear to you. Demanding ETA, like I could *give* a meaningful ETA without those reports . . ."

Wish they'd stop breathing down my neck.

Again I bobbed my head sympathetically, but I had no clue what he was talking about. ETA? Eight-oh-three'd? Was there something I was supposed to be saying in response

81

here? Should I look concerned? Cheer him up? What do you want from me, Dad?

Times like this made me think how much simpler life would have been if Dad had been a Hearer like the rest of us. Then he would have understood what he was putting me through right now. And maybe I'd have understood him better too. It seemed like he lived in his work world more and more each year, venturing into our living room so rarely that when I did spot him perched on the couch, reading, he looked like a stranger. I glanced at the mug and plate balanced on his printer. Was that breakfast, lunch, or dinner the night before? And why couldn't I shake the feeling that *I* was a stranger in *here*, and when I left his office, Dad would be relieved to see me go?

"I think I'm going to go lie down," I said, and started to explain about the headache, but that's when I realized it had gone away on its own. Maybe it was the fresh air outside. Well, that was one good thing at least. Dad didn't ask for more info. Just nodded and tapped his keyboard to wake up the screen. "Thanks again for the necklace," I added.

"Of course. Happy birthday, honey." The lower half of his face wrinkled into a pained smile. I smiled back, but suddenly—not for the first time, either—all I could think of was how much older than Mom he looked. Even though they'd been prom king and queen of the same high school class at Lincoln.

Even weirder, I couldn't have told you exactly why he looked so ancient. It's not like he had marionette wrinkles and a turkey-gobbler neck like Granny Rowan had had, or a long white beard like Grandpa. Though Dad's jawline had sagged a little since our early family portraits, everything about him said "distinguished." The silver at his temples made him look smart and serious. Even the crow's-feet around his eyes seemed to add to his authority. Wait, that was it—his eyes. They looked old, inside.

Geez. What an awful thing to think about your own father.

Sometimes I was actually *glad* Dad couldn't Hear.

8

An hour before the party's official start, Parker burst into my room wearing the raspberry red minidress we'd found together last Sunday at the mall.

"Ta-da!" She spun, arms out like a figure skater. "So? What do you think?"

The satin hugged her waist, making her curves more dramatic. Her hair, always in a ponytail at school, now fell in soft, flick-tipped waves around her shoulders. Curled lashes, juicy lips, and shimmery chocolate brown eye shadow gave her an air of sophistication.

"Wow," I said.

"What kind of wow is that?" Her forehead got those

vertical wrinkles it gets when she's waiting for a teacher to pass back graded tests. "Good wow, or Waverly-overdid-it-on-the-makeup wow?"

"Park, you look beautiful."

She beamed. "Thanks . . . hey, you do too! Quint's jaw is going to drop."

I gave a little shrug. She was just saying it to be nice; I was dressed down in a sky blue V-neck sweater with a jean skirt and ballet flats. I wouldn't be dropping any jaws, what with my overly pink complexion and pouffy hair (which is the exact shade of mouse brown celebs refer to as their "natural hair color"). Parker, on the other hand, would surely have to help Ben pick *his* jaw up off the floor after he saw her.

An odd lump was welling up in my throat. I tried to ignore it. I'd never been jealous of Parker's being pretty, never.

My hair was sticking up in the back. "Jeez, I better run a brush through this mess."

"Relax. We have plenty of time before anyone shows up." Parker reached for the copy of *Cosmo Girl* on my night-stand. She flipped through the mag while I fiddled with silver hoop earrings and slid on a hint of clear lip gloss. My standard "dress up" routine. I shrugged at my reflection on the wall. I looked . . . normal. Better than this morning, but nowhere near Parker's league.

I fingered my sleeves. Cozy fleece, perfect for a comfy evening reading in the front of the fire. Only what the hell was I thinking, buying it for a Friday night party with guys? I glanced at Parker behind me in the mirror. Any guy looking at both of us would zone in on her and blot me out of his memory . . . at my own birthday party. Mentally I ran through my closet, but none of my outfits were exactly electrifying. I'd never tried to do more with my look than fit in, be "cute."

Maybe I didn't think I *could* do better. There was my freakish height, the aforementioned pouffy hair. I brushed on mascara; maybe my eyes could be pretty, despite their drab olive color, grayish green or maybe greenish gray . . . at any rate, not a shade that poets spilled much ink about.

Icka once said that if I'd been shorter I could have been a career shoplifter or another petty criminal. No witness would notice me for long enough to fill out a description. Har har. Part of me actually missed the ugly costume— I'd never have a reason to wear something that attention-grabbing again.

Waverly had broken it down to us how high school parties worked. You told people to show at eight, but only the most clueless of freshmen arrived on the dot. Most people knew they were supposed to trickle in between eight thirty and nine. So I wasn't worried (much) when the doorbell didn't ring until eight twenty-seven. Still, that sound made us race down the hall, past Icka's closed door—the light was on, but hopefully she'd stay inside reading or painting all night—and down the stairs.

My heart sank when I saw Quint standing on the door-mat, a six-pack of Dr Pepper cradled in his arms. I'd almost forgotten my promise in Waverly's car.

Inwardly I sighed, but outwardly I put on a welcoming smile. "Hey, Quint!"

"Hey." He looked nervous. *Wish I wasn't the first one here.*

"You two go sit down!" Parker's elbow nudged me. "I'm going to see if your mom needs help in the kitchen." She raised her eyebrows as if to say, "Flirt with him, damn it!"

Each of us settled on one end of the couch, like a 1950s couple from some old TV sitcom, waiting for The Dad to come down and grill The Hapless Date. Quint even looked the part of a sitcom guy, with his blond crew cut like a baby chick's down, his classic 501s paired with a black T-shirt.

"Augh." He smiled and gave an exaggerated sigh. "Dr. K *sucks*."

Believe it or not, this broke the ice between us. It was our class motto, repeated daily under people's breaths and reflected in their Whispers. As if by magic, Quint had spir-ited us back into safe familiar territory, lab partners bitching about our sucky teacher. For a minute or two, the conversa-tion bounced along. I just did what I always did, Listened for Whispers and looked for ways to give people what they wanted. But then, inevitably, the science class venting hit a lull, and Quint leaned closer. So close I could smell the alcohol in his hair gel.

"Great sweater," he said, crossing and uncrossing his

legs. *I hope she liked the chocolates.*

"Thanks." Uh . . . was Quint just being nice here, or was he—for some unfathomable reason—flirting with me? Well, I thought, no harm in being nice back. "Hey, thanks for the yummy chocolate," I said. "That was really sweet of you. Oh!" I cringed and laughed at the unintentional pun.

"You have such a cute laugh," he said. Okay, so he was absolutely, positively flirting with me! But just as I thought that, I Heard his mind Whisper, *I wish I could like Joy the way I like Rob Keillers.*

My chest literally stung, as if someone had snapped a rubber band right over my heart. It wasn't like I had a problem with Quint being into guys. No, the problem was, I'd just Heard him wish he was into *me*, and I could never make that wish come true. Yee-ouch.

Over the years, I'd learned I couldn't respond to every Whisper with my name on it. I'd accepted that fact . . . sort of. At least I no longer cried under the covers. Mom didn't have to give me pep talks reminding me of all the nice things I'd done for people, and how I wasn't a failure at all. But still, the first moments always hurt like hell.

Move on, I told myself. Change the subject, that always helps. But to what? I fingered a small hole in the neck of my dull fleece sweater, the sweater Quint had politely complimented. Suddenly I thought of Parker's dress, and how when Ben told her that she looked beautiful later he'd really mean it; he'd say it in a husky voice, looking into her eyes. . . . A wave of self-pity washed over me. Wasn't this supposed to be the one night a year when *I* stood out? And yet I was sitting on the sidelines in my rags, like a clueless Cinderella with no fairy godmother. And of course no prince. "I should have bought a dress, at least," I blurted out. Quint stared at me—my outburst had startled his mind into silence—so I went on. "I just wish I'd worn something more . . . I don't know, special."

"Hmm, lemme think." He rubbed his chin. He was back in problem-solving mode, like in class. Out of flirt mode. (Thank god.) "Okay," he said. "You know what would make that outfit killer? Sexy boots."

"Ah." I shook my head. "See, I never wear boots, because they always have heels. And heels add height."

"Hey, nothin' wrong with being tall," Quint said. "When you showed up in class today in those shoes, *everyone* looked up . . . it was like a supermodel walked in."

I blinked at him. Supermodel, me? Now he was laying it on pretty thick . . . but where was he going with all this flirting?

I want Joy to be my girlfriend, Quint Whispered. *I just want people to think I'm normal, like her.*

Right. Normal like me. What a joke. But as far as *he* knew, Joy Stefani was typical to a T.

Could I make Quint's latest Whisper a reality by becoming his girlfriend? I pictured myself dating him . . . and found the idea not repellent. After all, it probably wouldn't be too different from being Quint's lab partner: lots of joking around, good conversation, the occasional thoughtful present. He was nice, smart, good-looking—all the qualities Parker had rattled off in the car. And since she thought we were such a fab match, I'd be making her happy as well. A two in one.

Footsteps clomped up the front steps. The door burst open and all four upperclassmen guys Parker had invited were standing in the doorway. Ben's white smile lit up the entire room, and I felt my torso leaning toward his brown bomber jacket like a hungry flower leans toward the sun.

"Be-en!" Parker dashed out of the kitchen and pounced on him, flinging her arms around his broad shoulders. His grin widened, and his friends all whistled. I looked away, feeling stung.

"Cool necklace thing," Quint said, reaching out to touch the pendant, all faux casual.

His cold fingers brushing my collarbone clinched it for me. No sparks were ever going to fly between Quint and me. I didn't get anything out of his touch, while being three feet away from Ben made me light up. If nothing else, my feelings for Ben had taught me what attraction was . . . and wasn't.

"You know something?" I told Quint, rising from the couch. "You're damn right about those boots. Stay here, I'll be right back!"

Five minutes later, I'd turned my closet inside out searching for the knee-high silver vinyl boots that Icka had bought me last Christmas. The moment I'd undone the newspaper Icka used as wrapping paper, I'd Heard her hoping she could borrow them. Which made me suspect she'd bought them for herself all along.

They were secondhand but still shiny, with three-inch chunky heels. I'd never worn them once. They weren't exactly my style. But it was my birthday, for god's sake. I could ditch the practical flats for one night at my own party, right?

Crap. Where were those boots? A lost mitten and a long-widowed argyle sock were the only secrets my closet was giving up today. Was it possible Icka had "borrowed" them without asking and not returned them? Of course it was.

I marched down the hall but hesitated a moment before knocking.

On the one hand, I'd said I was done with her.

On the other, I never said I was done with my boots—which she *stole*.

Scarlett was parked in front of the closed door like a sentry, blocking some of the light from inside. "Shoo, Scar." She didn't budge. "Why do you like *her* so much, anyway?" I added under my breath. On some level, it had always bugged me that the dog slept with Icka instead of with me. "She's not even letting you in. Not very nice." I rapped twice. "Icka! I need my boots back. *Now*."

And, you know, maybe part of me just wanted to see her too, see that she was okay after our big fight.

But mostly I wanted the boots.

I banged on the door. "Icka!" Nothing. She was worse than Dad. "*Ick*-ah!"

Downstairs, the doorbell rang, and then rang again, over and over, like an alarm. Guests were arriving in car-sized clumps, and the soft hum of conversation was now a solid buzz.

I realized I'd never actually heard Icka come home. Was she having another political debate with the poor schmoes at Starbucks, berating them for their company's failure to serve direct-trade coffee? Was she holed up in the library with her sketchbook, staying out of my way like I'd asked her to? Or—I didn't want to think this, but—was it possible she was still somewhere out in the woods, drunk? With Icka, nothing was out of the question.

In frustration, I shook the doorknob from side to side like people in movies do for some reason with locked doors when they know full well they're not going to give way.

It gave way.

I barged in, groaning as the familiar stale smells hit me. Paint and dust and smoke, coffee grinds and turpentine. There were windows, in theory, but centuries ago the Vampire Icka had hung mud brown fabric over each pane.

Her room was, also, an unmitigated pile of filth.

Now before you think I'm judging it based on perfectionist standards, we're not talking about just an unmade bed and overfull hamper. We're talking sci-fi and fantasy paperbacks bizarrely grouped into stacks by the foot of the bed, like a staircase for an elf. Olive green paint spattered on the ceiling. Giant, unframed paintings of dead birds and insects hung crookedly from the wall with thumbtacks, occasionally interrupted by posters from old grunge bands like Nirvana. Every square inch of Granny Rowan's antique cherry roll-top desk was covered with a bumper crop of canvases, crumpled notebook pages, magazine cutouts (for her angry psycho collages, no doubt), and a sticky travel mug with the remains of a latte still in it.

I desperately didn't want to look under the bed and was thrilled when I spied the silver toe of one of my boots inside her closet. To rescue them, I'd have to wade through a knee-high sea of books, paint supplies, and other junk. It would be worth it. My silver boots did not belong here. I cringed and cursed my way to the closet, but after dislodging my right boot from a nest of coiled phone wire and putting it on, I could not for the life of me find its mate. Not even when I dug into her pile of Doc Martens and Japanese comic books and paint bottles and other junk like an archeologist. I hit bare floor, but no treasure. Icka had no car, no friends, no boyfriend—where could she have hidden my damn boot? Did she squirrel it away in her locker, out of spite? It would be exactly her brand of petty evil. I stared at the forlorn odd boot on my foot and imagined Icka's smirking, superior mouth as her hand slammed the locker shut. I wanted to scream.

I did scream.

I hope nobody's hurt!

"You okay in there?" A broad-shouldered male figure

93

peeked from the other side of the door. "Hey." Ben Williams was ducking under the doorway, grinning at me. "Looks like I found the birthday girl."

"Oh!" My voice came out trembly and high, like Mickey Mouse. "You're here!" I blushed at how stupid I sounded, stating the obvious. Of course he was here, how else could I be looking at him, talking to him? But Ben Williams wasn't *supposed* to be here in Icka's room. He was supposed to be flirting with Parker. If she came in and saw us alone in a bedroom . . . "I was just about to go downstairs," I said, ditching the squeaky voice this time.

I wish we could stay up here instead, Ben Whispered. My heart skipped. Then his gorgeous green eyes took in The Fortress of Ick. "This your room?" *I sure hope not.*

"Oh no no no. This pit," I said, "is my older sister's room." I hopped on my socked foot toward the bed. "I was just looking for my boots, which she villainously stole." I was hamming it up now; I wasn't even upset about the boots anymore. All I could think of was that Ben didn't want to go downstairs. He wanted to be here, in this smelly disgusting room, with me! "Part of me thinks she buried the other one in the backyard," I added, "and another part of me doesn't even want to know w—"

"Aha!" Ben narrowed his eyes and charged across the laundry sea. My jaw dropped at the view: He *was* wearing the butt pants! From the top closet shelf, he picked up two old computers' logic boards. Between them was the left silver boot.

"Oh my god! How did you see that?"

"The hardware was what caught my eye," Ben admitted, holding up the boot. "Your sister was in my computer class last year, and she'd always take home junk our teacher was going to toss."

"Yeah, well, garbage is sort of a hobby for her." I sank onto the bed and waited to feel the familiar swirl of embarrassment, worry, anger, and defensiveness that came over me when someone I didn't know well dissed Icka.

But he gave me a thoughtful look. "That must be hard for you," he said. "Having a sister that's . . . you know . . ."

"A freakazoid?" I suggested.

"I was going to go with 'different.'" He held up sarc quotes like bunny ears on either side of his head and grinned.

I grinned back. "How about 'interesting?'"

"'A challenge?'"

"'A unique challenge.'"

We both chuckled at our collection of euphemisms. All we were doing was joking around, I reminded myself, just like we had so many times at lunch. Only there we'd been in public, in a group, with Parker inches away. Here we were alone . . . and everything seemed so much more intense. Or was that just my wishful thinking? Normally I didn't even like for things to feel intense. I was the only one of my friends who hated roller coasters, and I had zero interest in ever getting drunk. But this was different. I didn't feel like I was crashing out of control. I just felt brighter, more alive. I finally understood where the expression "turned on" came from.

What Ben did next went beyond the world of lunchtime wit. He slowly sank to his knees, slid the boot along the floor, and guided my left foot into it. "Only one maiden in the land will fit this slipper," he said with mock seriousness. With both hands, he smoothed the material up my calf. I was barely breathing by the time the zipper, and his hands, reached my knee. "Guess you're the one," he said, and smiled so I could see his canines, which were just a little sharp in a sexy way. *I hope I can steal some more time with her,* he Whispered.

My hands were sweating. It wasn't just my imagination: Ben was Whispering about me, flirting with me, and I wanted him to. I'd never felt like this before. Sure, I'd pined in silence for guys who never noticed me. And with those who did, I'd tried to make a fire without feeling any spark myself. But now I could suddenly understand the hunger, the shared urge, that made two people go ahead and kiss. I could picture myself leaning down, crushing his lips with mine, tasting his soft, full mouth . . .

Not that I ever would, of course.

I sighed. Parker was my best friend. So I couldn't be The One.

"Hey." Ben frowned. "You okay?"

I nodded. Oh, this wasn't fair. Not only was Ben hot and fun to be around, but he was turning out to be a thoughtful person too. I forced myself to speak. "Maybe . . . we should get back to the party now."

"Yeah, okay," he agreed. *I hope I didn't just blow it with her.*

That's so not it, I thought miserably. If only you could read *my* mind.

I didn't move, and neither did he. I stayed at the foot of Icka's bed, staring down at my boots (why hadn't I ever worn them before?), and he sat in front of me, facing the door, where unfortunately Icka had seen fit to hang one of the paintings from her gross insect series. A giant winged cockroach.

"That roach is so . . . lifelike," Ben said at last. I giggled. "No, seriously, I didn't know your sister could paint so well."

"She can do everything well," I said, rolling my eyes. "Everything but pass for human."

"Sounds like my little brother." Absently, he encircled my booted ankle with his hand, sending tingles of electricity up my leg. "He cuts class and gets stoned every day so he won't have to deal with life."

"That sucks." I blinked. "Wait a sec. Is your brother a really tall freshman named Jamie or James or something?"

"Whoa, how'd you know that?" Ben laughed, sounding embarrassed. His hand was off my ankle. "Williams is a pretty common name, and we don't look *that* much alike . . . do we?" So it was him! *Please don't tell me everyone at Lincoln knows we're brothers.*

Boy, I knew just how he felt; the last thing I wanted was for everyone at school to mentally associate me with Icka. "It was a lucky guess," I assured him. "He's in my government class. Well, when he shows up."

97

"Which is, let me guess, never." Ben sighed. "Jamie tends to . . . avoid places filled with people, you know? Almost like he's afraid of them." I nodded. "Part of why we don't hang out at school," Ben added. "Or, well, anywhere."

"I never hang out with Icka." Ben and I had more in common than I'd ever realized. "She's not afraid of people. She just hates them."

"See, I can't wrap my mind around that," Ben said. "Hating people *or* being afraid of them." Now both his big hands were encircling my ankles, gently massaging them. I was sure he could feel my pulse through the boot's vinyl. "I'm pro people, myself."

"Me too." *Ba-boom, ba-boom, ba-boom.* Remember Parker, I told myself. "So . . . you want to get back to the party, where the people are?"

"Not at all."

"Me neither," I said.

We both laughed.

I just want to stay right here in this disaster of a room, and kiss you.

He moved up toward me, and I felt my face tilting down toward his. All thoughts of Parker flew from my head as I inhaled Ben's warm scent. If I'd wanted to lie to myself right then, I could have said I was just responding to a Whisper, granting a wish, like at the eighth-grade dance with Erich Grossman, who slow-danced like a wounded ferret and smelled like Right Guard. But Ben Williams smelled like soap and leather and cotton and also like a *guy*. His square

98

jaw was a movie star's jaw. His lips tasted stingingly sweet. I was granting a wish, all right. My wish.

Where did Ben go off to? Hope he didn't leave or something.

Parker! The sound of her Whisper made me pull back from Ben before our kiss was much more than a peck. He blinked at me in confusion, then the door burst open and Parker's slinky outline appeared.

"Oh, there you are!" Her eyebrows knitted as she took in the sight of us, me three inches away from her crush. "Both of you . . ."

9

Parker gazed down on us from the doorway, her beauty cool and composed. Did she know what I'd done? Did she suspect? Terror made me lightheaded as I Listened anxiously for confirmation of my doom.

But all I Heard was *I wish this dress was three inches shorter* and *Ooh, I want to sit next to Ben.*

I let myself exhale. Huh. She didn't suspect a thing.

"Okay, what are we all doing in Icka's room?" Parker flopped down on the floor directly in front of Ben and leaned back to snuggle with him. I Heard him Whisper, *Damn, if only someone hadn't walked in right then . . .* but after a moment or two he put his hands on her shoulders and began to knead them.

"Joy was in here looking for her shoes," he said, sounding calmer than I felt. Then again, he wasn't actually dating Parker—I was the one guilty of betrayal, not him.

Parker glanced at my shiny silver feet and did a double take. "Whoa," she said. "Vinyl. That's so not you."

How do you know it's not me? I thought, feeling irritation cloud my remorse. If I had it in me to make out with my best friend's crush right under her nose, then I wasn't sure I knew what was me anymore.

"Phew, this room reeks like Icka." Parker turned back and touched Ben's arm. "Don't you think?" She gave me a knowing look. "Ben had a class with her."

I nodded. I was feeling very strange. From the moment Parker had sat down right in Ben's lap, I'd felt something tighten in my chest. Jealousy—no, possessiveness.

I had no rights to Ben. If I was any kind of decent friend, I'd swear him off right now. Pluck out this new selfish part of me by the roots, like Mom pulled pigweed from her garden. But there was only one problem. I wasn't sure I wanted to. Because kissing Ben was the most amazing feeling I'd ever had. And if I hadn't been selfish, it never would have happened.

I can't wait to be alone with Ben, Parker Whispered, and I clenched my jaw, wanting and not wanting to be helpful.

A soft moan escaped Parker as Ben's huge hands rubbed her neck. She sounded like Scarlett moaning to be let out, I thought, then felt bad. Parker hadn't done anything wrong;

I had. Now I was thinking snarky thoughts about her, on top of everything?

What the hell was happening to me? The contents of my own mind scared me lately. Meanness, selfishness, disloyalty. No wonder Icka claimed to be horrified by my Whispers.

Using the mattress for support, I pushed myself to my feet. I had to get out of here.

"I'm, uh, going to see if Helena's here yet," I mumbled in excuse.

The staccato tramp of my heels on the hardwood staircase shocked me. Icka was the one who clomped and stomped down the stairs, not me. In the dim downstairs hallway I heard snatches of loud conversation and Whispers carried from the living room:

"Oh my god, awkward . . ."

"Watch, this is how Bree dances!"

Dude, I wish he'd stop boring me with his football stories.

Hope she's not still mad about that joke.

"You two lovebirds or something?"

My party was entering full swing without me. I slipped into the kitchen without being seen.

Mom glanced up from loading the dishwasher. "Honey, what are you doing here? You should be enjoying your party."

"Mom, where's Icka? She did come home, right?"

Mom smiled. "There's no need to worry. Jessica will

be home tomorrow, and—"

"Tomorrow?"

"Well, yes, she's visiting Pendleton U this weekend. Don't you remember?"

I blinked. Pendleton was a small private art college in Portland. It was the only school that went out of its way to woo Icka, hinting at scholarships and inviting her to shadow a freshman student. "But I thought she told their recruiter she'd rather join the Young Republicans than set foot on a private school campus."

"She did," Mom said patiently, "but remember what she said a few days ago at dinner?"

I squinted. Tuning out Icka's dinnertime rants was an art I excelled in.

"How she might be willing to give it a try," Mom prompted, "if we'd all shut up and stop pressuring her?"

"Really?" That did sound like something Icka would say . . . and, if she had to be in downtown Portland, maybe that's what she was referring to when she said she had to go. "I guess I just haven't been paying attention lately."

"Well, you've been busy with your birthday plans. But that's okay," Mom added quickly. "Birthdays are *important*. I know how much you've been looking forward to today." She plunked a spatula in the dishwasher with finality. "Now go, have fun!"

Did her voice sound strained? For someone who was promoting fun, Mom didn't seem like she was enjoying herself much. Her posture was straight as a pencil, her smile was all lipstick and no twinkle. Was something bothering her—being away from her older daughter, maybe? I lingered, Listening for Whispers. "She's only going to be gone overnight, right, Mom?" But the moment I spoke, the crown of my head suddenly pulsed with familiar pain.

"That's right." Mom grinned and snapped her fingers. The sound sent waves of pain through my head, and with it a crunchy noise crackled through my mindscape, on and off like radio static: "Convenient . . . can't . . . party . . . this year . . . Go . . . fun . . ."

Whoa. What the hell was happening? This was worse than just a headache. "Ma . . . someth . . . pening . . . me . . ." I could barely hear myself over the static.

Mom's eyes looked worried as she put her hand on my shoulder. Her mouth opened and closed, but I couldn't understand her reassurances.

"Help me," I tried to say. "I can't Hear you, I can't Hear anything, it's just noise." My palms were now cold and wet with sweat. Icka's warning ran through my head: "I've figured out why you're getting all those headaches. . . . You're about to turn into me." Had *she* ever gone through this?

Or had Aunt Jane, when she lost her Hearing? As soon as my mind went *there,* my heart started booming like I was running wind sprints in P.E. It felt like something truly terrible was happening. I thought of the kiss, my selfishness and disloyalty . . . maybe I deserved something terrible. "Mom . . . I did a really bad thing," I whimpered, feeling as sick and weak as when I had had mono the year before.

But Mom shook her head. "No . . . tie . . . rary," she assured me. " . . . ain . . . ear . . ."

Oh, god, I don't understand anything you're saying! I heard my words only in my mind.

Sympathy crinkled the corners of Mom's eyes. She reached into the cabinet and pulled out a bottle of Tylenol. " . . . own . . . urry," she said. "Doe . . . urry . . ."

Don't worry. I told my heart to stop pounding. I clung to her words like they were a life raft. I could see Mom's lips form the word "migraine." I wasn't dying, it just felt like it. Though my head still throbbed, the static was becoming more intermittent, fading away. But my pulse just wouldn't slow down, like my body was still warning me of danger. I choked down two red-and-blue gelcaps, dry.

Mom patted my shoulder. "A little better now?"

I heard her clearly that time.

"Migraine headache," Mom said grimly. "I'm concerned your stress is getting worse. We need to sign you up for a teen yoga class to help you rela—"

"Was it just another stress headache?" It seemed so much worse. "Headaches can fill your ears with static?"

"Absolutely, they can affect all your senses." Mom stroked my hair. "It seems like the worst of it's passed."

I nodded numbly. Mom must be right. A small part of me understood that I just didn't have the strength to keep thinking about it, not tonight. I didn't have room in my panicky, lustful, guilt-ridden, aching head.

I stepped back into the crowded living room, where I filled a glass with pink lemonade, just to have something to do. The static *and* the pain were gone now, but my head felt sore, tender. I couldn't help wondering—had static-filled headaches ever happened to Icka? I almost wished she were here right now so I could ask her . . . but no, wait, I wasn't talking to her. With good reason. The memory of our fight made my chest feel like it was on fire. Now that I thought about it, if it hadn't been for Icka's stupid "warning" bracing me for the worst, maybe a little static wouldn't have freaked me out of my skull.

Across the room, I spotted Parker and Ben standing next to each other in a cluster of her Youth Service Committee pals. Parker was switched on. Her face glowed as she babbled on about her plans to revive the Lincoln High recycling club. Ben nodded along, but his drifting eyes made it clear to me he wasn't quite as into glass and aluminum as she was. The new selfish part of me was pleased to see Ben looked bored by Parker's save-the-world-through-transcript-padding ambitions, though I'd personally always admired her for being so motivated. Every so often Parker would touch Ben's arm, just for a second. Each time she did it, I felt the same dull ping, like someone was flicking rubber bands at my chest, right below my throat.

Even though the smell of food was starting to make me nauseous, I edged over to the food table . . . just so I wouldn't have to watch the Ben and Parker Show anymore.

Joe Rabinowitz turned to slide his bulky frame toward me. "Heeeey, birthday girl!" Somehow Joe's voice always came out sounding both squeaky *and* sleazy, but he wasn't a bad guy at heart. He was passionate and smart, one of those computer geniuses who would one day become cool, in college or maybe grad school, or let's face it, at age thirty-five. Right now, though, he needed help to carry on a conversation. It was like he expected the whole world to read his mind and draw him out of his shell . . . which meant he and I got along fabulously.

"Hi, Joe!" I greeted him with my award-winning Sweetest Smile.

He grabbed a jumbo shrimp in each hand and grinned back.

Then we both waited.

After a moment of silence, I realized I was waiting for Joe to Whisper something as he always did at this juncture, and Joe was waiting for me to move our witty repartee along a safe, amusing path, as *I* always did. And that's when I first became aware of it: the silence.

Not literal silence; people were still talking. Whisper silence. No one at the party was Whispering. How was that even possible?

Joe stared at me, clearly getting anxious. But I had no idea what was going through his brain. I scrutinized his face. Bobbing square head with black overgelled hair. Dead blank moss green eyes. Game-show host smile, horsey teeth, thuggish chin. Did he always look that creepy and strange? I couldn't relate to him at all. What should I say?

"So," I began brightly, "uh, how are you?"

"How *am* I?" He blinked like I'd just asked the rudest possible question. My heart sank. What did I do wrong here? He just kept staring, slightly shaking his head.

I broke the pained silence after thirty seconds to chirp, "Well, I'm doing really well, myself! Feelin' great. Good day. Good day for a birthday."

"Excuse me," he interrupted my rambling. "I have to go." And he turned on his heel.

From the corner of my eye I saw Jill Johnson picking at the veggie plate, frowning intently, as if she were searching for something in particular. I Listened in, half expecting the static to return. Instead, silence. Weird. Gah, what was Jill looking for? It was driving me crazy. Her long, pale face, framed by auburn curls, gave away nothing about what was going on inside her head. When you came right down to it, without Whispers, what did you have to go on to under-stand people? Memories. The past. Suddenly I remembered all the times she'd Whispered about chocolate cravings in the middle of French class. And luckily, the box from Quint in my backpack still had three truffles in it. "Hey, Jill," I called out, "want a piece of chocolate?"

"Like junkies want heroin." Jill sighed and held up a baby carrot. "But I can't do sugar, I'm trying to lose ten pounds." With a snap, she chomped the carrot in half and added with a full mouth, "Way to rub it in my face what I'm missing."

I cringed. I was just trying to be helpful. "Sorry."

Stunned, I fled back into the kitchen. Mom was putting candles on fifteen of the pink-frosted cakes. "Joy, what are you doing back here already?" Did her voice sound a little sharp?

"I can't Hear anything," I said. "Any Whispers."

"Sweetie. Tonight is all about *you*." Mom adjusted a candle's position and covered over the first hole with frosting. "May I suggest you take a break from Listening in to other people so much, just this once?"

"But it's just so dead quiet out there." I heard the childish fear in my own voice, but I couldn't stop myself. "What if . . . what if there's something wrong with me? With my Hearing? What if it's changing or . . . going away?"

An odd look crossed Mom's face. Impatience? If so, I didn't blame her. I was sounding like a real worrywart, as bad as Helena on school picture day. "Sweetheart, I really think you're worrying way too much." She was bustling around, fiddling with oven settings. "There's absolutely nothing wrong with your Hearing, you just need to relax."

"I guess, but—"

"We put a lot of work into this party, didn't we, and after I promised you I wouldn't let Jessica ruin it, I think it'd be a shame to let your fears ruin it. Don't you think?"

Slowly I nodded. "You're right." It was incredible how Icka had gotten to me with her "warning" and now I was seeing disaster everywhere. Interpreting every coincidence as a sign of doom. Well, I wasn't going to let her destroy my birthday party from afar by making me paranoid. That wasn't fair to me and Mom and all my guests. "I'm going to go have a good time."

"That's the spirit! Here, take a sugar cookie with you."

She pressed the warm cookie into my hand and gently pushed me toward the door.

I bumped smack into Quint in the hallway.

"Hey, you!" I'd completely forgotten about him. Beaming a cheesy smile in his direction, I said, "Check it out . . . you were totally right about the boots."

"Nice." He didn't smile back but folded his arms across his chest. "I was waiting on that frickin' couch half an hour. Did you walk to the mall, buy those boots, and come back?"

"Sorry . . ." I winced and mentally added ditching him to my growing list of not-nice actions. Exhibit Q. "I didn't mean to take so long." Think of a vague excuse to spare his feelings. "I got held up by some drama." Quint shrugged, his mind giving away nothing. I squirmed. It was hard to reconcile his icy demeanor with the sweet boy who'd showered me with candy and compliments earlier. There had to be something I could say to bring that Quint back. I thought of his earlier Whispers. Maybe he still wanted to flirt with me.

"Quint?" I dropped my eyelids halfway, made my voice lower, breathier. "I'm *really* glad to be talking with you again. Let's go sit on the couch together like before." He raised his blond eyebrows as if to say, You must be joking. "This time I won't take off," I added quickly. "Promise. I'm all yours," I'd never flirted so brazenly before, flipping my hair and tossing off cheesy lines. But all I could think of was making things okay, making Quint smile again, making him like me again like before.

He swallowed, then shook his head. "I think maybe you *are* drama," he said, and stalked away.

I dug my nails so hard into my palms they left red half-moons. The phrase "made a fool of myself" kept repeating in my head.

It went on like that for another two hours. I would approach someone, or they'd approach me, and I would have no clue what to say or do. The awkward silences piled up around me, wounding the vibe of the room till I would be forced to take a chance—make a guess at what was the right thing to say—and then screw things up even worse.

By midnight, I was so on edge that when the living-room lights dimmed suddenly, I actually gasped and wondered if I was losing my vision as well. I felt extra stupid when I saw Mom gliding out of the kitchen carrying my birthday cupcakes with all the candles lit. Everyone started singing "Happy Birthday" to me, and at the end they burst into spontaneous applause. I hung my head. After yelling at my sister, kissing my best friend's crush, and acting like a jerk all evening, I was getting applause.

I heard Ben's deep voice urge me, "Make a wish!" For

a crazy moment, I thought about wishing Ben would kiss me again. Then Parker at his side added, "And don't tell us what it is!" and it was that way she'd added onto Ben's sentence . . . it spelled "ownership" as clearly as if she'd kissed him in public. I could wish that Parker would stop liking Ben, but even then she'd already liked him so long it'd be awkward for me to date him. I'd have to wish she'd never liked him in the first place. It seemed dumb to waste a birthday wish on something impossible.

The whole room was staring at me. I was taking too long. I could hear the buzzing of human voices but no words, nothing clear. No Whispers. I couldn't think of what to wish for. I just tried to concentrate on blowing out all the candles, even though without a wish there was no point.

Guests started to drift off soon after that. Instead of presents, I'd asked people to donate in my name to Heifer International, this organization that buys farm animals for poor families all over the world. (Of course, half the people got me presents too because people never listen about stuff like that.) Mom had gone to bed, so Parker read off the grand total of how much my friends had contributed to H.I. for my birthday present: $385.

More applause and I heard people say nice things about me, which made me feel uncomfortable because I knew now they weren't true:

"Oh my god, Joy's such a sweetie!"

"She cares about helping people."

"I can't believe she gave to charity instead of getting presents!"

I saw Ben looking at me with admiration in his eyes. I didn't know what he was thinking, but I bet it was some version of "What a sweet, kind, unselfish girl."

Nobody here knew me at all.

10

Seconds after the last guest left, Parker kicked off her heels and tied Mom's frilly retro apron over her dress. Armed with a Hefty Cinch Sak, she zipped around our living room, loading the bag with plastic cups, plates, cans, and napkins.

I trailed behind her, halfheartedly dunking a cup here, a can there. "How can you have so much energy still?" I complained. "It's like being friends with Wonder Woman." My cheeks were sore from holding up my smile all evening.

Parker shrugged at the compliment and went on stacking cake plates. Her mind stayed silent, closed. I stared at the back of her head, a strange fear pounding in my chest. What did that shrug *mean*? Had she gotten suspicious about Ben?

Was she irritated at me for some other reason? Without my Hearing I felt as helpless as a person suddenly blind, at the mercy of those around me.

"Thanks for everything you did today," I told her. "You made it a great birthday."

"Hey, you're my best friend."

Right, I thought. And I should start acting like it. How many kind words cancelled out a betrayal? How much praise and admiration would I have to heap on her before I'd feel less guilty about wanting to kiss Ben a hundred more times? I had a hunch it didn't work that way, but after making a fool of myself all night I was almost scared to say anything that *wasn't* positive and harmless. "This place looks a hundred times cleaner," I said, bending to DustBust under the couch cushions. "You could put Merry Maids right out of business."

Parker bit her lip. "Must be in my *blood*," she muttered.

Shit. I could have kicked myself. Before saving up the money to open her nail salon, Parker's mom had been a maid. It was one of those things she didn't know I knew, an example of how my Hearing had brought me closer to my friend than she herself would let me get. I'd been so concerned with trying to get on Parker's good side and not making a fool of myself, I hadn't stopped to think how my compliments would make her feel.

Normal people lived in blissful ignorance of how often they stuck their foot in it. Maybe I would too, I thought. Maybe that would be the silver lining, if I was—gulp— losing my Hearing forever.

Which I *wasn't*, I reminded myself. Mom had said it was nothing to worry about. I tried to re-center my thoughts on positivity, but the silence was like empty space, and my mind was all too eager to fill it up with scary thoughts.

We tidied, vacuumed, and loaded the dishwasher without another word.

It wasn't until we were in the bathroom brushing our teeth and washing off our makeup that Parker turned to me and asked, "So what'd you and *Quint* talk about?" She said it casually, but in a sly tone, as if Quint and I were having a torrid affair. Was she hoping we were? Or had she changed her mind about matching us up, like Quint himself had, apparently? Without my Hearing, I didn't want to commit to anything.

I stalled by swishing mouthwash around for forty-five seconds instead of thirty. "We just talked about science, and, you know, some other stuff."

Parker nodded patiently and smiled. "And . . . ?" she prompted. "Any sparks?"

"I don't know."

"Well, is there *potential* for sparks?"

"Um." I looked away. Was there any harm in conceding "potential"? It just meant possibility. Leaving the door open. "Sure," I said, shrugging. "There's potential."

Parker beamed. "I knew it! Call him tomorrow and then call me."

It almost sounded like an order, and I felt myself bristle, just like I had when she told me the silver boots weren't "me." Calm down, I thought. That's just how Parker talks, she's direct. I usually like that. Besides, I have no right to be mad at *her*. I was in the middle of forming a noncommittal open-ended reply when she gasped and grabbed my arm. I felt one of Parker's famous subject changes coming on.

"Oh my god, I *have* to tell you my ideas for the recycling club!"

"Yeah, tell me!" I said, happy to be off the hook about Quint. Though, I couldn't help thinking there was something odd about extolling the virtues of recycling when we'd just packed a landfill with soda cans.

She breezed on. "So. I was thinking Ms. Phelps for adviser. . . . Weekly meetings . . . one activity per weekend. And we can meet on Tues—no, wait. Wednesday? No . . ." She frowned. "Yeah, Tuesday or Wednesday."

Normally I didn't second-guess Parker's plans. But it occurred to me, as it must have been occurring to her, that there was no way she could fit running a new club into her already tightly packed schedule. But I didn't want to sound unsupportive. So I just kept swabbing my face with a toner-soaked cotton ball.

She squeezed toothpaste onto her brush. It was purple, like almost everything she owned. "Whatever," she said as if to herself. "*I* don't have to be at all the meetings."

It was my turn to frown. "You don't?"

"Mmm-mmm!" She brushed, spat, rinsed, and finally said, "See, that's the coolest part of the whole plan. I wouldn't be the club's president. You would."

I shook my head, probably harder and more times than strictly necessary. "I'd like to help you, I mean, if you want me to, but—"

"Joy, I want to help you this time." She smiled at me. "I know how to run a club, so I could advise you, but you'd be the official president. You need something like this," she said flatly. "No offense, but . . . it'd be good for you to polish up your transcript. I mean, how are we going to be roommates at Stanford if you don't get accepted?"

I stared at her. I couldn't see myself as president of anything: running meetings, breaking tie votes, making speeches . . . the thought made my heart race in an unfun way. And I'd never cared about puffing up my transcript with activities because Mom had always made it clear she'd be perfectly content if I went to U of O, like she and Dad did. But none of that mattered. What I felt more than anything else was an immense sense of relief. Parker wanted to be roommates. College roommates—Mom was still friends with hers, Icka and I even called her Aunt Joyce. Parker wanted to be my friend for life. Everything was still okay between us, better than okay. Even though I'd kissed Ben. The universe had taken away my Hearing, maybe, but it was giving me a second chance to be a good friend.

"We *will* be roommates at Stanford," I assured her. "I'll get all A pluses if that's what it takes. I'll even do that stupid SAT prep course my dad wanted Icka to take."

"I'll loan you my PSAT book," Parker said, grinning.

Two magazine quizzes later, she settled into my bed—I

always take the sleeping bag when she comes over because she can only fall asleep in a real bed—and pulled the covers up to her nose. I lay inside the too-warm bag trying not to make noise even though I felt like tossing and turning. As Parker drifted off to sleep, her breathing the only sound in my head, I started to feel alone, and scared.

I'd tried to relax and enjoy my birthday party, tried not to think about Hearing, but alone in the dark I could no longer deny my fears. Something was wrong with my Hearing, had been wrong since the sledgehammer headache with its crunching static took over my mind. What the hell was happening to me? The thought of losing my Hearing, permanently, was almost too much to think about. When Aunt Jane returned from her decade in the woods, she'd lost more than just her Hearing. She'd lost everything. Would I lose all my friends, lose people's respect? When I grew up, would I be unable to cope in a job or a marriage?

Hearing was how I knew how to relate to people. What to say. What to do. How to be normal. Back when I could only Hear clearly by touching someone, I'd been awkward and shy around everyone but family. Would I have to go back to being *that* Joy?

Wait a minute. What if I could still Hear by touch, right now?

Slowly I rose to my knees and crawled over to Parker's sleeping form. A ribbon of moonlight lit up her small, sharply pretty features. Her face had grown so familiar to me, and yet asleep she looked like a different person.

Her twin, perhaps. Relaxed jaw, unlined brow, and those intense eyes turned to off. My hand snaked out and touched the top of her head. I felt the heat of her body, her life stirring behind those closed eyes . . . but no sound.

I sighed.

"What the hell are you doing?" Parker's eyes were no longer closed.

I stepped backward as if from an angry dog. Busted. "Sorry, I just . . . erm, you know."

"No, I don't know. You've been acting really weird tonight, Joy! What's wrong with you?"

"Uh . . ." There was almost no rational reason for me to be standing over her sleeping body, holding her head. So I picked the one thing I knew would excuse me, my Get Out of Jail Free card from the Bank of Parker. "There was a spider."

It worked almost too well. She screamed like a banshee and danced madly across the room in her nightshirt. "Where? Ew, ew, where did it go? Did you kill it?"

"No, it ran off." I waved vaguely toward the back wall, but she'd already flipped on the big light and was pacing.

"We have to find it, okay?" she pleaded. "Joy, you have to kill it, Joy. I cannot sleep—like, ever again—unless you kill it for me." She hugged herself. "*Please* don't let it get me!"

"Don't worry," I said, feeling like the worst friend in the world. "I'll kill it for you."

"Thank you, Joy!" Parker sounded about six. Guilt stabbed at me for the second time tonight. Not only had

I betrayed my best friend, but now I'd roused her from sleep and whipped her into a frothing hysteria. Even Icka wouldn't have sunk that low.

For the next few minutes, I conducted an FBI-level investigation in search of the alleged spider . . . while Parker chewed on her French manicure in the doorway.

"Are you sure it was *on* me?" Was that suspicion in her voice, or just terror? God, how did regular people survive without Hearing? "Wait." Her eyes narrowed. "How could you tell in the dark?"

"I know I saw something . . ."

That's when I spied him, a baby daddy longlegs in the far corner, behind the bed. He was just chilling, trying to look inconspicuous. No way was I going to kill this cute little guy. He wasn't even a real spider. Not to mention, I wasn't real big into killing stuff in the first place, though I wasn't as extreme about it as Icka (who for six weeks ate nothing but fruit and nuts so the green blood of dead plants wouldn't stain her hands, as she put it).

"Maybe you just *thought* you saw something." Irritation was definitely back in her voice. "Imagined it. Trick of the light."

I stared at the daddy longlegs. It stared back at me. I swallowed. "Found it."

"You did? Oh, thank god. I can sleep now."

I prayed she wouldn't come and look, and maybe I could pretend I'd killed it. But the funny thing about Parker is that as much as she fears spiders, she always wants to look at them too. She tiptoed over.

"Oh my god . . . it's huge and gross."

I bit my tongue.

She dashed to the bathroom and returned with a wad of toilet paper, which she handed me with a wide-eyed expression of respect and gratitude.

The daddy longlegs didn't have the sense to move before I smushed him with the tissue. As I carried the little murder victim to the toilet for his ceremonial flushing, I told myself he was probably almost dead from starvation anyway. I probably did him a favor. I scrubbed my hands and tried hard not to think of Icka and her ravings about plant blood.

Parker had already tucked herself into my bed again. When she saw me, she clasped her hands to one side and with a faux Southern drawl cried out, "Ma-a-ah hee-roe!" Then she cracked up.

Now that I'd saved her from giant spiders, things between us seemed back to normal. Even though things within me were very far from normal.

I wasn't aware of falling asleep, only of waking up.

And what woke me was the unmistakable sound of dreaming Whispers. I should explain. When people dream, they express longings just as much as when they're awake, only most of the time it doesn't make any sense outside the dream.

I want to rule the ocean, Parker was Whispering as I came

to on the floor. It was daylight. *I wish I was Queen of the Indian Ocean and ruled over all the sharks.*

I breathed a sigh. I was back, really back. I could have hugged Parker, but it probably would have woken her up, and I didn't want to have to kill anything this morning.

I could really go for a banana split.

My ears perked up. That was actually something I could get her. We still had all kinds of stuff from the party: ice cream, whipped cream, nuts, cherries. I knew we had bananas because Icka was always going on about potassium. But just before I was out the door, I heard her Whisper one more time:

I wish I could trust Joy to stay away from Ben. I hope she knows he'd never actually go for someone like her!

I blinked. It was a dream, I told myself. People Whisper all kinds of things in dreams. I mean, she wanted to be Queen of the Indian Ocean.

But it wasn't just a dream.

And I'd never Heard Parker—or any friend—Whisper something negative about me. I mean, wishing I would walk to school faster was one thing, but nothing *really* bad. My stomach felt cold. She was right not to trust me. Until yesterday I didn't think I was capable of being disloyal, and deep down I still carried an image of myself as a model BFF. But Parker had seen through me. On a gut level, she sensed Joy Stefani wasn't as nice as she seemed to be, at least not anymore. I wiped my clammy palms on my pj bottoms.

The universe had given me back my Hearing, but now it was taking away my friendship.

No.

I was the one who screwed things up. I had to own that, even if it was too late to change it.

Yet, even as I mentally punched myself for what I'd done to my best friend, it was her second Whisper I kept coming back to, like poking at a sore tooth with your tongue. Ben wouldn't go for *someone like me*? What did that mean? Okay, I wasn't a showstopper like Parker, but did she think there was nothing worthwhile or attractive about me? If she thought I was such a boring loser, why'd she want to be my best friend? Why'd she want us to be college roommates, friends for life?

Even worse—I swallowed—was it possible she was right about me being a loser? Other than my Hearing, which no one knew about, was even one single thing about me special? What *did* Ben see in me? What was there to see?

My heart was pounding in my throat so loud I was worried it would wake Parker.

I escaped down the stairs.

11

Maybe I was spoiled. Okay, so I was *definitely* spoiled. But I'd gotten so used to seeing Mom in the kitchen Saturday mornings—frying eggs or sipping chamomile in her robe while Dad drank coffee, or reading one of her inspirational self-help books at the table—that I actually felt a twinge of panic when I saw all the lights were still off downstairs. No kettle on. No smell of coffee. The oven clock read eight thirty-seven.

Nervously I drummed on the counter. Where was Mom? I needed her. I'd left Parker dreaming upstairs, but her cell phone alarm would go off in twenty-three minutes. Even though I knew Mom wouldn't exactly be proud of me for kissing Ben and making Parker not trust me, I needed advice on how to deal with it now. Besides, Mom was the only one who could explain what was happening with my Hearing. Last night my Hearing had flickered out for hours after that awful headache. She'd said it was all just stress, nothing to worry about, but I needed more than assurances. I needed to understand. What exactly had happened to me last night? Could it happen again?

I padded down the hallway toward Mom and Dad's bedroom. Icka could mock me all she wanted for leaning on Mom, and judging from yesterday maybe even *Mom* thought I clung to her too much, but what else was I supposed to do? There wasn't any book on Hearing, no site on the Internet, no one else on earth I could trust to help me. Mom was it.

I knocked on their door like when I was a little kid and had a nightmare. Desperate? Pathetic? I was beyond caring. "Mom?" I called. No answer. "Dad?" I pressed the top of my head to the door and Heard nothing. I turned the knob. Their California king bed was made, a department-store-esque display involving a dozen decorative pillows.

Back in the kitchen, I spied the magnet cow clipped to a note in Mom's round, heart-dotted-i printing.

Joy,
went to go pick up Jessica from Pendleton. Just as a reminder, we probably won't be back by 11, so

make sure Dad doesn't work through brunch with Gram and Grandpa. —♡ Mom

I sighed. Brunch with Grammy and Grandpa Stefani—I'd forgotten all about it myself. Normally I looked forward to seeing them, but the timing was all wrong. Without Mom's soothing presence, I'd get caught in the crossfire of Whispers between Dad and his parents. He never made the slightest effort to please them, always leaving her to smooth things over. Now I'd have to take on that job, and in my present state I wasn't sure I was up to the challenge.

Anxiety froze my fingers, just like yesterday after the fight, so I filled the kettle halfway and twisted the burner's setting to high. Trust yourself, that's what I'd told myself on the quad. It sounded so right, but where had trusting my own instincts gotten me? I'd double-crossed my best friend. Trusting myself wasn't as cool as it sounded, for the simple reason that my self wasn't trustworthy. Which brought me back to the problem of Parker, Ben, etc.

The teakettle whistled. Still deep in thought, I tipped boiling water into a mug and tossed in a packet of mango Ceylon.

What would Mom do in this situation?

Not be in it.

Okay, but what if she was, somehow. What if she was, say, switched into my body in a bizarre *Freaky Friday*–type incident?

I stopped in midstir. I *knew* what Mom would do if she

were me. After all, I'd been hearing—and Hearing—her advice all my life. I didn't need to ask her to know she'd rate a three-year friendship over some cute boy with great lips. Mom would work hard to repair the damage with Parker. Mom would back away from Ben. Mom would be a true-blue friend. The answer was simple . . . so simple it made me wonder why I'd been making things complicated in my mind. Piping-hot tea burned my taste buds, but it was my fault for being impatient to drink it. Maybe Quint was right: *I* caused the drama in my life. I was the drama.

I dropped an ice cube in my mug and winced as my mind hit rewind and fast forward on last night's events: ditching Quint, kissing Ben, lying to Parker, making a fool of myself. The more I looked back on all I'd said and done, the more it felt like I was watching some other person. A selfish, self-centered girl who stepped on other people's toes and didn't care about the consequences. Who only focused on her own desires.

But I *wasn't* that person. Not at heart, anyway. I was a Hearer, someone who tried to make the world a happier place. Hurting people made me feel sick with regret, queasy and achy. Sure, choosing my selfish desires had brought me stolen, golden moments with Ben and that sweet kiss . . . but was any kiss worth this guilt hangover? The answer was no.

It was time to start acting like myself again. That's what

Mom would say if she were here. That's what I felt in my gut.

A couple minutes later, I'd sliced a ripe banana lengthwise and was scooping ice cream into a fancy crystal bowl. Parker liked butterscotch, so I spooned a generous dollop over her sundae, then squirted on whipped cream and arranged three maraschino cherries on top.

When I presented it to her at her bedside, Parker stirred, sat up, and broke into a huge grin.

"Oh my god, Joy, what the hell is that?"

"A feast," I said, "to celebrate the founding of *our* recycling club."

Parker's jaw dropped. "You're going to do it? You're in?"

"I'm so in!"

She bounced from the bed and hurled her arms around me. They were still toasty warm from being under my comforter, and her hair smelled like her green apple shampoo and the soft rose-scented perfume she was wearing last night. After squeezing me tight, she grabbed one of the spoons in my hand and clinked it against the other. "Long live the recycling club!"

I repeated after her, thinking that whatever hassles and stress this club entailed, it would be worth it for how happy it was making Parker.

"Mmm, butterscotch!" She took her first enormous bite. "I love butterscotch."

"I know." I grinned at her.

"God. If I had mutant metabolism, I'd eat ice cream every morning."

"Totally, same here." Not true—I'd eat chocolate cake—but the details didn't matter as much as rebuilding unity with Parker.

I'd love to know why Joy's being such a freak lately.

Freak? The smile fell off my face.

"What." She stared at me.

"Nothing."

God, I wish she'd stop being so damn secretive.

I felt a painful tug. As always, part of me wanted badly to please her, to give her what she wanted. But stop being secretive and a freak? I'd never Heard such a barbed tone in her Whispers before, ever. Besides, I didn't want to *imagine* what she'd think of me if she knew my secrets.

"Joy, why aren't you eating any?"

I took a tiny bite of ice cream, careful not to spoon a cherry or hog too much whipped cream. My mind kept helplessly replaying Parker's words, spinning them over and over. She was the closest friend I'd ever had. Of course I knew her better than she knew me, but that's just what happens when you Hear people's Whispers; you get to know them more than they could ever know you. I'd long ago learned what my sister couldn't, how to be friends with people on unequal terms. The trick was to give them so much they never noticed what you were holding back. But Parker had noticed, and I had no idea what to do to fix things.

* * *

"So what are you doing today?" Parker asked, after she'd showered and changed into one of her work outfits: a camel suede pencil skirt and jacket with a cream silk shell underneath. Ever since Parker turned fourteen, her mom let her be the Saturday receptionist at her nail salon in the mall.

"Not much." I tried to cover the shake in my voice with a yawn. "Brunch with my grandparents. Then probably homework." And a long, long, long talk with Mom.

"Oh, that sucks." *Wish I could afford to sit around today.* I winced. Parker worked from ten to four, scarfing a protein bar during her ten-minute break. As long as she stuck to sale items and outlets, the job meant she could afford a designer wardrobe and fit in with girls whose parents handed them charge cards. Girls like me. Say something nice, I told myself. Change the subject, make her feel better. "I was thinking," I said. "Since I have free time today, I'll jot down all my ideas about our club."

Her face lit up with pleasure . . . and surprise. "You actually have ideas? I mean, already?" she added hastily. But I Heard her Whisper, *Hope she does come up with something! How great would it be if I didn't have to think of everything for once?*

I swallowed hard. It hurt to Hear that, but deep down I knew Parker was right. I'd made a habit of depending on her to take the lead. Running this club could be good for me, and not just because it'd bring me and Parker closer. "Oh, I have tons of ideas," I assured her. "For recruiting, for

131

fundraising, for . . . processes," I finished vaguely. Okay, so I didn't have clue one about leadership, but I resolved to do some research on the internet that very afternoon.

Parker grinned at me. "You're really into this, aren't you?"

Into regaining your trust and being roommates at Stanford? Absolutely. "We are going to save the planet together!" I told her.

"Woot!"

We high-fived just as Waverly's car honked outside.

Shoot, I'd love to hang here and brainstorm with Joy instead of going to work. . . .

I had to concentrate so I wouldn't beam from ear to ear.

Parker gave me a one-handed hug so she wouldn't wrinkle her work outfit. "See you at four!"

"See ya!" I echoed. The four of us, me, Parker, Bree, and Helena, had been meeting at the mall on weekends since school started. There wasn't that much else to do in Beaverton on a Saturday afternoon, and besides, Parker's mom gave us discounts on pedicures.

"Oh, by the way!" Parker ducked her head in the doorway. "Are you going to call Quint?"

Crap. I was wondering when she would ask about him! "Uh . . . I might," I said, ducking my head as if I was shy about a crush. How fake. But it was better than having her suspect the truth.

"Oh, yay Joy!" She clasped her hands together as if praying for us to work out. Then she made the phone sign with her thumb and pinky. "Call me with a full report, okay?"

"Sure thing!" I grinned, and waved good-bye.

A full report?

Why did that sound like she was my teacher or my boss or something?

I sighed. Maybe I was just being dramatic again, like Icka, making life more complicated than it had to be. I loaded my spoon with gooey, melted sundae and tried to enjoy the simple things: the sweet taste of ice cream, the warm feeling of making someone else's day a little brighter. There was nothing I could do about the complex things anyway.

At eleven sharp, I was pacing the living room in a pastel blue cotton dress and the strand of pearls Grammy had given me when I was born. Dad trudged in from his office in rumpled jeans and a sweatshirt only a second before car doors slammed outside and I ran to the door.

"Joy Marie!" Grammy Stefani's round body was lumbering up the front steps. She held out thick, silk-draped arms, though she was too far away to hug me. "Happy birthday, sweet girl."

Grandpa, spry and lean, bounded up the steps in half the time it took Grammy and extended his hand to Dad, who shook it. "Hey there, Bobbo!"

I stifled a giggle as Dad gritted his teeth. Not only were Grammy and Grandpa the only two people on earth who remembered my middle name (I guess it helped that Marie was Grammy's first name), but they were also the only people who called my father Bobbo. He was Robert. Robert C. Stefani, J.D., and anyone who tried a Rob or Bob or Robby or Bobby on him was consistently corrected. But he never tried to correct Grammy and Grandpa. They called him Bobbo all the time and he just gritted his teeth.

"Now where are my blondies?" Grandpa asked, pretending to search around the room for Mom and Icka.

I actually saw Dad roll his eyes. It always seemed to bug him the way his parents made a big deal over my mom and sister having blond hair.

Dad explained Mom was picking up Jessica from a college visit.

"College visit!" Grandpa repeated, nodding with pride as if merely visiting a college was a great achievement. "That Jessica's got a brain that could take her places in this world." *But I hope she's smart enough to stay home instead and be a good wife and mother,* he Whispered.

I blinked. Grandpa thought women belonged at home?

"And you!" Grammy lunged at me with one of her supertight hugs. "You get more gorgeous every time I look at you!" Yet as she made this declaration, I Heard her mind Whisper, *I'd like to see Joy Marie lose five pounds.*

I paused in midhug. Lose five pounds? Had I Heard right? But I wasn't even overweight . . . was I?

And I wish she'd wear a little makeup, cover up that sallow complexion.

My hand flew up to my cheek. Sallow? I caught Dad

studying me and put my hand down. Did I look particularly pale today? It was true I hadn't slept well the past two nights.

I excused myself and marched up to the bathroom, where I applied a coat of foundation and loose powder to what suddenly struck me as a puffy, washed-out, chubby-looking face. I decided it wouldn't hurt me to try one of Helena's "eating plans" just for the week. Only fruits, veggies, and lean protein. The next time Gran saw me, she'd have no If Only Whispers.

My diet met its first challenge a minute later, when Grandpa gifted me with a box of See's caramels. "That's my favorite," he said, smiling. "Go on, open it up and have some!" *Hope she likes it . . .*

I glanced at Grammy and hesitated. If I ate fattening candy, she would disapprove. If I didn't, Grandpa would feel hurt. What was I supposed to do here?

"Let's not spoil Joy's appetite for lunch, Papa," Dad cut in, snatching up the chocolates and setting the box on a high shelf.

"Come on, one or two won't make a difference," Grandpa put a wiry arm around me. "How am I supposed to spoil my granddaughter, eh?"

"We can all have some after lunch," Dad said smoothly. "Speaking of which, we should probably head for the restaurant if we want to avoid the noon rush."

"That's our Bobbo!" Grandpa sighed audibly. "Always having things his own way."

I stared at Dad. I'd never, ever heard him talk about "spoiling appetites" before.

Grammy and Grandpa's favorite brunch spot was called Frannie's, and as usual it was packed with senior citizens, as if some special homing beacon alerted them and only them to its existence. I picked at my wilted Caesar salad and wished I had yummy pancakes and eggs in front of me like everyone else did. Like Grammy, I thought suddenly, who was shoveling in waffles without a Whisper about the state of her own figure. I pushed away the mean thought. They were happening more and more often. I was going to have to watch myself.

"Joy Marie?" Grandpa was talking to me. "You ever thought about getting highlights?"

For a moment I thought he was talking about a subscription to the kids' magazine I used to browse at my pediatrician's office.

Then I realized he meant dyeing my hair.

"Well, I . . ." Again, I hesitated. Till yesterday I'd never considered changing my appearance to look more eye-catching, but like I said, my hair *was* "natural hair color" colored, and the thought of spicing it up intrigued me. Would Mom even let me get highlights? And what would Icka say? That I was copying her, that I was being a sheep/sellout, or both?

Everyone at the table was looking at me to answer. Unfortunately, I didn't know what Grammy, Grandpa, and Dad wanted to hear, because I'd tuned out and missed the opening of the conversation. Was Grandpa talking about how great I'd look blond like my sister, or was this a discussion about how girls were growing up too fast and using too many beauty products in a vain attempt to copy pop stars?

"Oh, what a lovely idea!" Grammy piped up, solving the question in my mind. "With a few gold highlights, you'd look just like a cover model!"

I glanced at her warily. I already knew she thought I needed work.

"Joy's hair is Joy's business." Dad wiped his mouth with finality and laid the folded napkin by his empty plate. "Besides, she looks beautiful the way she is." At that, he suddenly cringed and I Heard one of his classic random-sounding Whispers: *I hope I can find another great secretary to replace Betty.* I barely had time to process Dad's rare compliment before I had to wonder, Was he just phoning in this entire brunch while he thought about hiring staff?

"Well, of course Joy Marie looks great now!" Grammy backed off with a nervous laugh. "Whoever said she didn't?"

"We just thought it might be a nice birthday present," Grandpa added, in what I was starting to think of as his hurt voice. "A trip to the salon for blond highlights."

Dad shrugged. "Only if she wants to." Oh, great, he was passing the buck to me!

"Well, Joy Marie?" Grandpa asked. "How would you like a nice present courtesy of the Stefanis?"

My hand shook as I speared a hunk of dry chicken.

"Um . . . I . . . ah . . . I'll ask Mom if I'm allowed to."
Brilliant! Passing the buck to *Mom*.

"What a good girl you are!" Grammy cried, and ruffled
my dull hair. "Asking Mommy's permission . . . Why, we
should have thought of that ourselves, Grandpa." (Grammy,
for some reason, called her husband Grandpa around Icka
and me, like we hadn't figured out his name was Walter.)

"That's right," Grandpa/Walter said, laughing ruefully.
"Grandparents can't just give the presents they want to these
days, they have to ask the parents' permission for every little
thing. It's like living under fascism."

Whoa. Fascism? Had Grandpa just compared my parents
to Stalin and Mussolini? Was he trying to pick a fight?

Dad took a slow breath, then pushed his plate of salmon
Benedict forward. "Well, I'm stuffed," he said in a friendly
way, as if Grandpa hadn't said any of that. "Are we ready for
the check?"

"*I'm* certainly not done yet!" Grammy said, though she'd
all but licked her plate clean. "Besides, we're in the middle
of a lovely conversation."

"That's right, you have to learn to be more patient,
Bobbo." Grandpa was wagging his finger, scolding Dad like
he was an eight-year-old boy.

But Dad just held up his hands and smiled. "Okay, sorry,
my mistake."

Oddly enough, his apology took the wind out of
Grandpa's sails. His argument "won," he had nothing to
do but sit there clearing his throat and futzing with his

napkin. For five incredibly long, awkward minutes, no one said a word, but I could Hear Grammy and Grandpa Whispering.

I so want Bobbo to lose that gut.

I wish he'd spend more time with us.

How I long to see the girls in church.

Would have been nice if he'd dressed up to show us respect.

Hope next time we come all this way, more than half the family bothers to show up.

Wish Kelli had taught the girls a lady never crosses her legs above the ankles.

Automatically I uncrossed my legs. Then, after a moment, I recrossed them.

"Check, please!" Dad flagged the waitress, and this time no one stopped him.

Back home, when Grammy and Grandpa finally shuffled into their old blue Buick, Dad and I waved good-bye from the street, breathing identical sighs of relief. Then Dad turned to me. "I'm in the mood for vanilla hazelnut coffee," he said. "Shall I make you a mug too?"

I had never been into the bitter taste of coffee, but I said, "Absolutely." Sitting across the table from Grammy and Grandpa, it had felt for once like Dad and I were on the same team, and I didn't want our bond to fade just yet. Besides, it was so rare he gave me a signal of what he wanted me to do. I trailed him to the kitchen counter, watched him measure grounds into a fresh filter. Side by side, we read the newspaper as we waited for the coffee to brew. It felt like we were on the verge of spending actual time together.

"So, was it just me?" Dad switched off the coffeemaker and filled my mug from the pot. "Or were my parents driving you insane as well?"

"No, it was fun," I said automatically, but it felt hollow. Why was I bothering to put a cheery spin on what we both knew was a crappy afternoon? I was like a robot. A lifetime of training had made perky optimism my default setting. I frowned and took my first sip of coffee in years. It wasn't as bitter as I remembered. "Actually," I said, hesitating. "To be honest, brunch kind of sucked."

Dad drained half his coffee, then slowly nodded. "I love them a lot," he said, "but their demands and expectations can be hard to take sometimes. I can only imagine what it must be like for—"

"They kept Whispering about me," I blurted out. "And about you too. They wanted us to be, like . . ."

"Totally different people?" he suggested calmly.

"No. I don't know. Maybe." I sighed. "They didn't used to be like this! When I was little . . ."

Dad looked right at me. "Honey, they've pretty much *always* been like this."

I shook my head, not wanting to believe him, but my chest ached with the sudden horrible realization. If Grammy and Grandpa hadn't changed, if they'd always been pushy and controlling, then that left only one possibility: I was the one who'd changed. My Hearing had grown, matured, just like Icka warned me. I was Hearing things I'd never Heard before. Things I didn't want to Hear. Things like Icka Heard.

"Are you absolutely sure about that?" I set my coffee down. "I mean, like you said, you can't Hear." I hadn't meant the words to sound so harsh.

"Hearing's not the only way to know something, Joy," he said, not sounding offended. "You can use logic, inter-pret the evidence. In my own way, I've been listening to their Whispers all my life." *I wish you could understand what it was like for me.*

My heart skipped a beat. Dad just made a wish, about me. *To* me.

He must have seen my eyes widen because he grabbed his mug and turned. "Lots of work to do," he muttered.

"Dad, wait!" I touched his arm and Heard, *I hope I never make you feel like they make me feel.* "You *don't*," I said.

He winced, then his face relaxed. "Oh," he said softly. "Well . . . good."

"But Dad?" My voice shook at the very thought of say-ing what I was thinking.

"Yes?"

I took a deep breath and decided to trust myself. The last time I had Heard him Whisper about me, I was five; next time I could be thirty-five. I couldn't afford to miss this opportunity. "Sometimes you make me feel confused," I admitted. "And, well, frustrated." Dad cocked his head to one side and narrowed his eyes, listening. "The thing is, I never know exactly what you want from me."

He stared at me. "Want from you?"

"Yes! Tell me." Finally! Why hadn't I thought of asking years ago? "I need to know," I said. "How can I do it if I don't know what it is?"

"But Joy," he said, sounding frustrated and confused himself, "all I want is for you to be happy."

I blinked. There it was again, what Ben's stoner-boy brother had Whispered to me. Now my own father was saying it, and it sounded nice, and I believed him.

So why didn't it make me feel any better?

Dad waited, eyebrows up, for me to say something. But I was having trouble untangling my thoughts, so I just smiled and said, "Thanks, Dad."

"Pumpkin, you never have to thank me for that." He set down his mug, squeezed my shoulder, kissed the top of my head. Then he slipped out the back door to his office, Whispering about defendants and depositions, whatever depositions were.

How could I grant Dad's wish for me to be happy, when what *made* me happy was granting wishes—and Dad's were so far out of reach? I couldn't hire him a great new paralegal or buy him a BMW. Everything he wanted was out of my hands. So how was I supposed to be happy around him?

The phone rang, startling me. I picked it up, glanced at the caller ID. "Oh, hey, Aunt Jane!"

"It's me, honey." Mom's voice was a thin coat of cheer

142

painted over exhaustion. "I called to say I won't be coming home tonight."

Adrenaline pumped through me. "But I have to talk to you. What's going on? Didn't you and Icka—"

"Your sister's not with me," Mom said. "I have no idea where she is."

12

"Joy? Hello?"

I blinked over and over. "You don't . . . know where she
is?" Oh my god.

"Oh, honey, don't worry," Mom said quickly. "I didn't
mean she was lost at sea or something!" Her chuckle echoed
hollow in my receiver. "Jessica's off doing her own thing
today, that's all. Is your Dad home?"

"Wait, what do you mean she's off doing her own thing?"
Panic alarms were going off in my head. The last time I saw
Icka was when I told her to get out of my life, forever. I
hoped that was coincidence—but with Icka, you just *never
knew.* "Weren't you supposed to pick her up?" My mind

was suddenly flashing pictures of that small purple figure disappearing into the woods. . . . "Wasn't she supposed to be waiting for you, at Pendleton?"

"We-elll, as a matter of fact, she *was* waiting for me." The same odd chuckle as before. What was going on here? "She just wanted to let me know," Mom went on, "that she wasn't ready to come home yet."

I felt my jaw relax. "Oh." So Icka was okay—Mom had seen her—but she was just mega-avoiding me. She'd rather hang around some preppy private school today than deal with me. *That's* how much I'd gotten to her. I settled back into a wicker breakfast chair, propped my socked feet on the table, and grinned. I should have told Icka off years ago!

I was totally unprepared for what Mom said next.

"Jessica can't get enough of Pendleton! Her heart's set on going next fall."

My mouth dropped open. For real. I shut it, but it just opened again, like a door in a haunted house. What Mom was saying was impossible. The thought of Icka liking a place that had other humans in Hearing distance, that actually hurt my brain. Ditto with setting her heart on something (assuming she had one). "Seriously?" I managed to say. "But . . . but . . . she so didn't even want to go in the first place. Icka hates school. She hates people." And people hate Icka, I added to myself. Icka equals hate.

"Maybe she's starting to get over it," Mom suggested, as if we were talking about something simple, like a kid kicking an aversion to broccoli. "She told me she was having

145

too much fun to leave and she'd like another day to enjoy herself."

"Fun, she really said fun?" I twisted my hair. "Are you sure she wasn't being ironic?" A crazy idea popped into my head. What if Mom was just *telling* me Icka was okay so I wouldn't worry?

"Honey, she was grinning from ear to ear." Was that pride in Mom's tone, or exhaustion, or something else? I stumbled to my feet and paced the cordless around the table. What if Icka had never even made it to her college visit and was still freezing out there in the woods behind school, all alone? I gripped the white kitchen bar to steady myself. Mom wouldn't flat-out lie to me. This was why I hated the phone: it was so easy to get confused without my Hearing.

"I just . . . I can't believe she liked it." I swallowed. "I mean, she can't stand being forced to Hear other people."

"Try thinking of it this way," Mom said. "Your sister's getting a fresh start, away from us, away from the kids she's known for years. Maybe with these new folks she's not already expecting to Hear the worst."

"Yeah, but still." Though when she put it that way it *almost* made sense. Almost.

"Not to mention?" Mom added coyly. "From what I could see, she and her freshman hosts are fast becoming *best friends. . . .*"

The word "friends" broke me. Crushing the phone to my ear, I speed walked into the living room, socks skidding on the parquet, and pounded up the stairs to make a bee-line for my bed. My comforter still smelled like Parker's shampoo. Friends. I could imagine Icka shivering in the woods, squatting in a rat-infested warehouse, or stumbling drunkenly into a stranger's car—and doing it all just to mess with me and Mom. But having *friends*? "She can't have friends!" I blurted out. "I mean, what kind of losers would like Icka?"

"I like her." Mom's soft voice shamed me. "And more importantly, I love her and want her to be happy." I cringed and curled up in bed, remembering all the times Mom had hoped and wished for Icka to have friends. I'd Heard her Whisper it year after year, when the only people singing around her daughter's birthday cake were Mom, Dad, and me. Mom had held out hope all this time, encouraging Jessica, loving her even when she was hard to love. If I wanted to be like Mom when I grew up, I had a depress-ingly long way to go.

Finally Mom said, "I'd like to chat more, sweetie, but I'm here at Aunt Jane's, and it looks like I'll be staying for dinner tonight, so—"

"What? *Why?*"

She lowered her voice. "Honey, Aunt Jane's not doing so well today."

I stared at the white ceiling. "What's she processing this time?"

"Joy!" I couldn't blame Mom for sounding shocked at my resentful tone; I didn't normally argue with the time she spent supporting her sister. But this time *I* needed Mom's support. What if I lost my Hearing again today, or picked up more Whispers like the ones from Grammy and Grandpa? Mom always knew what to do, how to make me feel better. My stomach was suddenly clenching at the thought of facing the day alone, without her advice to see me through.

I heard Aunt Jane's familiar low voice calling Mom in the background. "Hey, Kel?"

"I have to go. She really needs someone to talk to."

"Well, what if I need to talk to you too?"

"Joy," Mom said, more gently this time. "Your aunt is truly alone in this world. I pray you never know what that feels like." A chill ran down my back when she said the word "alone." Alone, a-lone: like a disease, like a death sentence. I glanced around my neat, all-white room. What *would* it feel like, to be holed up all alone with nothing but my own thoughts ringing in my head . . . for the rest of my life? "You have your friends," she reminded me. "And you can always talk to your father about family stuff."

I started to say I might as well be alone with just Dad in the house, but then I remembered the talk we'd just had about Grammy and Grandpa. I slipped my finger around my topaz pendent. Maybe Dad *was* becoming someone I could talk to. Maybe Aunt Jane did need Mom's support more than I did. Maybe I was being selfish, again. Still, something just didn't feel right.

"I'll be home with Jessica late tonight," Mom promised. "And tomorrow you and I will have a super-fabulous mother-daughter time, okay? I'll make those scones with the vanilla beans! Bye, hon!"

I shrugged at the phone in my right hand and wondered exactly when I had entered this parallel universe in which everyone in my family had changed into someone else.

I was still puzzling over the weird phone call at four P.M. when the 38 bus pulled up to Macy's. Outside my rain-speckled window, gusts of wind were shaking skinny mall trees that were already lit up for Christmas. As I shuffled to my feet behind a gaggle of pantsuit-clad grannies, my pocket buzzed with a text.

It was Bree, our unofficial event planner if Parker was busy. Rain sux. Meet @ SB not McD. I groaned to myself. SB. My least favorite of our serious-rain fallback meeting spots, and not just because it involved a trek across the mall.

Coffee was a stimulant. It made people's thoughts race, made them talk faster, made them Whisper more and louder. Listening in was habit for me, but sometimes the Whispers at Starbucks got so distracting I couldn't focus on what my friends were saying.

I dug my blue plaid umbrella out of my backpack and prepared to flash my bus pass.

I wish I'd stuck it out in veterinary school. I glanced up in surprise at the grizzled bus driver. He stared dully back at me. "You have a good one, miss."

"You too." I tucked my pass back into my wallet. Weird.

In all the times I'd ridden his route before, I'd never Heard him Whisper about anything but traffic.

I opened my umbrella. It jammed—halfway open, half closed. I pushed harder and heard the plink of a tiny metal piece hitting the concrete. Nice.

Ahead of me, one of the older ladies sneezed and Whispered, *Oh, dear, too bad I forgot to pack tissues.* I rushed to pluck a minipacket of Kleenex from my purse and hand it to her. When she smiled and thanked me in a nasal voice, I felt a little better for the first time since Mom called.

Talking to Dad sure hadn't helped. All he did was glance up from his screen for a moment to say he was glad Icka's first college visit went well. Then, he asked how I felt about us ordering Chinese tonight and "each doing our own thing." Translation: Without Mom around to enforce the dinner ritual, he planned to wolf down a few bites of beef chow fun and go right back to working till he passed out in his expensive chair. I'd stared at his face, Listened in for Whispers, but Dad had clearly failed to grasp the bizarreness of the situation. Then again, Dad had never grasped what a big deal it was for Icka to be friendless in the first place, so what did I expect? It's not like he had any friends himself. Well, he had coworkers—he played racquetball at the gym with other lawyers from his firm—but that hardly counted.

A goth chick in a corset was holding open the door to Hot Topic for her identically dressed friend as I approached, and I felt hardness in the pit of my stomach when I glimpsed who was inside. Two of the stoners who'd made fun of me on my birthday lurked by the register, browsing Urban Decay makeup with bored (or maybe stoned?) expressions. I looked for Ben's brother, Jamie, and was glad when I didn't see him. Even if he was a pothead and a thief, he was still too nice for that crowd. I'd Heard his thoughts, and I knew.

By the time I'd trudged down to the ultracrowded Starbucks, my hair was a heavy, wet mop and my mood matched the weather. I surveyed the mobbed cafe from outside. Frustrated mom with screaming toddler, check. Stressed white-shirt corporate guy with BlackBerry, check. Awkward, mismatched couple probably on blind date, check check check. Okay, prospects did not look good. With the Whispers this crew would generate, I'd be lucky to come off as spacey rather than retarded.

Still, I couldn't help smiling when I spotted the back of Helena's brown wavy hair and Bree's bouncy curls.

I bounded up to the tiny, overloaded table for two on which they'd managed to crowd a mound of muffins, cookies, and drinks. "I am *so* glad to see you guys!"

"Hey, Joy!" Helena waved her calorie-free San Pellegrino in salute.

Bree snapped her phone shut and grinned. "Pull up a chair, hurricane hair."

I giggled. "My umbrella broke."

"Oh my god, poor you!" *I hope she gets a new umbrella that's not ugly plaid.*

I frowned. I liked plaid.

A commanding whine drummed its way into my thoughts just then: *Want truck. My truck. All my trucks. Mommy give trucks now.* I forced myself to look away from the crying two-year-old across the room. Tune it out, I told myself. Just let it go, you don't have to Listen to that.

"Did you hear me, Joy?" Bree sounded impatient. "I said we bought you a venti white mocha!" Her sharp chin pointed at a gargantuan paper cup topped with whipped cream.

"Oh, wow, you guys, thanks!" I sat down and took a long, sweet drink. Warmth coursed through me. Being with my friends was just what I needed right now. "You guys wouldn't believe what a weird day I've had," I began. Their eyebrows arched, but before I could tell the story of Icka's newfound coolness, a heavy stream of Whispers bombarded my brain.

I wish he'd stop crying, for the love of—

Hope they'll ask me out to dinner too.

I need you to pick up that phone. Pick up.

I hope she doesn't guess the mocha was really for Ben and Parker.

I looked up. Helena was toying with her bottle cap, trying not to look at me. I frowned again. Why was I catching so many Whispers in here without even trying to?

"So tell us already." Bree drummed her lavender fingernails on the table. "It better be good because we have some *really* good gossip for you."

"Well, my mom called and—"

I just want to slap that woman's kid.

Please don't let this be my last chance at love.

"And she said, um . . ."

I wish fat people didn't post ten-year-old pics of themselves on the internet!

Why can't they put in less goddamn syrup?

If only I'd never gotten pregnant with that loser's baby.

I stared at the young mother, a sweet-faced brunette in a flowered skirt. Had she really just wished her kid unborn? What was going on here? I'd never Heard Whispers like these before. Sure, I'd Heard the crazy old vet on the bus wishing his Rottweiler could bite all the invisible spies who were trailing him, but he was, well, crazy. Ordinary, sane people didn't sound like this. Did they?

What was happening to me?

You are so screwed. I thought of Icka's smug smirk under haunted eyes: *I know why you're getting all those headaches.* But Mom had said my Hearing was already mature, and she'd never given any sign she thought the headaches were connected to our power. Was it possible Icka knew something Mom didn't?

"Earth to Joy. You look like you need protein." Bree pushed her muffin across the table. "Here, take half my marionberry. It's fortified." *Hope Parker doesn't end up ditching us.*

I glanced up, triply distracted. "Um . . . is Parker not coming or something?"

"She just called me," Bree said, casually emphasizing the

last word. "She and Ben were supposed to be here by now but . . . let's just say there was trouble."

Why can't he say "please mommy" instead of "gimme"?

"Trouble?" I said, trying to focus.

Bree leaned in conspiratorially. "So they're down at the Nature Company because Parker wants to show him these amber earrings with a mosquito in them—"

I should have gone for decaf.

Wish I'd never married that snake.

"—cuz her birthday's coming up, whatever, and then suddenly Ben's phone rings—"

I wish you'd pick up, you son of a bitch! Pick up.

"And it was the police on the phone!" Helena cut in, excited.

"Well, mall security," Bree corrected. "As in rent-a-cops." She always liked to remind us she had more street smarts than us because she was from L.A. "So, anyway, it turns out Ben has, like, a brother . . . who's a total JD."

"Shut up!" Helena pinched a piece of muffin between her thumb and forefinger.

Truck. Milk. Up.

I wish I could drop this kid in the dryer sometimes.

Bree mistook my shocked face for a response to her story.

"Yes, my naïve friend, it's true." She patted my arm. "So this little thug gets himself into a fight, in the middle of Hot Topic. He knocked over a whole rack of leather pants, then

154

chucked a bottle of Punky Colour hairspray at the other guy's head."

"Um, freak show . . ." Helena averted her gaze as if it was all happening here and now.

"Can you even believe Ben has a brother?" Bree's green eyes were glittering from the gossip high. "Even *Parker* didn't know."

I swallowed. It must be a different brother, I thought. Jamie wouldn't hurt anyone. "Well, if my brother acted like a retard?" Helena said. "And threw goth hair products? I'd definitely tell people I'm an only child."

She and Bree snickered.

"So, Ben's like, 'Sorry, I gotta go,'" Bree continued. "He rushes off to go bail out his hood brother. And Parker's like"—Bree mimed picking up a phone and lowered the pitch of her voice to imitate Parker—"'I'm going to follow him to Hot Topic.'"

"Oh my god!" Helena pressed her palm to her chest.

"I know, right?" Bree slammed down her espresso. "Obviously he didn't want her tagging along, but she's *so* used to having her own way. . . ."

"Yeah, well." Helena stretched her long legs, jostling the table. "We all know Parker can be kind of a—"

Hope I made a good impression.

Hope I never have to see his ugly mug again.

"Um, Joy, what are you looking at?" Bree scanned the left side of the room after me.

"Nothing. Sorry." My eyes were glued to the well-dressed, middle-aged man and woman shaking hands, smiling. Only instead of smiles I saw one desperate grimace, one plastic mask.

Bree's empty Frappuccino cup sailed over my head into the trash can, startling me back to attention. "—and if it was my brother?" Bree was saying, "I'd let his hairspray-throwing ass fry."

"Parker says their dad's really strict or something," Helena shrugged. "Ben's fake ID says he's eighteen, so he might be able to pass as the kid's guardian, so their dad won't find out."

"Ben's kind of a hero," I said.

"I know," Bree agreed, "and they're totally perfect for each other. It's sick."

"Wish *I* had a boyfriend," Helena said out loud.

Bree's eyes went saucer size and bored into mine. *Please make her shut up before she gets on one of her self-pitying rants.*

"Guys just don't go for heavier girls, you know?"

Bree snorted. "Oh my god, Helena, you're a size five."

"But I'm short, so—"

"*Joy* has a boyfriend," Bree interrupted, digging her elbow into my arm. "Remember that freak in government who gave you a flower? That was so classically funny, right?"

I shook my head. "It wasn't that big a deal."

"What freak gave you a flower?" Helena poked at her stomach mournfully. "No one ever gives me flowers. . . ."

"Can we talk about something else, you guys?" I was feeling pangs at the memory of Jamie's eyes meeting mine after I trashed his offering. "It wasn't really all that funny."

"What?" Bree squinted at me, her clear green eyes suddenly stone. "Oh, yes, it friggin' was, Joy. I was there, hello?" *I wish she'd just let it go and stop challenging me.*

Whoa. I'd never Heard Bree sound irritated like that at me. What had I done to piss her off so much? I felt a flutter in my stomach, shrugged, looked down. "All right, it was *sort* of funny, whatever."

"Hilarious."

My face burned. "Right, okay. Hilarious."

Bree smiled at me. I took three giant gulps of my drink, tried not to care that it was Parker and Ben's. It was still warm and good; making a Whisper come true felt good no matter what. *I hope Parker never comes back,* Bree Whispered. *I want to be the queen bee and have Joy as my little fan girl.*

I choked on my mocha.

"You okay?" Helena jumped to her feet. "Do I have to do that Heimlich thingie from P.E.?"

"No," I croaked. "I'm okay, I'm fine. . . ."

I wish I could take on that whole table of girls, yeah, starting with the blonde.

I gasped. "Whoa!" Mystified, my three friends followed my alarmed glance to the elegant fortyish businessman whose mind had just Whispered that. Was he a threat?

Should we call the police? Or was he just a bored perv with a laptop?

"Stefani?" Bree narrowed her eyes at me. "Are you freaking out?"

"Hey, don't turn into your sister."

"Don't start drawing bugs. Take away her napkin."

Nervous laughter. In my mind, Whispers were taking over, piling on top of each other. The strangers:

Wish I knew enough karate to kick his ass.

I'd like to give her a tonsil massage.

His bags better be packed by the time I get home.

And the friends:

Too bad someone forgot her ADD meds.

I hope she didn't find out what Ben said about her.

I stood, feeling dizzy. "Be right back. Bathroom."

"Okay, *bye!*" Bree said, in an overly sweet voice, as if I was crazy.

Here's hoping she comes back normal.

I wish I knew how many calories were in a bite of muffin.

I shambled into a stall just as sour acid seared the back of my throat. Crashing to my knees, I vomited half a venti white mocha into the toilet. Tears stung my eyes. I gripped the side of the bowl to push myself up. Then I flushed, scraped at my mouth with a smear of tissue, and moaned softly.

Parker's little fan girl? That's how people thought of me?

I couldn't go back. Couldn't go back to the table.

Was that how Ben thought of me? Last night . . . we

connected, it was real . . . he even opened up about his brother. But what was he *really* thinking when we kissed?

My chest ached, but I couldn't stop myself from asking those questions.

"I wish I'd never Heard any of this," I said out loud, and the tears started falling. "I didn't want to know . . . I just didn't want to know!"

No wonder I'd been so quick to brush off Parker's unkind Whisper this morning. No wonder I hadn't wanted to see my grandparents for who they were. I didn't want to know, not about my friends or my family or the rest of the world. I'd rather be clueless, clueless and happy.

Isn't that what I'd been before, happy? A happy little idiot.

The long, rhythmic sobs I was making scared me. They didn't sound like me. I wasn't a crier. Icka was the crier.

Was this what she felt like?

Was this what my life was going to be like, from here on out?

"Get ready. You're about to turn into me."

I rocked back and forth on the cold, hard black-and-white floor.

All I wanted to do was shut this off.

Anything was better than feeling like this. Bring back the headache, the static, the thunderbolt pain. Turn off my Hearing, this time for good. I'd rather spend the rest of my life not knowing what people wanted—not knowing when I was hurting people or being used or making a fool of myself—than spend another minute back in that café.

I stopped rocking. My palms felt clammy, my fingertips stiff and cold. Had I just wished to be rid of my gift, the one and only thing that defined me?

Oh god . . . I *did* wish that.

And I *meant* it.

"Oh, please make this new Hearing go away," I said, but the words were lost in sobs and I only Heard them in my head. "I wish I could make it go, make it all go away. It's just too much, I can't, it's all out of control, I just can't. *Take it. Please. Make it go away. . . .*"

I wish I'd never Hear another stupid fucking Whisper as long as these cigarettes let me live.

"Icka!?" I jumped to my feet. The voice Whispering in my mind was unmistakably my sister's. But what was Icka doing *here*?

I want to kill my Hearing dead, and kill me too if that's what it takes.

"Icka, how did you get in here?" Heart hammering, I spun to face the door, but only my own pale, frazzled reflection greeted me in the mirror. "Hey . . . where'd you go? Where are you?" I passed through each of the two stalls, slamming in the door. I was alone.

This had never happened. I'd *never* Heard the voice of someone who wasn't within a few yards of me.

Was I imagining it?

I pivoted and faced the sink again, forcing myself to gaze in the mirror. My hair poufed wildly in all directions, my

eyes looked bloodshot, and my skin was tinged with gray-
ish green. Slap a hospital gown and straitjacket on me, and
I'd be all ready for my tranquilizer shot. Had the stress of
Hearing so much awful stuff severed my link with reality?
Or maybe—I felt a surge of hope—maybe *all* the voices I'd
Heard today were only figments of my deranged mind, not
real at all?

I stared into my own eyes. They looked worn, pained,
but still sharp. Not that blank, floating, untouchable look
I'd seen in some of the homeless downtown. I sighed, and
my reflection sighed with me. Much as I wanted things to
be different, I couldn't wish myself insane to make them
so. No matter how bad things got, at least I could trust my
own judgment.

And my judgment said, *"I Heard Icka."* How . . . now
that was another question. I was at a mall in Beaverton,
she was on a college campus in Portland. My Hearing had
grown stronger, that no longer seemed in question. But how
much? Was I suddenly so scary powerful that I could pick up
Whispers from thirty miles away? In which case, wouldn't I
also be Hearing the millions of Whispers between us?

I heard the squeak of sneakered footfalls at the exact
same moment I noticed the *things* in the mirror. To the
right of my reflection, by the door. A gleaming white
row of . . . were those *urinals*?

I gulped. I'd been so upset I'd zombie walked into the
men's room!

The door creaked open, and for a pulse the café crowd

roared into my mind. I dove into the end stall just as the door slammed and male voices—familiar ones—took over the room.

"That's the last fuckin' time I try to bail you out of trouble." Ben's voice was preternaturally cool. "You almost cost me Frosh Number One. That makes you officially not my problem anymore." Acid churned in my stomach again. *That's* what Ben sounded like? He thought of Parker as "Frosh Number One"? To hide my girly blue sneakers from view, I climbed—quietly as I could—onto the toilet seat, and stooped forward to peek through the crack between stall wall and stall door.

Jamie's head was bent toward his brother, the bone-straight bangs covering his right eye. He was wearing black jeans and a black T-shirt that said ONLY USERS LOSE DRUGS. "I said I was sorry." His low-pitched voice sounded as soft as it did in his Wishes.

"Whatever. Just don't come home tonight." Ben wasn't even looking at him, he was too busy doing a post-rain hair check, adjusting stray locks that were the same chestnut brown as Jamie's hair, but shinier, brighter, kissed by the sun. "That's free advice," he went on. "Give Dad a day to cool down . . . maybe two." *I want him to stay away as long as possible.*

Jamie stuffed his hands in his pockets and stared at the floor. "The thing is . . ." *Wish I didn't have to ask.* "I kinda don't have any money."

Ben laughed. "I'm not giving you shit, you little parasite," he said. "Go sleep over with one of your drug buddies. Or learn to work your sensitive side, charm some chick into being your sugar mama. Works for me!" He grinned hideously to examine his perfect teeth, then gave himself a smug nod of approval. Ugh! My pulse drummed through my face. I lied to my best friend and endured torturous guilt for *this* self-centered asshole?

"Someone's in here." Jamie turned to squint in my direction, his face suddenly anxious, twitching. No way could he see me through the tiny cracks, I reassured myself. Not unless he had X-ray vision. *I want out of this room!*

"You're such a tool." Ben reached out and flicked Jamie's forehead. "Of course someone's in here, they're probably just taking a shit. Who cares?"

"Are you really not picking this up?" I blinked. Picking *what* up? Jamie glanced toward the door, then lowered his voice so I could barely hear it. "Someone in here is seriously upset."

13

I froze. How the hell could he possibly know how I was feeling? I wasn't even crying anymore when they walked in!

Ben exhaled noisily. "Dude, just block it. Tune it out." I held my breath. Block *what*?

"I can't." Jamie was clenching his teeth, having trouble forming his words. "I'm not . . . like . . . you."

Pick it up. Tune it out. Block it. Were they talking about . . . ? No. They *couldn't* be talking about Whispers.

Mom had always told us our family were the only ones with the gift, and it only appeared in girls. Then again, when I thought about it logically—why had I never done that before?—it was impossible for Mom to know that for certain. What if another family had the gift and Mom just didn't know about them? Even within our family, we certainly weren't in touch with every branch. What if somewhere down the line, hundreds of years ago, the gift mutated so boys could have it too?

In other words, there was a chance that Ben and Jamie could Hear. That it wasn't just our family. That everything I thought I knew was . . . wrong. I rocked back against the wall, struggling to catch my breath. It felt like a soccer ball had slammed into my stomach.

"Holy shit." Jamie's voice went ragged with panic. "Too intense." *I gotta get out of here.*

I forced myself forward and pressed my face to the gap in time to see him leap for the door. Ben lunged after him. Whispered curses went off in my mind.

He needs to get the hell back in here, before those girls see he's my brother—

Let me go, asshole—

Why can't he just act normal *for once!*

Jamie gripped the door handle and pulled. A burst of crowd noise. Then Ben was grabbing his shoulders, using his full weight to drag Jamie off balance, slamming him against the wall beside the urinals. Jamie groaned as the back of his head smacked the tile, and I winced. Ben wasted no time in pinning him.

"Where do you think you're going?" Ben was barely even out of breath. "I told your worthless ass to wait in this john . . . till I leave with Frosh Number One."

"Ben, let me go!" Jamie's eyes were wide. "You *know* what's going to happen to me." Happen to him? Could Hearing my Whispers somehow . . . harm him? And why didn't his brother seem to give a damn?

"Nothing's going to happen." The way Ben was pinning his right shoulder looked painful. "Come on, it's way past time you grew a pair and learned to face this." *I want my brother to pass as normal. I want to be able to stand next to him in public.* I cringed. Did my Whispers about Icka sound as shallow and selfish as Listening to this asshole?

"It's getting worse," Jamie begged. "I can't ignore it, okay? I've tried to before and—"

"You have to *learn* to ignore it, man. Picture a thirty-foot stone Wall around yourself, like Dad says. It works."

"For *you.*"

"Will you stop being such a wuss?" Ben grinned his arrogant grin. "This is going to work for you too." I clenched my fist. He wasn't even listening to his brother's terror. "It won't kill you, it'll make you stronger. Now take a deep breath."

I wish I were stronger. . . . It boiled my blood to see Jamie struggling like this, just to be what that conceited jerk wanted him to be. He inhaled through his mouth like a drowning man gasping for air. Then he blew out a sigh.

"See that?" Ben relaxed his grip on Jamie's shoulder. "It's already getting better. Piece of ca—"

With a wet crack, Jamie's right fist smashed into Ben's

perfect nose. My heart triple-skipped.

A dark ribbon of blood trickled down from Ben's nostrils to his T-shirt before he could tip his face up to stop it. I felt a sick satisfaction, as if the blood had roused some angry spirit I didn't even know lived inside me. Groaning, hands over his face, Ben let go of Jamie and started to back away, but Jamie lurched at him again, fists swinging wildly. The boy who gave me the lily and wanted me to be happy was gone. This Jamie was nothing but rage.

Want to get rid of this. A punch slammed into Ben's gut, and he sagged. *Don't want this power anymore.* Slammed into his throat. *Want to be free of this.* Slammed into his jaw. *Want to be someone else.* Slammed into his ribs.

My stomach was flip-flopping. Angry satisfaction had turned to horror. Oh my god, why wasn't someone walking in to use the restroom?

Ben's body slumped sadly, his head still tipped back, right thumb and forefinger stopping the blood from his nose, other hand protecting his eyes. He wasn't even trying to match his brother's crazy new energy. He was just taking it, punch after punch, resigned to weathering the storm.

My eyes stung with tears, and I closed them. I couldn't watch someone pulverize a face that looked just like his own. How had I ever missed seeing that these two were brothers? They even had the same square jaw. . . .

Low sobs from outside the stall.

I couldn't let this go on. I had to go out there. Try and stop Jamie from killing his brother, whatever the cost was.

Besides, if they could Hear my voice, they already knew who I was anyway.

"Stop hurting him!" I yelled, and jumped down from the toilet.

The instant I opened the stall door, I wished I could have taken the action back.

Because Jamie had already halted his attack—no brave interference from me was needed. He'd backed several feet away, in fact, and was crying. Ben was no longer hunched over, protecting himself from the rain of blows. He and Jamie both stared at me like I'd suddenly grown an extra head.

"Joy?" Ben's mind ran wild with Whispers. *Okay, she better not have heard what we were talking about.*

"That was *you*?" Jamie wiped tears from his cheeks. He looked disoriented. *I wish it wasn't Joy of all people, seeing me like this.* "I just wanted to leave," he said, as if to himself. Then he ran out the door.

I stared at Ben, more confused than ever. If the two of them could Hear, why were they so shocked to see me? And if they *couldn't* Hear, what was going on?

"So, Joy, heh, whatcha doing in the men's?" Ben cleared his throat, attempted to put on his confident game face, but he was bleeding and his jaw was swelling up, so the effect was just kind of goofy.

"I . . ." What could I say? "I had to throw up, so I ran into the first bathroom I saw."

I'll say one thing: Ben's look of warm concern was a

lot more convincing than, say, Bree's. He really had the charm thing down. "Well, I sure hope you're feeling better," he said, hoping no such thing. "And I'm very sorry you had to be a witness to the Ugly Effects of Drugs on Today's Youth." He said the last few words in an ironic TV announcer voice.

"Drugs?" So that was going to be his excuse. "You mean, Jamie was high?"

"Ohhh, yeah. Boy was flyin'." *Hope she buys this.* Ben turned on the hot water, soaked a paper towel, and squeezed it before applying it to his face gently. "He's been experimenting with heavier shit lately," he told me. "It's making him act crazier than usual. But he's come down from it now, thank god."

"Thank god," I echoed, disappointed. What really happened? I wanted to know the truth, craved it so bad it felt like hunger. But I couldn't blame Ben for covering up. Whatever his secret was, it was a family secret.

I stood dumbly, watching him soap and rinse the front of his T-shirt. The iron smell of blood mixed with coconut-scented liquid almost made me gag again, but I had to stay. To let these awful smells and images seep into my memories of last night's kiss, record over them. This broken version of Ben was the real one. I wanted to memorize his face. To never be fooled by it again.

"Meh." Ben scowled at his beat-up reflection, and I thought I might have seen a crack somewhere in his thirty-foot stone wall. In that moment I could have asked him, maybe, almost. About his family. About his gift, whatever it was, and how he'd learned to manage it. I could even have asked him if he ever really liked me, if we connected at all back there in Icka's room. But then Ben rinsed his mouth and spat, did his stupid teeth-checking grin in the mirror, zipped up his brown bomber jacket all the way to his neck. "Hey, I appreciate you not saying anything, 'kay, Joy?" A nod, a cocky grin. *I hope she calls me when she's feeling better.* Unbelievable. He just assumed that I'd swallowed his lame story about the drugs, that I was too sick or too stupid to have caught what had really happened. That I would fall right into line and into his arms again, no questions asked.

"Don't worry," I said, then paused. Was I really going to say this? "I won't tell on you to Frosh Number One." I saw him flinch before I turned and walked out.

14

Gross Businessman was still leering down his latte, Whispering his gross lust for teens.

"Oh my god, we thought you died or something." Helena had worried the label off her empty San Pellegrino. "Parker's here, waiting in line," she added in a hushed tone, like she was trying not to tip off the paparazzi.

"Guess who *you* just missed seeing?" Bree tossed me a wicked grin. "Your boyyyy-friend!"

I shrugged and averted my eyes from the venti cup containing the milky sweet stuff my stomach had just rejected. Someone had moved my chair—for Princess Parker, I guess—and tossed my messenger bag on the floor. Its strap was caught under Bree's chair leg.

"No, seriously, it was him," Bree went on, apparently tired of waiting for my reaction. "Emo boy just ran through here, *crying his eyes out*." She puffed out her overly glossed bottom lip and trailed index fingers down her cheeks to show tears. Helena giggled. "All right, Joy, fess up now. Did you break up with Jamie and hurt his wittle feelings?"

At that, both of them cackled till they were out of breath, as if a person crying was the funniest joke in the world. As I gazed at their happy, reddening faces, I felt this weird sense that I was . . . alone. I'd always pictured "alone" as "not around people," like Icka on her mermaid rock or Aunt Jane in her rain-forest cabin. But this version of aloneness, surrounded by people you used to think were friends, this was even worse.

"Good-bye," I said. They just looked at me strangely, like I'd just spoken a line that wasn't in our script. "I'm going home now," I continued. "I just threw up."

That got a reaction. My so-called BFFs all gasped and shrank away.

Ew, I don't want her to breathe on me with her sick germs.

I hope she stops acting psycho when she's well again.

At their total lack of caring, I felt a strange satisfaction. A sense of letting go, like it was okay for me not to care about their feelings either.

Helena and Bree gazed at me with identical simpering faces of "concern."

"Feel better!" they chorused.

Like you give a damn how I feel, I thought. Hypocrites. My hands shook, the blood thumping in my ears like a battle drum. Blood calling for blood. I bent down, grabbed my messenger bag with both hands, and yanked it, so hard that the strap trapped under Bree's weight nearly tore off.

"Joy, what are you doing?" Bree was on her feet, glaring. I scooped up my bag, perversely pleased that I'd made her do just what I wanted her to without saying a word.

Helena cleared her throat. "Um . . . whoa?" *She can stop being rude anytime now.*

Why the hell should I? I thought. Being super nice and polite sure hadn't won me their respect. Maybe rudeness was underrated. I swung the bag across my shoulder and started hoofing it toward the exit, doing my best to ignore the Whisper storm behind me. Maybe storming out was underrated too.

"Joy!" Too late. Parker was waving madly from near the front of the coffee line. Her camel suede jacket looked rumpled, and her eyes looked tired, probably thanks to last night's fake spider attack. But she was grinning as if seeing me was the best thing that happened to her all day. "Joy, come here."

No way, I thought. She sounded like she was calling her puppy. And the pathetic truth was that on any other day I would have bounded over to her, wagging my tail. But for once this dog had a wish of her own: getting away from all these other people and their Whispers, pronto. So . . . why weren't my legs moving? I glanced at the door, glanced

173

back at Parker. What was wrong with me? Why did it take so much damn effort for me to *not* grant her desire? Was I that well trained?

The Whispers in the room began buzzing thicker, a hot, heavy stew of sound pouring over me. From the red-haired supermodel type at the bar: *I would rather they'd just told me I was adopted.* From a preschool girl in pink overalls: *And I want ten more Bratz dolls, and a TV for my room. . . .* From the sweet-faced lady knitting by the fireplace: *I hope he leaves that hussy not one red cent.*

I must have had a pretty weird look on my face, because Parker slipped out of line and strode up to me. "Hey . . . you okay?" Her hawk eyes zeroed in on my rain-soaked hair nest. "Um, Joy? Do you need to borrow a hairbrush?"

Normally, her implying I looked sloppy would have crushed my confidence. Today it registered like a gnat sting after a thirty-foot cliff dive. "I just barfed up your favorite coffee drink," I said, and prepared for her to pull back in disgust, like the others.

But she gasped, "Oh, *no!* That totally sucks, poor you." Then she whipped out her iPhone. "I'm calling Waverly. She can give you a ride home. You shouldn't have to take the bus when you're sick." Her hand reached out to squeeze my shoulder. *Hope Joy gets better soon.*

A lump rose in my throat. Why did Parker have to be nice to me right then? If I was going to bounce out of here and quit being Joy the Fan Girl, then I needed the strength of my anger. My battle drum. Don't you dare be nice to me, Parker, I thought, trying to call its energy back to me. You don't even think of me as an equal! I Heard you! (*There* it was: *ba-boom, ba-boom.*) Ben wouldn't go for someone like me? Well, news flash, Ben thinks you're fresh meat, he kissed me, *and* I know your mom used to be a maid!

What would happen if, like Icka, I just gave in to the urge to blurt out painful truths? Powerful truths, like poison inside me. I'd vomit them all over Parker, put the poison into *her*. Melt down her steady gaze. Throw her perfect posture off balance. Force her, for once, to feel like I felt.

"Forget it, don't bother calling anyone," I said. Parker stopped in mid dial and squinted at me. "I just . . ." I swallowed, tried again. "You . . . I . . ." And suddenly I knew I didn't have it in me. I was no Icka, much as I right then wanted to be. I didn't know how to attack. What to say and how. Where to start. I'd never fought with Parker. Not even about something small. How many times had Parker remarked it was amazing how we always seemed to think alike? How was I supposed to smash her reality, when I'd never even questioned her movie pick? "Just . . . you know . . . don't worry about it, Park." I hunched my shoulders. "My bus is coming in four minutes anyway." Trained dog.

Parker hesitated, glanced back at the line, which was longer than ever. "Well, okay . . ." she said. "But you'll call me as soon as you get home, right?"

"Sure," I lied, and told myself she had no right to act like some big boss and demand I check in with her. Because if I let myself see that she cared about me, it would only make walking away harder.

That was all pure bullshit about the bus. I had no clue of the TriMet schedule. Plus, no way was I planning to board some Whisper-filled public bus. But I had this feeling Parker wouldn't have been down with letting her poor sick fan girl walk two miles in the drizzling cold. And that was all I wanted to do: go outside, where no one else was stupid enough to be, and slowly make my way home, where I could lock myself in my room and lie in bed, safe in a Whisper-free cocoon . . . for the rest of my life.

To escape the bustling mall, I cut through a foul, putrid-smelling Dumpster alley behind Whole Foods. Holding my nose was a small price to pay for not Hearing Whispers. On Meridian Avenue, cars zoomed by me as I trudged past strip mall after boring strip mall. Whenever I'd hear a car door open in one of the parking lots or spy someone about to dash out of a store, I'd speed up . . . till they were out of Hearing range. As I dashed across the street to avoid a lady with grocery bags, it occurred to me that I was using up a lot of extra energy, trying to get from point A to point B without Hearing a Whisper. But it would have been even more taxing to have to Listen.

Come to think of it, maybe that was why Mom's side of our family—the Hearing side—didn't seem to include a whole lot of success stories. Maybe Hearing *was* a curse.

Even Aunt Sadie, the famous poker player, had ended up hooked on barbiturates. And Blithe, the deaf-mute painter who'd Seen people's "most secret longings," had died in an insane asylum. Mom's own mother, Granny Rowan, had worried her face into a mess of wrinkles early, doing whatever she Heard Grandpa Rowan wish for. When he died, back when I was in second grade, she only lasted six months before she went too. Her whole life was granting other people's Whispers. Even her *Whispers* were about other people's Whispers, as if her mind was all reruns, nothing original. . . . Wait.

It hit me like a sugar rush. I'd only Heard Granny with my weaker child's Hearing.

What if there'd been more to her? A whole, complicated person, hidden behind those anxious gray eyes? Behind those ritual warnings: *I wish you'd be careful biking in the street.* I was just a kid. I saw wrinkles and bicycle anxiety. No one had told me there could be more to a person underneath. And now Granny was gone; I'd never know her.

I dragged one foot in front of the other until I finally hit greenbelt, and then houses.

Rainwater had soaked through my sneakers by the time I turned onto Rainbow Street. Upstairs, the round lock on my bedroom door made a satisfying click when I jabbed it with my finger, ten times harder than I needed to. I peeled off my sodden socks and stuffed the ice blocks that were my feet into magenta fun-fur slippers. Then I remembered the slippers were a Christmas present from Bree. I kicked them off into the wastebasket and pulled on some mismatched socks and the silver boots I wore at the party. Then I went to draw my curtains shut.

Unfortunately, these were the white lace curtains Mom talked me into "choosing" when I was seven. The stupid things were so filmy that shutting them made practically no difference. In the twilight, from my bed, I could still make out the small shapes of the Marshall twins playing and splashing in the puddles in the backyard behind ours. Once I knew it was them, I could even make out some of their Whispers: *I want to play GI Joe.*

I want to play hide and seek!

I want to kick him.

My phone rang. I lunged across my desk to grab it. Mom, please be Mom. But when I recognized Parker's *"Eine Kleine Nachtmusik"* ring, I dropped it on the carpet like a hot lava rock.

Okay, so much for shutting out the world.

Then a lightbulb went off in my head. Leaving the phone where it was, I marched down the hall to Icka's room.

As always, it was tomblike in there. Cool, dark, still. Reeking of moldering corpses. I sprawled across the organic hemp bedspread and stared up at the mocha brown fabric covering the window wall. Now I finally got it, the point of that fabric. In the silence I could hear my own breath, first loud and fast in my chest, then slower and calmer in my belly. I felt blood returning to my icy fingers and toes. I was seriously beginning to rethink the whole idea of aloneness, real aloneness, being the worst thing in the world. There were much more painful experiences out there, especially for someone who could Hear. Icka had known that. For years now, she'd been trying to tell me how bad it was. By the end, she'd been screaming at the top of her lungs. Why hadn't I listened?

Scarlett whined at the door. I opened it and she waddled past me, heading for the foot of Icka's bed. "Scar, no, you can't jump that high," I said, reaching out for her. "I'll pick you up, okay?" But she dodged me and shuffled onto a short stack of books, then up a slightly higher stack right in front of it, and finally onto a plastic milk crate in front of *that* before clearing the bed. Huh. Here I'd thought all that stuff was just mess, typical Icka mess. But apparently it was a dog staircase.

Scarlett's cold nose nudged my hands, like she was starving for attention, which, come to think of it, she probably was. "You actually miss her, don't you?" I patted the cinnamon-colored fur on Scar's neck. "If you could think in words, you'd wish she was here." I lay back in the semi-darkness, and the dog nestled her warm head in my lap. I closed my eyes.

A bright light went on. "Wish you'd finally wake the fuck up, Joy-Joy!" said a sarcastic voice.

Icka. Through bleary eyes I saw her standing over my bed—her bed—in clothes I'd never seen before, a pink tie-dyed peasant skirt and checked lumberjack flannel, gleefully mismatched. "I can't wait to be free like Aunt Jane." To my groggy ears it felt like her voice was washing toward me from every direction, like surround sound in a theater. "I want to start fresh, be a whole new person like Aunt Jane said I could." Her white face loomed over me, Granny Rowan's solemn all-seeing eyes . . . and no mouth. *Just hope these guys can help me find oblivion.*

Speechless, I looked down at her feet, avoiding the ruined face that so resembled mine. She was wearing the silver boots. They shone like the moon. But, no, wait, *I* was wearing those boots now. Or was I still—

I wish you'd wake up and find me. I don't want it to end like this. Her bony hand reached out for mine, but before we could touch she seemed to fall away. Gasping, I instinctively reached out to her from the bed, but all I connected with was cold, slimy seawater.

Then the bed was gone. Icka's room was gone. I was far away, standing on top of Haystack Rock at Cannon Beach. Staring down at the stormy sea as her blond head vanished under its waves.

15

I shot off the bed. "What's going on?" I yelled. "Icka, are you there?" Scarlett barked sternly, as if to say, "It's bad enough she's gone and left me, do you have to rub it in?" But I kept going, shouting at empty air. "Where are you, Icka? What's going on? Can you hear me? What do you mean, oblivion?" The air wouldn't answer.

Icka's game, her stupid Hope and Faith game from years ago, hadn't worked. I'd never Heard her once. Not when she injured herself at the construction site. Not when she lay across the tracks. So how could it be working now?

Where was she?

Was she in *real* trouble?

Back in my room, I picked up my phone with shaking hands. There were two fresh texts from Parker: where r u?? and r u ok??? I ignored them and hit speed dial one.

"You've reached Kelli Stefani—" I punched star star. "Mom," I croaked. "Call me back, it's about Icka! I think she might be . . . in trouble." I winced. Saying Icka might be in trouble was like saying Kobe Bryant might have scored a few points in last night's game. "She could be in danger," I amended. Let Mom think I was jumping to conclusions, being a paranoid worrywart like Granny Rowan. I should have called right after I Heard her in the bathroom. How could I have been so selfish, so caught up in my own stupid problems that I never bothered to check if my sister was all right? I didn't want to waste time waiting for Mom to call back. Aunt Jane's number was stored in the kitchen cordless. I stuffed the cell into my sweatshirt's gigantic middle pocket and ran downstairs.

Dad was sitting at the breakfast table, phone tucked between his ear and shoulder, the Lotus Garden menu spread over a place mat in front of him. "Just a moment," he said to the order person, and turned to me with a smile. "What do you think, should we spring for sweet-and-sour tofu?"

Normally I would have been amazed and thrilled that he remembered my favorite dish, but now I was just twitching to get on that phone. I shrugged. "Sure, whatever."

The second he hung up, I grabbed the receiver and hit pound six.

"Hey there, fellow suffering human," said Aunt Jane's somber voice.

"Hi, Aunt Jane, it's—"

"If you're stuck hearing this stupid message, it means I'm busy creating art or doing my Zen meditation. Or, maybe I'm just feeling a bit antisocial today."

If Dad hadn't been watching with concern from his chair, I would have pitched the phone at the wall. Instead, I waited for the beep. "Aunt Jane, *please* have Mom call me back ASAP. It's Joy," I added, and hung up. Then I stuffed the phone next to my cell phone in my sweatshirt pocket.

"Honey?" Dad raised his eyebrows.

"I'm fine," I said reflexively. Ever since we grew past the Hear-by-touch phase, Dad had left all Hearing-related talks to the expert, Mom.

"You know." Dad swept invisible crumbs off his knees, all overly casual. "Whatever it is, *I* might be able to help. I do give counsel for a living. . . ."

I shook my head. "Thanks, but this isn't lawyer-type stuff. It's—" I almost said, "Family stuff," then caught myself. "Girl stuff."

"Oh." He seemed to slump. "You mean your gift." *I wish I knew the magic words to make it easier.* I squinted at him. Did Dad already know what was going on? *Wish she hadn't Heard Mother and Father judging her, always demanding perfection—*

183

"What?" I blurted out. "Oh my god, that's so not it." Dad blinked. "I don't even care about the Grammy and Grandpa thing anymore." He flinched. "I mean, that's *your* big issue, not mine."

"Okay, okay, you've made your point."

"Sorry." My fingers played with the braided place mat. "Does it, um, weird you out when I do that?"

"Maybe? A little?" Dad rubbed his jaw, then after a moment he sighed and smiled. "All right, yes, a lot." I crushed my thumb into the hard braided material. Ouch. "But I guess if you girls can get used to Hearing Whispers," he added, "the least I can do is get used to it too, right?"

"Dad . . . that's the thing," I said, trying to keep my voice calm. "I'm not sure if I *can* get used to Hearing this much. My power's been changing, or maybe it's growing, I don't know. It's all just so weird."

Dad puckered his brow and leaned closer. "Weird how?"

I hesitated. Could I really do this, open up to Dad about Hearing stuff like I would have with Mom? But he was so clueless. Then again, he was here and she wasn't. "I Heard Icka," I blurted out.

His lips formed a horizontal line of doubt. "But how is that possible? We know for a fact that she's in Portland, and even your mother can't Hear past fifty feet or so."

"All I know is, I Heard her." I filled him in on what happened in the men's room. And then of course I had to explain *why* I was in the Starbucks men's room, that I was throwing up. And *why* I was throwing up—what I'd Heard.

184

(I left out all the stuff about Ben and Jamie—poor Dad was already looking overwhelmed.)

"Pumpkin, you've had a truly rough day," he said. "But . . . Hearing your sister from another city?" He shook his head. "That's outside the realm of plausibility." Yep, saw that coming: lawyer speak. His face had taken on that same inflexible blankness it gets when he's working. A logic trance, Mom called it. When Dad's mind got stuck like this, she'd just smile and wink over at me. Whereas Icka wasn't fazed at all; sometimes she'd even (in her blunt, bitchy tone) point out some little hole in his train of reasoning and instead of being mad, he'd be all impressed.

Maybe I could impress him into taking *me* seriously.

"What about the story of Faith and Hope?" I said, folding my arms across my chest. "Isn't that historical precedent?"

"More like hearsay," he said, smiling. "Honey, that's just an old family legend. A bedtime story. I'm pretty sure one of your great-aunts made it up."

"So what, you think I'm making it up too?" So much for being intellectual. I felt like a frustrated three-year-old. This whole conversation was a giant red illustration of why I never opened up to Dad.

"Of course I don't think you're *lying*." Dad held his palm out, traffic-cop style. "However. You had one heck of a bad day. You threw up earlier. You've been getting headaches. Odds are, you're coming down with something, sweetie." He glanced down at the open menu as if it contained his case notes. "Remember that time you

185

thought you were floating over your bed?"

I rolled my eyes. Come on, that was in second grade. I had a 104-degree fever. This wasn't the same. But how could I dispute his logic? "Dad. Forget probability and evidence and all that lawyer stuff for a second. What if I *didn't* imagine it, and Icka's in some kind of danger?"

"Now, that is two separate what-ifs," he said, calmly. "Even if you did Hear her—big if—there's absolutely no evidence to suggest she's in danger. Mom saw her just this morning."

"But that was hours ago!"

"True, and if anything had happened, we would have had a call from her freshman host, or the RAs in her dorm."

"RAs?"

"Resident Advisers. Not to mention the Pendleton campus has a crime rate next to zero, not counting bike theft."

I blinked. Dad was throwing so many facts at me it was hard to keep them all straight. Let alone argue.

"We both know Jessica has a tendency," Dad went on, "to express herself in, shall we say, strong terms." I had to nod. Couldn't argue with that. "If she had a fight with her new friends, or got homesick, or maybe changed her mind about this being the perfect school . . . that would easily account for what you Heard." Again, I couldn't help but nod. He was making intelligent points. Points I hadn't even thought of. Points that should have been, in theory, reassuring. So why wasn't I *feeling* reassured?

"It's just that she sounded so desperate," I said, almost timidly. "She kept talking about getting rid of her Hearing. On purpose . . . and I didn't even tell you the scariest part. Just now, I fell asleep upstairs and had this dream about her . . . what?" Dad grimaced slightly, and I knew I'd lost him at the word "dream." "It felt really real!"

"Tell you what," Dad said, rising. "I personally see no reason to worry. But if it'd make you feel better, why don't you give Jessica a call in the dorms? Just to say hi."

I stared at my father. Where had he been all these years? Me, call Icka to say hi? What made him think I even had a phone number for her? Was he really not aware his kid was the only teenage girl in America who spurned cell phones? And that, as she and I were no longer what you'd call close, she hadn't bothered to fill me in on her weekend plans . . . much less supplied me with contact info? Not like the subject came up during my big You Are Kicked Out of My Life speech.

Would I call her if I could? The answer came in a heartbeat. It'd be worth me looking like a wishy-washy moron, worth every iota of awkwardness, to hear her bitchy voice on the line . . . and know she was safe.

But I didn't have the phone number. All I had was a clueless dad who wouldn't listen to anything *but* reason, and a mom who wouldn't even call me back.

Before I could update Dad on his daughters' lack of a sisterly relationship, the doorbell made me jump about a foot.

Ever serene, Dad glanced at his Rolex. "Golly, Lotus was fast tonight!"

I rolled my eyes inwardly. Dad's bad sense of time was legendary in our family. It was seven fifty-one, not even ten minutes after he hung up with Lotus Garden. Unless the guy had *teleported* over here, it couldn't possibly be him.

So who was it? I had a sneaking, sinking suspicion. Hint: I was known as her fan girl, and in the past hour she'd left me two voice mails and two urgent-sounding texts. If only Mom was home, I could have asked her to cover for me, say I was too sick to come to the door. But I'd never asked Dad to lie for me, and now wasn't a good time to start: I didn't want him to see me as someone who went around making things up.

I sighed. "I'll get it."

"Thanks, hon!" Dad flashed me a smile. From his posture as he stood, you could tell he thought our talk had gone swimmingly, that he'd solved all my problems using the awesome power of logic. "Cash is on the table out there," he added. *I hope they remembered the wonton soup this time.*

I trudged into the entryway. Well, I'd have to deal with Parker sooner or later . . . at least having something so much bigger to worry about put my issues with her into perspective, right? I leaned forward to press the top of my head against the cold metal door. Please god, please let it be the Lotus people. . . .

From outside, a low, shy male voice Whispered, *Hope this is the right Stefani.*

16

I never thought I'd feel relieved to see Jamie Williams on our porch. But seeing his stupid ONLY USERS LOSE DRUGS T-shirt through the peephole, I let out a leaky-balloon sigh.

Thank god, it wasn't Parker! I wouldn't have to deal with her just yet. Score one, me, finally.

Except . . . what the hell was Ben's brother doing here? Bringing me more funeral flowers? Part of me still ached to know how he'd sensed my distress earlier—did he really *Hear* me? But as Ben had made clear, I wasn't on the family-secret access list anyway. Anyway, Jamie was probably just here to ask me out, not clue me in. I sighed. Harsh as it sounded, the smart thing to do was shake him off. The way he was going, just being seen with him at school would be social suicide, the fast track to turning into Icka 2.0.

Polite but firm, I repeated to myself as I undid the deadbolt and slipped out sideways onto the porch.

Outside it was sprinkling still, and the air smelled like wet grass and pine needles. Jamie stood unsmiling under the porch light's glow, the dark night all around him. His eyes seemed to bore into me. For the first time I noticed they weren't green like his brother's but cider gold. Before I could begin my brush-off, he said, "You know, I thought about this a lot. And I'm not okay with you thinking I'm a drug-crazed psycho."

My heart beat faster. He hadn't come to ask me out, but to set the record straight about this afternoon . . . maybe even tell me his secret! Was it possible—just possible—Icka and I weren't alone after all?

"Hey." Frowning, Jamie waved his hand over me. "You seem kinda distracted," he said. "If it's a bad time—"

"No, no, I'm fine." I splashed on a smile. "So what were you going to say?"

But he tilted his head forward and peered at me with those piercing eyes as if to say, Are you *sure* you're fine? Was I Captain Obvious, despite my smile, or—unreal thought—did he know I was an emotional mess because I was Whispering *straight into his mind*? What if he could Hear me longing to know his secret?

The idea of a stranger Hearing my innermost thoughts

was suddenly real enough to unnerve me. I backed up onto the welcome mat and shoved both hands into my sweatshirt pocket, jostling the two phones, which clattered together. The phones. Mom still hadn't called with news about Icka. I hadn't called Parker back.

"You look really worried," Jamie said. "I should probably go." He turned, then turned back. "Just tell me one thing. Is it . . . the thing you're worried about . . . is it what you saw in there? I mean me? At Starbucks?" As he spoke of the fight, he seemed to slouch and went from meeting my eyes to watching two moths worship the lamp. *God, I hope she's not scared of* me.

Scared? He thought I was worried he'd beat me up? Maybe Jamie *couldn't* Hear what I was thinking. "Believe me," I said. "It's nothing to do with you."

"Really." He folded his arms across his chest. "Talking to a violent nutcase doesn't freak you out at all?"

Why did he not seem to believe me? "No—I mean, you're not a . . . Ben said it was just a bad trip," I finished lamely.

"Yeah, well, Ben makes shit up." He looked me in the eye. "He doesn't want people knowing about . . . about my condition."

"Condition?" The word threw me. "You mean, a medical problem?" Was there really some disease out there, like a liver defect or kidney sickness, that made people unable to stop punching their siblings?

191

"Not medical, exactly," Jamie admitted. "It's more like, I'm different."

"Different how?"

"You know how."

Drawn by an invisible magnet, I took a step closer to him. Tell me.

Please let it be true. He bit his lower lip. "Like you."

Now my heart was really pounding. He suspected me, as I suspected him. All my life I'd feared someone would notice I wasn't as normal as I pretended to be. But I never thought it would be someone like him. His tone wasn't accusing, it was inviting. Inviting me to open up. But why should I trust him? "Me?" I forced a laugh. "I'm, like, really average and boring. Sorry to disappoint you."

Jamie rolled his eyes. "Come on, don't give me that I'm-just-a-cheerleader act. I've been noticing you since school started."

"Seriously, there's nothing special about me." Did he say noticing me, all year?

"I think you're amazing," he added, ignoring my protest. "The way you control it, without any Walls."

Walls, that's what Ben was trying to teach him about . . . by force. What were Walls meant to block out, Whispers? But acting normal meant stowing my curiosity. I wrinkled my forehead. "I have *no* clue what you're talking about."

"How the hell do you do that?" He shook his head as if I'd said something funny or impressive. "You lie easier than most people *breathe.*"

For a moment I just stared. I couldn't possibly have heard right. He didn't just call me a liar. Then I felt the searing ache of my throat tightening, closing up.

"Joy, wait." He took a deep breath as if struggling to compose himself. "Just let me explain."

I pushed my pouffy hair in front of my face, allowed my features to twist into pain. He'd called me a fake. A phony. The only person who'd ever called me out like that was Icka, but she was at least family. She knew we'd both had to learn to lie, to hide our secret. Jamie wasn't family, wasn't even a friend. He was a stranger humiliating me. And I was done sending him mixed signals. "Get the hell off my porch," I heard myself say. The words were half lost in my lump of a throat.

"I swear, I didn't mean to insult you." His voice broke as I spun toward the door. *I wish I'd told her everything from the start. . . .*

Slam.

Inside I blew on my stiff fingers to warm them. The dimly lit hallway's smell of Lemon Pledge felt sterile. Stuffy. And, as always in the silence, Mom's grandfather clock took only about three ticks to drive me nuts. But at least no one in here was calling me a liar.

"Hon, who was that out there?" Dad called from the kitchen.

"No one," I yelled back. "Just Girl Scouts!"

Crap, did that count as a lie? I cringed. So maybe I wasn't a stickler for brutal honesty. But honesty was overrated.

Sure, I put on a happy face even when I wasn't feeling great, pretended to be thrilled by so-so gifts, and giggled at jokes I didn't find funny, all out of politeness, out of kindness . . . to make people happy. Why was that such a crime? Even Mom did it. At least I didn't lie to make people miserable, like Icka. Or tell the *truth* to make people miserable, like someone else I could name.

And yet . . . I'd slammed a door on him. I, polite, kind Joy Stefani, slammed a door in someone's face. It was beyond disappointing. I'd proved my pure niceness was an act, plus I'd done exactly what Icka would do. Worst of all, my short-lived fury didn't even come from the same place as hers, the frustration of walking through a hostile world alone, day after day. Mine came from shame.

Hadn't I spent all afternoon mourning the fact that no one outside my family understood me? And here this guy had—somehow—found me out. He saw through my carefully crafted shell. And I didn't like it.

I wish I hadn't screwed that up.

I almost jumped. So Jamie was still within Hearing range. I'd been cruel to him, but he hadn't gone away. Why not?

I want to talk to her. I have to know if she's like me.

Oh. I held my breath, waiting to feel wretched stomach pains because I failed to cater to someone's Whisper. But nothing happened. No pain, no regret, just the hall clock loudly chiming eight o'clock. I could hide in the house and pretend all I wanted, but deep down, in that same place in my mind where I Heard Whispers instead of silence, I knew the truth. Jamie and I had something major in common. As different as we seemed on paper, I *was* like him.

I took a deep breath and opened the door.

He was sitting on the porch swing, his face calm and contemplative. "You don't have to say you're sorry," he said, waving away the formality. "Just sit here, okay?" He stood and offered me the seat. "Just listen."

I sat in the splintery old wooden swing.

Jamie paced in front of me. "This is all so strange," he said. "I mean, I came here wanting to tell you everything and then suddenly my curiosity got the best of me and I was trying to push you to tell me about *you*. Then I realized . . . I was feeling *your* curiosity."

That stopped me. "You can feel my curiosity?"

"Oh, yeah. It's practically knocking me over." He was watching me closely. "You want to know about me? Well, now you know. That's it. That's my condition. I can feel . . . I *have* to feel . . . what other people are feeling." He leaned back against the railing.

"Wow." Now *I* had to stand and pace. So he did have the gift . . . or some kind of gift. But I didn't quite get what he meant. "How . . . how do you do that?" I said. "You get some kind of message or signal about their feelings and that's how you know what they are?" I had to tread carefully here. Not seem like I understood too easily how his ability worked.

But Jamie seemed surprised. "No," he said, frowning. "I just feel it. The emotion goes through me like a wave.

That's what we call them, in my family, Waves."

"Waves?" I repeated dumbly. Were Waves totally different from Whispers? All this time I'd been thinking he was either a Hearer or normal. I'd never considered there could be a third category, a gift Mom hadn't even known about. "So other people's feelings are Waves to you."

He nodded. "Sounds stupid, I guess. But it's the best way my dad could come up with to explain it to a kid. Waves rise up out of other people, all the time. From here." He touched his chest. "Happy Waves, sad, confused, lonely . . . of course, with a Wall you don't have to feel most of those. They'll just break and bounce off you."

"Okay, you keep talking about Walls. What *is* a Wall?"

"It's just a way of setting your mind, so you're protected from Waves. Supposedly. All the men in our family can do it, except me."

"Except you?"

He shrugged as if it didn't bother him, but I wasn't convinced. "I'm more like an open window than a Wall," he said. "Other people's Waves get inside me, whether I want them to or not. And if they're strong enough, like yours were this afternoon . . . then all I can do is run."

Suddenly I remembered how he hadn't wanted to speak to me in front of the stoners because my presence made them mad. How he fled the classroom when Mr. Jensen spewed vitriol about politics . . . *he tried to leave whenever people got upset.*

I was trembling, and not just from the cold. He'd done

it, just blurted out the truth about himself. I couldn't do that, could I? I scanned the blue-black horizon as if for thunderbolts, but it was just a normal October night—even the rain had stopped. Mom's crystal wind chime jingled in the breeze. Pieces of my mind were also jangling against one another, spinning wildly. Friends aren't family, an old voice echoed. But the logical part of me knew my parents had only built up that "family secret" stuff to shield their daughters from social ostracism. Jamie wouldn't think less of me or spread a rumor about me if I told him. The anti-freak police wouldn't jump out from behind Mom's azalea bush and arrest me. So what was stopping me?

I was lost in my very own logic trance when I saw Jamie at the railing looking away, staring out at the street. *I hope this isn't the part where she points and laughs and runs to tell the story to all her friends.*

God. I'd gotten so caught up in my own feelings, I'd forgotten about *his*. A mistake he himself was incapable of making. Impulsively, I reached out and grabbed Jamie's hand. My palm was ice, but as his fingers closed gently over my hand it became the only part of me that felt warm.

"I don't feel Waves like you," I began. "But I'm not as avera—"

He interrupted. "Never? You don't call them something else or . . . ?"

"No."

"But you believed me. No one but my family's ever believed me before." He squeezed my hand once more, then

197

let go. "I was wrong, I guess." *I wish you had been like me.*

"You weren't entirely wrong about me, Jamie," I said, then shook my head. "I just can't tell you any more than that. I can't. I can't."

"Breathe."

I inhaled, studied the lines on my palm, exhaled. No doubt Jamie could feel the Waves of longing coming from me. The longing to open up, to be honest and real with someone, made me dizzy, like gazing into the void of an open airplane hatch. It wasn't just that we both had gifts, it wasn't just that no one had ever told me a secret of this magnitude. It was that I was desperate for someone to talk to. Someone who was there, unlike Mom. Who wouldn't tear me down, unlike my "friends." Who could believe me and take me seriously, unlike Dad.

"Can I tell you something," I ventured, "that *isn't* about being different?"

"Of course."

"You kept saying I seemed worried and distracted earlier. Well, I was. I still am. I think this has been the worst day of my life."

He nodded. "You were pretty broken up at the mall. What's wrong?"

"Everything," I said flatly. "But the one thing I'm most worried about is my sister."

"You mean Icka?"

Despite the seriousness of the conversation, despite

everything, I had the urge to giggle. Even Jamie, the most out-to-lunch freshman at Lincoln, knew who my sister was; she was so wildly unpopular she was practically a celebrity.

"Yes, Icka," I said. "She's visiting Pendleton U this weekend. But something about it just feels so *weird*."

"It was like that for me too," Jamie said, nodding, "when I realized Ben wouldn't be around next year. For the first time in my life, I'd be without him."

"I don't think it's just that," I said, frowning. I'd never even *thought* of that. "It's more like . . . I keep thinking about her being . . . in trouble. And—this is going to sound really stupid, but—I had this dream. That Icka wanted to do something . . . something dangerous and crazy." I sighed. "You probably think it all sounds stupid."

"No . . . a little vague," he admitted, "but not stupid."

"Maybe everything's fine. Maybe I'm just projecting because we got into a fight before she left—not a real, physical fight," I added. "I just know what I feel."

"Uneasy," he supplied. "Anxious. I would say almost frantic."

I stared at him, rapt. "It's so weird that I don't have to tell you."

"It's so weird that you believe me," he said. "You really think she's in danger." It wasn't a question.

"It's just a feeling . . . I can't ignore it, though."

He paused. "So . . . are you going to take Max, or TriMet?"

"Huh?" Now he'd lost me.

"To Pendleton."

"*Oh.*" I finally got what he was saying. "You mean, like hop on a bus to Portland and track Icka down?"

"Well, yeah, if you can't ignore this feeling."

"I can't, but . . ." I felt a blush spread through my face. I could see how he'd come to the conclusion that I should go out and find Icka all by myself, if I was so uneasy, anxious, and frantic. But the concept was so far out of my comfort zone, I hadn't considered it. Leaving aside our sisterly issues, going to Portland alone at night on public transit—surrounding myself with strangers and their Whispers—terrified me. But I couldn't tell him *that.* "I—I don't know the TriMet schedule!" That one was weak, since the internet could tell me in about two clicks. "Or—what room she's staying in," I added. But it was a small enough campus. I was running out of excuses. "Plus," I added, "high school girl wandering around the city at midnight?" Translation: I'm a scared little baby. "She'll be home in a few hours anyway. . . ."

"I could take you there," he said. "If you wanted."

I blinked. "Really, you have a license?" For a split second, I let myself picture it, driving to Pendleton together. Finding Icka, safe. Having her yell at us. Driving home free of anxiety, everything peaceful inside my head for once. It seemed just dimly possible.

Then he said, "Well, not a license, official, like a piece of paper blessed by our government, but I'm an *awesome* driver. And we could borrow some wheels too," he went on, getting so excited by his own plan that his voice got faster, lost its shy tone. "I could help you, watch out for you and stuff, two's always safer than one, right?"

I stared at him. Jesus. That was most certainly *not* what I wanted, to be hurtling toward city lights in a stolen car with an unlicensed juvenile delinquent. Groaning, I kneaded my face with my hands, wished I could hide my skepticism so he wouldn't sense it, so he didn't feel hurt. Why was he so eager to help solve my problems anyway . . . didn't he have tons of his own? "Come on, it's Saturday night," I said, trying to be tactful. "I'm sure you have better things to do than go surprise my weird sister in college."

He dropped his gaze, making his bangs fell back into his eyes. The shyness crept back into his voice. "Honestly, no," he said, laughing a little. "I can't think of any."

Then I remembered: He had nowhere to go tonight. Ben had warned his brother to stay away, to steer clear of their father. My god, where was he going to sleep tonight? A park bench? Behind a Dumpster? And *he* was worried about *me*? I felt like a spoiled, ungrateful princess.

"That's incredibly nice of you to offer," I said, trying to compose myself. "But she'd probably be home by the time we got there anyway. So let's leave driving to Portland as . . . Plan B." Or Plan Z, I thought.

"Wait." He lifted his eyebrows. "Do we have a Plan A?"

"Well, I'm sure my mom's going to call back," I said,

"and I'm just going to . . . you know, wait for her. It's all I can do right now. Legally." I felt warmth creep into my cheeks as I realized just how dumb my "plan of action" sounded. As dumb—as crazy—as his idea of stealing a car and tearing off to Portland half-cocked sounded to me. What was worse, being a scared momma's baby or being an outlaw freak? Two days ago, I would have been certain of the answer. No longer.

"Awright, well, the offer stands." He stuffed his hands back in his pockets and pivoted. "If you change your mind, I'll be at Denny's."

"Denny's?" I repeated.

"Free soda refills," he explained sheepishly. "They don't kick me out till one or two."

"But, wait, where are you going to go after two?" I said, cringing at the mom-ish tone of worry in my voice, but he was already down the steps and didn't turn.

I plopped onto the couch and mechanically made it through another round of calling Mom, calling Aunt Jane, leaving voice mail. Then I tried to watch the end of *Mean Girls* on HBO, but my mind kept wandering back to Jamie.

What would it be like to have his gift? To have emotion overwhelm you instead of being able to turn it down? And how did Ben control it with a Wall while Jamie couldn't? What about their parents, the dad who didn't want Jamie to come home tonight after fighting? Icka had gotten into her fair share of trouble—*more* than her share, she'd covered my share too—but I couldn't imagine my parents ever kicking her out. What kind of sense did that make: Your kid's drowning in problems, so you make him homeless too?

Maybe Jamie could at least stay at the teen center Mom volunteered at. He wasn't safe on the streets. What if someone stabbed him tonight for his wallet, or he witnessed a drug deal gone wrong, like on TV? Gang members could dump his body at a random construction site. He could even be stalked by a serial killer, one of the gross kind that froze people's body parts. Months later, his parents would ID them and the entire nation would concur that their son's grisly demise was *all their fault.* . . .

Okay, I was getting carried away. But at least worrying about Jamie and his problems distracted me a little from thinking of my own.

The Lotus Garden delivery guy arrived, and I busied myself filling two plates and depositing one on top of Dad's printer. (He hadn't even asked me who was at the door, but floated off to his office "just to check the docket for a minute." Yeah, right: We both knew he'd be in there till morning.)

I set my own plate on our antique living-room coffee table. A glass sheet protected the wood, and Mom used it as a way to display family photos. Granny Rowan's eyes peered at me solemnly from a long-past Easter picnic. Grammy and Grandpa mugged from a Venetian gondola on their silver anniversary trip to Italy. They looked so self-satisfied and annoying. I flicked at their faces with my middle finger, then felt childish. I was just punchy from boredom and worry.

At nine o'clock I surfed over to the Disney Channel to catch *The Princess Diaries*. The phones were still silent.

My stomach was on sour spin cycle, but I forced myself to take a bite of my favorite sweet-and-sour tofu. Back when she first went vegan, it had taken Icka months to convince me even to try it, and she was so thrilled when I got hooked on the stuff . . . but less pleased after I continued to devour cheeseburgers. Thinking about Icka, about the days when we'd been more connected, made my heart flip-flop. Like it had those times when I Heard her. Don't think about it, I told myself. What can you do anyway? Face it, you're not some kind of caped crusader superhero. You're a wimp. Taking on the puppet presidency of a recycling club makes you quiver.

Six-year-old Jess gazed up at me from the coffee table. She was cuddling with puppy Scarlett, both of them smiling. I remembered how she used to squeeze my hand to Whisper to me. *I want to fly over the Grand Canyon like a hawk!* What happened to that little girl . . . what happened to us?

The photo next to it made me cringe: me and my sister at the Seattle Space Needle. We were up on the observation deck, leaning awkwardly against the railing, me at ten with braces, her thirteen, already with the beginnings of that cynical sneer. A pink-and-mauve sunset glowing behind us, as if to illustrate the end of our sisterly closeness. We'd fought a lot on that trip. Our arms were only around each other because Mom told us to pose. What happened?

204

Don't look. Don't think. Just eat and watch TV and sleep . . . she's probably with Mom already, on their way home. Mom will come home any minute and everything will be fine.

I arranged a phone on either side of me like a good-luck charm and lay back on the couch, listening to Julie Andrews's comforting voice with my eyes closed. . . .

I opened my eyes. It was dark, and my body felt bleary, heavy. I was still on the living-room couch. On the cushion under my right calf, my cell was vibrating. Mom, it had to be. A wave of empty-belly nausea passed over me as I reached down to grab it and flip it open. "Mom, are you with Icka?"

"Ew, I'm not your Mom!" Parker's voice, Parker's laugh.

"Oh. Hey, Park." I was too groggy to hide my disappointment.

"Thanks, you sound *so* happy to hear from me!"

"Sorry, I was asleep." I sat up and pinched my wrist, willing myself to wake up. I had to be alert enough to weasel my way out of this conversation. Talking to Parker was dangerous—not to mention awkward—until I'd talked to Mom about how to handle her new Whispers. And my new feelings of resentment. "I should probably go back to sleep," I mused.

"Oh my gosh, it's only ten thirty," she said. "Are you that sick?"

"Yeah." I'd almost forgotten being "sick." "I think it's a flu."

"My poor little Joy."

I made a noncommittal sound and gritted my teeth. I was so tired of being talked down to, feeling like her puppy instead of her peer. Especially after Jamie, who took me seriously. . . .

"Well, I'm glad you got home okay. I was worried about you." She paused. "You never called me back."

I groaned. "I know, sorry about that." I *did* feel bad for ignoring her texts. It was the first time I'd ever done that. But the truth was, all I'd felt at the prospect of talking to her was dread. And then I'd had the dream, argued with Dad, found Jamie at the door. "I just had all this stuff to deal with at home," I said . . . and cringed.

"I thought you were *sick*." Her tone was accusing.

"I was—am." Crap; I was so sleepy I'd mixed up my excuses! "I was sick *and* busy," I finished lamely. "It was really the worst of both worlds."

"God, I wish you'd just tell me the truth!"

I froze. This wasn't a Whisper. She was speaking out loud. Criticizing me. I had the sudden urge to hit End Call, press the button over and over till my fingers bled, escape her disapproval. But as in a nightmare, I was rooted to the spot.

"It is so frustrating being friends with you sometimes," she went on, her tone clipped, no-nonsense. "I know you keep people at a distance, whatever, that's just your personality, but it's getting harder and harder to connect to you at all."

Listening to her complain about me, I felt numb. Like I

was floating above the conversation between our two telephones. She was frustrated with me. I was resentful of her. And I couldn't think of a single way to fix it. It was just the way it was.

"I care about you, Joy . . . but I don't see how I could be your friend, let alone best friend, if you don't start telling me what's going on in your head." She exhaled noisily. "Why don't you *talk* to me, and let me help you?"

"Because you don't know me well enough to help me." The words slipped out before I could stop them. They weren't angry or baiting, like Icka. Just an honest observation on three years of lopsided friendship. Three years of her talking and me listening. Of her leading and me following. Of her wishing and me granting. She was sick of it? Well, I was sick of it too. And even if there were no solutions, it was a relief to say it out loud. I fumbled for the coffee-table lamp and found its metal snap. The living room lit up.

"What are you talking about, I don't know you well enough?" She sounded guarded, but curious too.

"I mean, you're right." I was shocked by my own calm. "You're right that I don't let you in."

"Why don't you?"

"I guess I'm scared that if you knew the real me, you wouldn't accept me."

"You don't trust me?" She gave a hard laugh. "*You* don't trust *me*. That's hilarious."

"Parker, I'm sorry. It's not your fault at all. But there's

just some things about me I don't think you could ever . . . understand."

"Oh, really? Like what, like the fact that you have a little crush on Ben?"

My stomach turned to ice.

"It's okay. Everyone knows, it's so obvious. The way you look at him . . ." Dead silence on my end. "I just don't want you to get hurt, Joy." Her voice had turned gentle. "I'm sorry, but you're not his type. He told me. He thinks you're nice. He said you were the best friend type."

"What, and you just believe whatever he tells you?" I sputtered. Who would have thought it would sting so much to have Parker *not* be mad at me for Ben, *not* be the slightest bit jealous of me or threatened by me? She just thought my "little crush" was pathetic. A puppy growling and gnawing at a pants leg, harmless, even kind of funny.

"Of course I believe him. He's practically my boy-friend!" She seemed flustered. "No offense, but right now you sound like Icka."

"Well, it's better than being your lapdog," I shot back.

"My what?"

"I am not just the best friend type. I'm a person. I'm not a sidekick." My voice had crept up to higher speeds and registers. I didn't sound calm anymore.

"No one ever said you were a sidekick."

"You don't have to say it, Parker. It's obvious how you all see me, as a follower. A little *fan girl*. Admit it. You don't see anything special about me at all!"

"Oh my god. . . ." Parker sounded like she was dealing with a crazy person. "Where are you getting this from? I have never even suggested you're not special."

"But it's what you *think*!" The old unfair argument.

"Great, so now you're a mind reader?" She snorted. "First you claim I don't even know you, and now you supposedly know what I'm *thinking*? That's—that's just crazy."

"Maybe it is." I hugged my own shoulders with my cold hands. "Maybe I'm crazy. But can you honestly tell me you think of me as an equal?"

Parker hesitated. Then, "I just can't talk to you right now, Joy," she said. "You're acting like a freak."

Silence on the line. She was gone. It was over. Mom hadn't called back in time to help me. She'd never called at all. I'd had to go it alone. Would Mom have advised me to be honest like that and risk losing the friendship? Almost certainly not. And yet I didn't regret a word I'd said.

I sat there blinking and gulping, holding the dead, useless phone in my shaking hands.

Then I knew what I had to do.

Still shaking a bit, I pulled on my boots, stumbled to the coat closet, zipped up my blue puffy jacket, stuffed wallet (with forty bucks, all I had outside my savings account), cell, and keys into its pockets.

I ripped a page off the scented, pastel blue pad of notepaper Mom left by the phone. *Dad*, I scribbled. *Thanks for talking to me—I feel MUCH BETTER! Sleeping over at Parker's tonight.* ☺ *XOXO Joy.* I slapped a giant ladybug fridge magnet over it and wondered if Dad would even notice I was gone.

Denny's was only half a mile away, if you didn't mind braving dimly lit side streets where creepy child-abductor types could be lurking in any given laurel bush. I was out of breath by the time I pushed through the glass door. The frosted-hair, frosted-lipstick night-shift waitress greeted me with the stinkeye. "Will that be a table for one, *miss?*" she said, pointedly highlighting the syllable about my age. *Here's hoping this one can afford solid food.*

Jamie caught my eye from a corner table.

"Thanks," I said to stinkeye, "but I'm just meeting my friend," and before she could say (or think) another word, I marched over to where Jamie sat with a glass of Sprite untouched, resting on a place mat covered in doodles. "It's time for Plan B," I announced.

17

Jamie offered to let me wait at the Denny's table while he "picked up the car" (again, he was vague as to what *that* meant). But I was through with waiting.

"No thanks," I said. "I'm going with you."

The waitress hovered, hoping for a tip that wasn't in nickels. I drew a ten-dollar bill from my wallet and set it by his glass. We needed good karma.

In the near-empty parking lot, I found myself scanning each car as a possible target: a Civic, a Neon, a Mustang. The notion that we could soon speed off in one of them made my limbs buzz with a wild new energy. I'd never dared to break a school rule, and now, without blinking,

I was going to commit a felony! But I'd reached a point where even jail sounded less awful than sitting on the couch biting my nails, wondering if Icka was okay. "So how does this go?" I rubbed my hands together in the cold, feeling giddy. "I mean, what's your usual method, pick some old car with no club or alarm system, hotwire it . . . switch out the plates?"

Jamie gave me a weird look. "Uh, someone's been watching too much cable." His voice was a bit overanimated, bouncy like Tigger from *Winnie-the-Pooh*. Was he picking up *my* excitement? He seemed to notice too and backed several feet away from me. "Look, I don't want to cramp your style," he said, breaking into a grin, "but my plan was just to borrow *Ben's* car."

Oh.

"It's parked in front of my parents' house and I have a spare key." *I just pray we get it back before he notices it's gone.*

"Right, of course." I ducked my head and felt a blush come into my cheeks. I'd assumed he'd be willing to steal a car for me, and now he knew I was willing to steal one too. "Lead the way," I muttered.

"We'll take Meridian." He thumb-gestured left. "Fastest way to my parents' place."

Even through my embarrassment, I couldn't help but notice that twice in a row he didn't call it "home."

Cars whooshed by on Meridian Avenue, kicking up streaks of dirty rainwater at us as we bounded up the blocks. Jamie's legs were as long as mine, maybe longer, so for once

I didn't have to slow down my stride for the other person.

Waiting at an intersection for the walking guy to replace the red hand, he turned to me and said, "So you were ready to commit grand theft auto back there."

"Oh, come on, I was kidding."

He fixed those golden brown eyes on me. "Then why were you feeling excited?"

"Augh . . . that's *so* not fair!"

"I'm sorry." He held up his hands. "If it freaks you out, I won't say stuff like that. I'm not used to being able to talk about this."

"No, it's actually okay." I smiled, then bit my tongue, wishing I could explain that I was already used to Mom and Icka Hearing me, so his using extrasensory perception around me felt normal . . . in a weird way. Normal by not being normal.

We pulled off Meridian and into a pocket neighborhood of skinny tract houses. Their two-story sameness depressed me. Strange how Ben's million-dollar smile, his shiny car, his perfect hair had given me the idea his family was well off. Comfortable, at least. But the street he and Jamie lived on, Pomegranate Lane, could have used more street-lamps. Or a sidewalk. Only a sloping curb separated front yards—many smaller than my bedroom at home—from the potholed street. Several yellowing lawns were adorned with yard cars. Ben's silver Land Rover, squeezed between a rusty old truck and a green Kia, stood out as the block's pride.

"Craigslist," Jamie explained before I could ask, not that

213

I ever would have dared go there. "He saved up three summers' worth of lifeguard pay to buy this thing used."

I nodded. Made sense that Ben would never let his family's lack of funds mess up his image. But I didn't get why Jamie sounded so admiring. What was such a great achievement about buying a stupid car to impress people?

Wish I could work as a lifeguard. Or as anything. Wish I had a Wall.

Oh. For the first time it occurred to me: devastating as my new Hearing was, Icka and I were better off than Jamie.

"That's the house," he added, pointing with his chin toward a ranch house with an empty driveway and most lights out.

"Your folks aren't home tonight?"

I wish. "My dad's always home," he said. "That's why we're not going to get too close." He fished a set of car keys from his pocket and double-clicked a button to spring the passenger-side door. So much for hotwiring.

I hesitated. "It's Saturday night, why isn't Ben driving his detachable ego?"

"Because he's out with Gina. She picks him up in her Miata. Get in."

"Wait, Gina *Belle?*" The school president, my role model of unflappability? "Jesus, is there any girl at Lincoln he's not hooking up with?"

Jamie shrugged. "He's got this weird mojo . . . it's the Wall thing, women always fall for him. He can sneak a peek at what they're feeling, but he closes off before it can get to him."

I shrugged like I'd never noticed, never fallen for it myself.

Then again . . . had I really fallen for Ben? My crush on him was about a lot of things—some of them messed-up things, like being jealous of Parker or keeping my desires secret even from myself. But was it about *Ben*? I'd hardly known the real him anyway.

"Come on." Jamie was holding the car door open for me. No one had ever done that. "I want us out of my Dad's Wave-range."

As we pulled out of the parking spot, I thought I saw a shadow move in the upstairs window, but I told myself to relax. Odds were I was just imagining things.

I turned to Jamie. "Pearl Street," I directed. "We'll stop at my aunt's house first."

"Yes, ma'am."

He surprised me by being a smooth, expert driver. Once on the street, he obeyed every traffic law, even slowing at a yellow light Mom would have run. Made sense when I thought about it logically: If you were breaking a big law, you had to be extra careful to obey the smaller ones so there was no reason to attract a cop's attention.

He merged onto the freeway. Now we were just an anonymous car doing the speed limit in the anonymous middle lane. I gazed in wonder at the red taillights all around us. "We made it," I said. "We're actually on the freeway. I can't believe I'm really doing this."

"You know, I was pretty surprised you took my offer." He kept his eyes on the road. "Figured if you ever decided to go through with it, you'd have ten rides lined up in seconds. Boom."

"Yeah, well." I ran my finger along the glove compartment door. "I've sort of been reevaluating my friendships lately."

"Should we talk about something else?" he cut in. "I really can't afford for you to get upset while we're in this car together."

"It's fine." I sighed. "I've had a little time to get used to the idea that my friends all think I'm a pathetic, boring follower."

"A boring, average girl," he recited, "with nothing special about her?"

I'd almost forgotten that I described myself to him that way a couple of hours ago. I made a face. "It's different when I say it. They're supposed to be my best friends, right? Would a true friend think that? I mean, say that," I added quickly.

"Probably not. But it sounds like typical drama levels, for a popular clique. I've seen much worse."

I hated to admit it, but I knew what he meant. My friends hadn't done anything awful like cut up my clothes or feed me weight-gaining bars, like the characters in *Mean Girls*. But it was confusing to think they were just "typical" friends instead of good or bad ones. What was I supposed to do with that? It was easier to hate people or love them, I decided, than to feel something mixed up and in-between.

Jamie cut into my thoughts. "Well, at least you have your sister."

"Huh? What do you mean?"

"I mean if you'd steal a car for her, that implies you're pretty close, right?" He laughed.

"Or that I'm insane."

"I wasn't going to go there, but—"

"We're not friends, me and Icka," I said. "I stopped being her friend a long time ago."

"What happened?"

"What happened . . ." I shifted in my seat. No one had ever asked me before what happened between me and Icka. People just took it for granted that Icka was to blame for our estrangement. But Jamie wouldn't have assumed that; he didn't see me as a sweet, innocent angel. "It was me," I admitted. "I was about eleven when everything came together for me." I learned to use my Hearing to fit in. "I sort of figured out what other people wanted me to do. How to dress. How to act. How to talk, even." Suddenly my voice was getting lower and faster, like I couldn't get the words out fast enough. He didn't interrupt, just kept driving, listening. "By middle school I was a pro at acting normal. And people just forgot that I'd been this shy, spacey, nervous little kid. I was popular. I started looking at my sister the way my friends saw her. I had to . . ." I swallowed. "I had to move on from her. And it took so long for her to get it. To give up. She just kept on trying to be close to me.

217

She'd call my cell from home and ask if I'd be back in time to watch a movie with her. Once she knocked on my door with these giant oatmeal cookies and said she made one for each of us . . . I haven't thought about that in years."

"Joy, stop feeling guilty. It's not your fault Icka's messed up."

"But I shut her out. I hated her. . . . Yesterday, I told her that the world would be a better place without her in it."

He leaned left, glanced out his window, whistled under his breath, then turned back to me. "Ouch. But still, so what? Everyone gets mad at their siblings. Look at Ben and me. I punched him in the face, he pretends he doesn't know me at school. At home we still look out for each other. Wow," he said, "you *really* don't like him."

I shrugged and pursed my lips.

"He's not the greatest, but he's not Satan. And from what I can tell, you're not a bad person either, Joy."

There it was again, the uncomfortable space in between. Between good and evil. The gloomy gray. For the first time I could really see why someone would want to embrace being truly bad—at least then you wouldn't have to slog around in this confusing, icky middle ground.

"What if she believed me, though?" I traced my fingers on the numbers of the clock radio: 9. 4. 1. "That the world would be a better place without her. What if she decided it was true?"

"What if she did? Can't be the first time that thought's occurred to her. I guarantee it."

I stared at him. Was he implying . . .

"You're all shocked," he said. "But you shouldn't be. Come on, of course I think about it. The world would be a better place without some guy walking around who can mirror rage and hatred."

"But you can also mirror love and happiness. . . ."

He shrugged off love and happiness. "There isn't as much of that stuff floating around. You saw me today. What scares me most is thinking I could become a shooter."

I felt a chill. "You would never let that happen. I know you wouldn't."

"What if I couldn't stop it?"

I shook my head. "I don't know, but that's just not who you are. You're not a killer."

"You don't know me that well yet."

"Maybe, but I've been Listening to—" I stopped. I almost told him I'd been Hearing his thoughts. "I mean, look how you're helping me right now," I covered. "*My* world's better with you in it."

He smiled. "Hey, did you ever think that might be why I'm helping you?" he said. "So you'll say stuff like that, and make me feel better. Like you make everyone feel better. I'm probably a lot more selfish than you think."

I thought about all the times I'd called myself selfish lately. And how I thought I was being selfless when I gave people what they wanted, even though giving people what they wanted made me feel good in a way. But what Jamie was saying just mixed it all up, selfish and selfless. I wasn't even sure what the words meant anymore, or if it was possible to be one without the other.

A minute later, I spotted the exit for Aunt Jane's. From memory I called out directions: right at the first light, left at the top of the hill. I pumped my fist and let out a breath of relief when my navigation skills actually led us to a sign reading PEARL STREET LOFTS. "That's it! Now we just have to find parking."

"Your aunt lives in a loft?" Jamie sounded impressed.

"It's microscopic," I said, trying to dispel any illusions of Aunt Jane being cool and glamorous. Her place was not like in the movies, where supposedly starving artists enjoyed a 360-degree view of some gorgeous city skyline. "It's a five-hundred-square-foot studio, and it's filthy. No furniture," I added, then frowned. "Though she must have bought a futon recently if my mom slept on it last night."

"Wait, your mom's here too?" He quirked his eyebrows. *I wish I knew what else you're holding back on.*

"Aunt Jane needed some emotional support," I explained. "She's kind of a train wreck."

"Great," he muttered. *I hope I can handle that.*

I hoped so too. Suddenly I had a flash of doubt, misgivings about this whole track-down-Icka enterprise. If Icka *had* ditched her college visit to see Aunt Jane, wouldn't she have run smack into Mom? And how would Mom and Aunt Jane react to seeing Jamie, my new outlaw friend and (unlicensed) chauffeur? Should I leave him downstairs? No, I wanted him with me. Him and his Waves.

It was too late for doubts. I had to just go with my gut.

"Grab that spot!" A Jeep started pulling out of a sizeable space right in front of the building, a stroke of luck. "Trust me, I know this neighborhood. We could waste ten minutes circling."

Jamie parallel parked like a pro and we both climbed out.

Café Chanteuse, the funky coffee shop next door to Aunt Jane's complex, was absolutely packed with people who looked like grown-up versions of the path's denizens. I paused in front of the open door. The sign read: OPEN TILL MIDNIGHT FRI-SAT. On the corner stage, a purple-haired girl with a guitar was singing with her eyes closed. Sometimes the singers there have these soft, sweet voices you can barely catch over the espresso machine, but this one was belting out her tune so loud I felt the hairs rise on the back of my neck.

"Whoa, scary Waves coming out of that one," Jamie said, stepping backward.

I poked my head in to Listen, then regretted it as the storm crashed down on me:

I just want to be an artist, I just have to make it work.

Wish I wasn't wasting Saturday nights slinging coffee in this dive. . . .

I hope she realizes Lisa's never going to love her like I do.

We hurried past.

In front of Pearl Street Lofts, the modern-art fountain

sculpture put on its nightly light show in purple, blue, green, red, and orange.

"My aunt designed that," I said, waiting for him to say it was "odd" or "unusual," which is what Mom and Dad always said about it.

But he just said, "That looks amazing," and Whispered, *Wish I had a talent.*

I scanned the list of residents' names: JANE ROWAN, 4C. Before I could push the buzzer, though, a high, insinuating voice called out, "My my, is that Janey's *other* niece? With a boyfriend?"

A five-foot-tall middle-aged woman in a turquoise jogging suit was dragging a leashed basset. Doris, Aunt Jane's downstairs neighbor.

"Oh, hi, Doris! And Henry." I bent down to stroke the dog's velvety ears while Jamie sized up Doris. She was the same as I remembered her: still bitterly wishing she wasn't single.

Doris's trembling, peach-manicured fingers turned her key in the lock. "Well, come on in, Romeo and Juliet!" She motioned for us to follow her into the elevator, and after I'd ascertained her Wave-acceptability from Jamie's slight nod, we did. "So, what are you doing here?" She pushed her own floor-three button as well as floor four for us. "Introducing Aunt J to your boyfriend?" *Wish I had a handsome man to show off.*

"Actually—yeah!" It was a way better explanation than what I was really doing.

Jamie slipped his arm around me. I could almost hear him smirking.

"Well, you look good together," she said grudgingly. "Lucky he's tall. I can't abide short men. Just between you and me, I could never put up with a shrimpy Stuart!"

Jamie caught my eye, his face a question mark. I had to look away not to laugh. When she'd dragged Henry off, the moment the third-floor doors closed, we both exploded.

"What the fug is a shrimpy Stuart?" I gasped.

"Is that old people slang for—"

"I don't know!"

"I don't *want* to know."

We were still snickering when the elevator doors opened again.

Jamie stood there frozen in front of the door.

"What's wrong?"

"I can't be here." He punched the top floor, eight, and the doors closed.

"What are you doing, we have to—"

"Can't, can't, can't go there. Too strong." He was sounding like he did talking to Ben in the bathroom. "You were right about your aunt being a wreck."

"You mean, you can feel—Waves?"

He nodded, shivered. "Scared, angry, confused . . . I can't, can't, can't—"

"It's okay, it's okay," I said.

He was like a kid. I had this urge to comfort him, like smooth his hair or squeeze his shoulder. Until he slammed his hand against the elevator wall. "God fucking damn it!"

I shrank back, and he shrank away from me, mirroring me.

"I'm sorry," he said, sounding about five years old. He gave me a guilty look. *I wish I could stay with you and help. I wish I wasn't so damn weak. . . .*

"It's all right. Just head back to the car . . . I'll meet you there."

I left him on the eighth-floor hallway and stepped out of the elevator on floor four, alone. I started to walk down the hall to Aunt Jane's front door, then remembered Jamie's reaction and thought better of it. My Hearing was getting stronger. Maybe if I just tried to Listen from here . . .

Instantly I picked up a wrenched, choking voice:

If only Jane had talked her out of it somehow. . . .

Mom. That sobbing voice was Mom?

If only I knew where to look . . . where to start . . .

Mom's Waves were what Jamie was feeling. God, no wonder he ran.

My heart thundered against my ribs. So Icka was really gone; my gut feeling was right. I kept thinking I should go, I should run after Jamie. Before Mom catches me Listening. But I couldn't stop, like how I couldn't stop staring at Ben's swollen face. Was this the real Mom?

I don't ever want to see her again . . . Oh, god, I just want my baby to come home safe! Let her be safe, safe and happy, somewhere.

How could this quavering, hysterical person be my mother, my rock?

I never want them to know what I did. I just want them to be happy, I have to make them happy . . . get her back before they know she's gone.

We were the ones she didn't want to know, me and Dad. She wasn't even planning to tell us that Icka was missing, because it wouldn't make us happy?

If only it hadn't been Joy's birthday. I wish I could have canceled the party to go out and look for Jess. . . .

A chill ran down my spine. I remembered the calls from Aunt Jane that went to voice mail. Mom had known about Icka being AWOL yesterday afternoon. Did that mean Mom had valued my birthday celebration over searching for her missing older daughter? I knew one thing it meant: Icka had been gone over twenty-four hours. Where could she be? Not at Pendleton. She'd never been at Pendleton. She'd certainly never made friends there.

Mom had lied.

Lied to *us*, me and Dad. Her family.

I felt weak and leaned back against the wall, but the toe of my boot slid on the slippery floor and I found myself dancing to keep from falling flat on my butt. My boots were as loud as tap shoes in the echoey hallway.

"Please let that be Jess at the door!" Mom Whispered, and

225

suddenly a familiar sharp pain rocked me.

My face jerked backward as the bright red pain washed over my crown, scraping as it spread down to my forehead. Holding my head in both hands—as if to keep it from breaking apart—I threw myself at the stairwell door, pushed it open with my hip, and raced down the steps. The pain started to lift quickly. By the time I reached the ground floor my head was fine.

It was Mom, Mom who caused my headache.

How? And why? If Icka were here, we could figure it out together. That's what she'd wanted, for us to solve mysteries together. But now Icka was missing, a mystery herself.

I didn't stop running till I was outside.

A dark-colored Subaru was parked in the place of Ben's Land Rover.

My stomach felt like someone had kicked me with cowboy boots. Where the hell was Jamie? Was he so spooked that he'd fled? But I couldn't believe he'd just abandon me here. . . . Maybe the police picked him up for driving a stolen car. Maybe he ran into some really angry person packing a knife. Or a gun.

I'd only been standing there catastrophizing for about thirty seconds when I realized Mom could still be trailing me. I slipped into the café where I'd be less obvious to spot, and immediately I was enveloped in a fog of Whispers.

I'd be loving life if I could see that *pretty smile across the breakfast table for the rest of my days.*

I wish this pseudo-progressive coffee shop bothered to compost.

I was scanning the tables in vain for Jamie when I heard someone call my name. The barista, a slim, androgynous blond woman, was at my side. "You Joy?" Numbly, I nodded. She handed me a napkin with some writing on it: *Too many Waves in here. I'll be circling the block till you come out. —J*

I felt my shoulders drop and my breathing return to normal. "*Thank* you," I said, but the woman was already wandering back to her station, Whispering: *I wish Lisa could see how good we were together.*

I watched her amble away, thinking I should duck out of here myself before the Whispers got to me. But then something made me look just *past* her. To the right. At the fifties-style booths near the back of the shop. A middle-aged dude with a ponytail was sitting close to a woman with pouffy mouse brown hair much like my own, but running to silver. As the woman tipped her head back to laugh, I saw a button nose exactly like my mother's. Aunt Jane?

18

The fingers on Aunt Jane's left hand were intertwined with the man's, and she was so caught up in their eye contact she didn't even notice me till I was blocking her view of Purple Hair.

"Joy! What are you doing here, kiddo?" Aunt Jane jumped out of her chair, nearly tripping on her crinkly gypsy skirt. *Please, not another family crisis.* But she opened strong, patchouli-smelling arms to hug me anyway. Purple Hair finished her earsplitting rendition of Tori Amos's "Silent All These Years." "Stu!" Aunt Jane yelled over the applause to her date. "Meet my other favorite niece."

Stu? So the ponytailed guy was . . . Shrimpy Stuart?

He crumpled his napkin, stood to his full height of five and a half feet, and smiled at me. "Heard so much about you, Joy!" *I hope she likes me.* His T-shirt read CHILD-FREE: DEEDS NOT SEEDS.

I didn't smile back. Who *was* this guy? Aunt Jane wasn't depressed *or* alone. Did Mom ever tell me the truth about anything?

"So where's Robert?" Aunt Jane glanced around for my father.

"Dad's not with me," I said. "I came with a friend."

Her eyes went as saucer-wide as if I'd said I flew here in my Learjet. *I hope she's not on the same path as Jessica.*

More like hot on the trail, I thought. Purple Hair was starting to get worked up again with "Cornflake Girl," so I grabbed Aunt Jane's hand. "We need to talk," I said. "Outside."

She gave me another look of astonishment. Then she nodded at Stuart, snagged her oversized purse (which appeared to be made out of burlap), and motioned for me to follow her out the back door. It led into a cold—but thankfully empty—screened courtyard with black iron patio furniture and a carpet of Astroturf. On the two walls that weren't screens, a mural depicted sunny blue skies and sandy beaches, a whimsical protest against Portland's constant rain.

"Well, here we are!" Aunt Jane picked up one of the heavy wrought-iron chairs and settled her wiry body into it. "I guess you've got some questions for me, about your

Hearing?" She gave me a knowing smile, the sort of look Yoda might have given Luke Skywalker before their first lesson. "You came to me as an adult, without your parents in tow, that means you're ready for the truth. Go ahead, ask me anything."

My heart quickened at the thought of all the things I *could* ask. Like, had she ever Heard a Whisper from thirty miles away? Did she really lose her power on purpose? (How?) Was there a way to stop another Hearer from picking up your Whispers . . . and did it cause headaches? Did she know others with gifts?

But there was only one question I cared about right now. "Where's my sister?"

Aunt Jane's brow wrinkled, and suddenly she didn't look so much like Yoda anymore. She looked like Mom, a weathered, hippie version of her both older and younger at the same time. "So *that's* why you're here," she said, sighing. "Well, I suppose you're mad at me too for not holding her back, but how could I? I know firsthand how it feels to be ready. Ready to move on. Be free."

"She didn't just move *on*." I wasn't about to let her use her hippie lingo on me. "She ran away, Aunt Jane! We have to bring her back home."

"No." Aunt Jane shook her head emphatically, making her crystal earrings chime. "I'm not sure that's such a good idea, it could hold back her spiritual growth. Separation is a healthy stage of development," she went on. "Your sister's in a very exciting place, at the true beginning of her

230

life, metaphorically speaking—"

I cut into her psychobabble. "What place is she in, *physically* speaking?"

Aunt Jane frowned. *I do wish I'd pressed more about her plans.* "Well, she left my condo last night, around ten," she admitted, "so, at this point. . . ."

"She could be anywhere." I swallowed, felt nauseous. She'd been my last hope. "Have you and Mom even called the police?"

"Oh, the pigs." Aunt Jane rolled her eyes. I didn't even know adults did that. "Just between you and me, Officer Friendly and his crew, they wouldn't search too hard for a runaway who'll be eighteen in spring."

I shook my head, not wanting to hear this.

"She might choose to return someday." Aunt Jane was obviously trying to cheer me up. "When she's learned what it is she wants to learn on this journey. Of course I hate seeing poor Kelli in a tailspin. She's praying your sister turns around and comes straight home, but I think—"

"Mom's just sitting around, hoping and praying?" I was so angry I felt light-headed. "Why isn't anyone *doing something* to find Icka? She is *out* there somewhere and no one knows where, and you think it's fabulous. Mom's lying that she's in college. And Dad doesn't even know his own daughter's missing! What kind of family is this?"

"Wait a minute, Kelli *lied*?" Aunt Jane looked startled. "Your father . . . has no idea?"

I plopped into a chair, breathless from my tirade.

"But then how did *you* know . . ." She pushed up her glasses. "Why'd you come to me?"

"Because *you're* the one who told her to destroy her Hearing!"

"Destroy?" Her head snapped backward as if I'd slapped her. "No, we talked about healing, clearing up childhood patterns, a gentle process. Years of growth—"

"Icka's not patient enough to wait years," I said. "If she wants to kill her Hearing, she'll do it this weekend. She even found someone to help her, some *guys* somewhere. . . ."

"What?" She blinked. "How do *you* know all this? She called you?"

Maybe it was wrong of me, but part of me felt gratified to be shocking her with how much I knew. She wasn't the only one with the answers.

"No she didn't call me. She Whispered to me."

Aunt Jane stared at me. "Are you saying . . . ?"

"I've been Hearing her all afternoon. In my dreams, when I'm awake . . . just like in that old story you told us when we were kids. Hope and—"

"Faith. Oh, dear." Aunt Jane stood and her chair groaned as she pushed it away. She began to circle the table. "Oh, dear, oh, dear." *I hope I haven't made a horrible mistake. Please let Jessica find her way out of this danger she's in!*

"This is real, isn't it?" Now I was no longer enjoying shocking Aunt Jane. Now I was just plain terrified. "She's really in danger. How do we find her?"

"Not we, *you*. Joy, do you understand how rare this

232

is, how significant? Somehow you've opened up a deep connection with your sister. One that transcends distance. Your great-grandmother said it could happen when extraordinary need meets extraordinary understanding. Compassion."

I thought about that moment in the Starbucks bathroom when I'd wished away my Hearing, when I'd first understood what it must feel like to be Icka. The moment I'd first Heard her.

"She is reaching out to you for help," she said, and now I could see the fear in her eyes. "You're the one she wants to find her. And there's no time to lose."

"All right, but what can *I* do?" I felt around in my pocket for my phone. "I'm calling Dad for help."

"The hell you are!" She knocked the phone from my clammy grasp. It thudded weakly on the Astroturf. "Joy, think. The first thing he'd do is ground you and hire a private detective who'll waste two weeks poking around online, lurking in parked cars and digging through trash bins. Your sister's leaving a red-hot trail just for you. Follow it!"

The butterflies in my stomach turned to bees. "But . . . where do I follow it *to*?"

"Ask her."

"You mean . . . I can talk to her directly?"

"She can Hear your Whispers," she said, like it was obvious. Which I guess it was. It was just a whole new way of looking at Whispers. "Your minds are connected. You should be able to see what she sees, remember what she's remembering."

"Seriously?"

"You can't be thinking about other things, though," she added. "You have to focus entirely on connecting with her. Try it now."

Icka, I said silently, *I wish I could find you.*

All I Heard at first was Aunt Jane beside me: *I pray nothing happens to that girl because of me.* Me, me, me. Why was it so hard to think about other people without thinking about yourself too?

I closed my eyes and gathered up thoughts of Icka. The small purple figure disappearing into the woods. The mermaid on the rock. The lone plate of Tofurky on Thanksgiving. Icka. Jess. My sister. Have to find you, get you back.

Almost immediately, my body lurched forward as a warm orange light bathed my vision. My mind's eye flashed on two little girls toiling over a moated, turreted sandcastle, a sepia-toned photo that could just as well have been Mom and Aunt Jane as me and my sister. Queasiness like a wreath of cigarette smoke drifted up toward my head, and *blink:* I saw Jess's grip on my hand as we ran toward the shimmering waves. Blink: the zoo at age seven, trembling behind Jess, hiding from the play-fighting grizzly bears. Blink: arms around each other at the Space Needle. Then I was staring at the café courtyard's painted sky wall once more.

"What'd she say? Where is she?"

I was dazed. "I just . . . saw all these images. Memories, or something."

"No words at all," Aunt Jane said grimly. "Suggests she might not be fully conscious. Why don't you ask her to *show* you where she is now?"

I swallowed. "We can *do* that?"

Aunt Jane bit her lip. "You can do a lot more than fetch people what they want, Joy."

I closed my eyes again, concentrated: *Jessica, I wish you could show me where to find you.*

As if in reply, I got arms-around-each-other-at-the-Space-Needle a second time. The Space Needle again . . . wait. "The Space Needle's in Seattle!" I blurted out. Seattle, with its direct-trade coffee on every block, its weird art and green politics. Seattle, the birthplace of grunge music. "That's where she'd be! That's where she is." I took a deep breath. "I guess that's where I have to go."

I'd been the one to push her away. Crazy as it was, danger-ous as it was, I had to be the one to bring her back. Because even though I'd shut her out of my life, I was the only one in the family she was still talking to. Besides, Aunt Jane, unlike my parents, had faith in me. Of course Aunt Jane just might be crazy. But when it came down to it, who in our family was totally sane?

"Call in every hour, you hear me?" Aunt Jane swept her burlap purse off the table and turned toward the main room. *I just hope I'm not making another big mistake. . . . I hope*

235

this makes everything better, not worse. "I'm going upstairs to talk to your mother."

"Good luck sorting through the lies."

She turned around and smoothed my hair. "I don't blame you for being disappointed in her, Joy," she said softly. "God knows Kelli and I have had our differences. She doesn't get why I felt I'd be happier without my Hearing. And I don't get how she can go through life never looking below the surface." Or Hearing below the surface? I thought. "Then again, who am I to judge her?" Aunt Jane went on. "I chose not to have children myself because deep down, I knew *I* wasn't up to the challenge of raising girls who could Hear."

"I guess Mom wasn't up to it either."

"I wouldn't say that." Aunt Jane's eyes were shiny. "All I have to do is look across the table at my niece, and I know she did a damn fine job. Now we have to help her, because she's fallen down under the weight of supporting everyone."

Her words didn't penetrate my anger. Still, I nodded. It was the first time her hippie-therapy talk had ever made sense.

"And I'm going to help her with tough love," she added. "I'll tell her she has fifteen minutes to enlighten your father, or I'm calling him myself."

"Wait!" I grabbed her arm. "But what if they call the police?"

"I'm pretty sure you don't need to worry about that,"

Aunt Jane said. "Your mother would sooner run a PTSA meeting naked than explain to the authorities how she lost *two* teenagers." She frowned. "You dad might put a detective on your trail, though, or try to follow you himself. Don't worry, I'll give you a big head start before I tell them where you're headed."

"Wait, how could you give me a head start?" I was confused. "As soon as Mom Hears you, she'll know everything!"

"Oh, please." Aunt Jane dismissed Mom's power with a wave of her hand. "Even I can block out Kelli."

"*Block* her?" I blinked. "Are you saying . . . you can stop her from Hearing you?" Realization started to dawn on me. "How would someone do that?"

She hesitated, and I could see the wheels turning. Whatever it was, she'd assumed I knew already. If I didn't, should she be the one to tell me? "Well. A couple ways," she said finally. "Anyone—even a non-Hearer—can learn to control her own mind. By letting go of a desire, you change the subject in your brain. Meditation helps," she added. "Or training yourself to think of something else. Something harmless."

I leaned forward. "Is that what Mom and Icka do, they let go of desires they don't want me to Hear?"

Again she hesitated. I hated putting her on the spot like this, but I had to know the truth. "There is another way," she said, "but I don't recommend it. It can damage your emotional health." She sighed. "An adept like you can build a mental barrier and hide her Whispers behind that Wall, so no one knows what's going on inside."

"A Wall?" So my family had Walls too, like Ben and his dad? I asked the question I was pretty sure I knew the answer to. "Can those Walls cause headaches?"

"Can they ever. On both sides. When I was eighteen and my power was growing stronger every day, your grandma and I used to give each other *splitting*—" Suddenly Aunt Jane stopped and stared at me. "Wait a minute, are *you* getting headaches? Already?"

I nodded. "Getting them and giving them, I guess." Our house was a psychic war zone, and I'd never noticed.

"That means you're breaking through." Her tone was surprised, almost awed. "Joy. Your Hearing must be very strong if you can already do that. Of course," she added, "living in a house full of both kinds of blockers, you've clearly had opportunities to hone your power."

I almost had to sit down again. My head was spinning with terms I just barely understood. Blockers. Adepts. Hone your power. Breaking through. What else did Aunt Jane know that Mom couldn't, or wouldn't, pass on to us? And why had I never tried to talk to her before?

Then it hit me. Both kinds of blockers? My hand felt the smooth stone of my topaz pendant. "Dad," I whispered. It wasn't that he never thought about us, he just didn't want to burden us with his hopes and expectations. The way his own parents had done to him. "Did you teach him how—"

"When I was in the forest," Aunt Jane said, "your father filed my taxes for ten years. As far as favors go, I'd say we're even."

Outside the café, I barely had time to zip my jacket before the Land Rover rolled up.

I jumped into the passenger side.

"Whoa." Jamie reeled to the left, as if a magnet had pinned him to the inside of the car door. "You okay? Where'd you get all this energy?"

"Get back on the freeway," I told him. "We have to go to Seattle."

"Ah . . . no can do, Nancy Drew." He was slowly peeling himself off the door. His voice hit me back with my own resolve and urgency. "See, the thing is, Seattle is the opposite direction from home, and we *have* to return this here coach before my brother comes back from his date and turns me into a pumpkin. Which is technically Cinderella, not Nancy Drew, but—"

"This is more important, I swear!" I said. "I'll explain everything on the way, but we have to *go*."

He stopped. "Everything?" he said softly.

I took a deep breath. *"Everything,"* I said, and I meant it.

19

Confessing my secret to Jamie felt like flying down a roller-coaster track, my vision blurred, my stomach weightless as exit signs whizzed past. Halfway through, when I got to the part about how hard it is for me to *not* grant a wish, Jamie's right hand quit the steering wheel. It found my left hand, resting on my knee, and covered it, his long fingers flexing underneath to compress my palm. And he didn't let go for the rest of the story, and I didn't let go of his hand either, so he was sort of flying down the hill with me. When I got to the end—when he knew why I was throwing up and crying in the Starbucks bathroom, when he knew about my dream, and Mom's lie about Icka being okay, and Aunt Jane telling me *I* had to be the one to find her—he looked at me. Just looked. A brief glance too, because he was driving, but it was enough. I felt *understood*.

He didn't speak for seven exits. Then he said, quietly, "I always wondered why everybody around you was so happy."

"Were they? I'm glad . . . sort of." I smiled at the moon that seemed to follow us through the otherwise black night. "Mom always said our gift could make the world a happier place. I'm glad it wasn't *all* lies." I was almost afraid to ask my next question. "What about me? Was I happy?"

"Sometimes." He signaled to pass a Pepsi truck. "You just never stayed like that for long. You'd be smiling, but then you'd send out these Waves . . . out of nowhere you'd be scared, or uneasy. Couldn't figure you out. Thought you might even have the same thing I did, but in reverse or something." He shook his head. "Instead you have this totally amazing power."

I snorted. "Yeah, it's pretty awesome being me."

Chopin played on my phone just then. MOM'S CELL flashed on the screen. "Augh," I said. For the tenth time since Aunt Jane had spilled the beans to my parents, I screened her out by punching Ignore.

"I'm not saying your life's a picnic," Jamie said. "But look at *me*. I just wish . . . well, hell, you can probably Hear it." *I wish I wasn't broken like this.*

My limbs felt squirmy. The closer I was to another person, the harder it was to ignore their Whispers. Without thinking I suggested, "Maybe one day you can learn how to control it."

"Uh, don't go there." His tone had a dark, sharp edge to it suddenly. "You sound like my dad or Ben."

"No," I said, hurt, "I was just saying—"

"You think I haven't *tried*?" He chuckled, a sound of pain. "Trust me, I have tried so hard, so many times. . . . I can't put up a Wall, I'm just defective. It is what it is."

"But what if a Wall's not the only way?" I was reaching. "I mean, if they're Waves, can't you, like . . . dive underneath, or surf them, or something?"

"What the hell does that mean?" The edge was back.

"I don't know, okay?" I was starting to feel attacked. "I'm just trying to help."

"I've been dealing with this shit my whole life." He stared at the dark road ahead, his posture stiff, hunched. "Don't you think if there was some way out I'd have found it? Or maybe I'm just stupid and lazy, and I *like* being a freak." It broke my heart the way he recited this list of insults, like it was a mantra he'd been forced to memorize. Who had told him those things?

"Of course I don't think that!" I brushed his bicep, and felt his shoulder relax a little. "I just don't think you should give up hope. I didn't know half of what I could do till this weekend. Maybe you're still discovering your potential."

"Maybe." He shrugged. "Look, I know you're trying to

help. I'm just not used to . . . never mind."

"What?"

"Someone still having faith in me." He said the words quickly, sounding embarrassed now.

"Well, *get* used to it," I said. "I'm not giving up on you. Trying to solve other people's problems is in my blood." I paused. "Also, you may be the only friend I have left."

"Trying to solve people's problems for them . . . having no friends," he deadpanned. "Ever thought about how those two things might relate?"

I rolled my eyes and grinned. "Shut up."

Before I could attempt a better zinger, we were interrupted by my cell. For once it wasn't Mom's ring.

"Please be Icka!" I wished aloud, and scrambled to fish the phone from my jacket pocket. It was Dad.

I didn't want to talk to him, but it wasn't fair to keep him in the dark.

I sighed and flipped it open.

"Pumpkin?" I could hear the wind whipping of engine sounds in the background. "I'm driving to Seattle. To sync up with you."

"You what?" I held the phone at arm's length and gave it a sidelong glare, as if I suspected it of lying. Dad wanted to "sync up" with me? Not call the police? Not hire a detective? But join my search party? "So does this mean you believe me?" I ventured. "That I'm Hearing her?"

Dad was quiet for a moment. "I'm not sure *what* to believe

243

anymore," he admitted. "It seems I've been going on some faulty intelligence."

Faulty intelligence. I cringed, thinking about the lying note I'd left, the tense conversation he'd likely just had with Mom. Then again, Dad's being so out of the loop was partly his own doing—he'd always kept the rest of us at a distance; understandable, perhaps, but now he was paying the price. A gloomy thought popped into my head: What if my parents ended up divorcing over Mom's not being honest with us, or Dad's not being there for us? I couldn't help but notice he said, "*I'm* driving to Seattle," not "we." As if reading my mind, he added, "You know, our family has some things we need to talk about, later." He sounded almost stern, for him. "What matters now," he went on, "is both my girls coming home safe. I want you—and your friend—to check into the W Hotel downtown the moment you get to Seattle. I've booked a room for each of you. Wait for me there, understand? Do not go anywhere till I arrive."

I had no intention of waiting in my room. But I wasn't going to lie to him again. "Dad, I don't know how much longer I'll be able to Hear her. I'm sorry, but I just have to keep looking. With you or without you."

He exhaled noisily. "Well, I don't like this," he said.

I held my breath. Was he going to call the police on us?

"But I can see nothing's going to stop you, so there's

no point in arguing." A pause. "Promise to keep your phone on?"

"I will."

"And keep your wits about you."

"I will, Dad."

I hung up feeling like, for once, Dad's Vulcan-like ability to bury his emotions was a good thing.

Three A.M. found us in South Seattle, at an all-night Shell station. We were the only customers. At the register, a pretty Indian girl in charcoal sweats had spread her textbook on the counter and was praying she'd pass her microbiology midterm.

Jamie had been Whispering about food for the past hour, so we headed straight for the glass case that housed gas-station cuisine: the standard nukeable breakfast bagels, energy drinks, frozen treats.

I just want a turkey sandwich, he Whispered.

"Second row," I replied, not feeling the slightest bit self-conscious for responding to his thought.

When the cashier didn't glance up from her cram session, I rang the bell and for once in my life didn't mind getting glared at. While I counted out cash for food and gas, Jamie ran outside to start the pump. Draining my wallet down to the last ten bucks made me nervous, but we needed fuel *now,* to keep going. And we had to keep going.

The images I had picked up from Icka since leaving

245

Portland had disturbed me—so much so that several times, Jamie had had to pull over and leap out of the car. He'd stand by the side of the road panting, catching his breath, praying for calm. A trip that should have taken under three hours had taken four.

In that time, I'd gotten a bit better at Whispering directly to Icka, but her responses had grown more jumbled: a mishmash of our shared memories, past wishes, and random sights and sounds and sometimes even sensations. As we'd driven through Olympia, I had flashed for several seconds on a gray courtyard swarming with young people who looked much like Icka: ripped jeans, dark jackets, silver-studded chins and eyebrows. I'd Heard no words but felt a sense of reaching out to the crowd. Searching. Was she yearning to belong? Had Icka come to Seattle hoping to find friends? Or was she searching the crowd for someone specific? The guys who were going to help her kill her Hearing.

It had been the last clear picture for a while. Soon after, I'd begun to see disjointed images. A spinning pink elephant. An IM chat window filled with endless repetitions of the letter "O." A stack of chemistry textbooks dancing. I saw a chorus of little kids hiss and spit like demons. Felt myself falling down a well; I hit the water and kept falling. Heard a young guy's braying laughter on a loop. Smelled the sweet, sickening, outdoor-concert reek of pot. Was the person she was searching for . . . a drug dealer? If so, whatever they'd hooked her up with had to be a thousand times stronger than weed. Sitting in the car next to Jamie, I'd worried that Icka's next dispatch of brain shit would set him careening off the road. Around the time we'd passed Tacoma, I got a crystal-like set of flashes. A dank ceiling peopled with lecherous gray shadow hands. I—or Icka—floated on a moldy mattress. My lungs screamed for oxygen. I wished desperately to turn on my side but couldn't. I understood these were Icka's wishes, Icka's experiences. What the hell was happening to her?

And then, after that, nothing. Not even static.

Behind the gas-station register, a laminated neighborhood map caught my eye. "Over half a million people call Seattle home," its cover boasted. I pulled it off the rack and plunked down my last ten bucks.

"Which one of these is the alternative neighborhood?" I asked the cashier. "Like, where would you see tats and piercings?"

She rolled her eyes. *I wish these kids would run along so I could study.* "Try Capitol Hill," she said aloud.

"Thank you."

"Or the U District," she added. "Maybe even Ballard and West Seattle."

I stared at the map, disheartened. I'd been expecting to comb one little neighborhood. The four districts she named looked enormous, each practically a town in its own right. For Jamie's sake, at least, I tried to think positive, but the universe had suddenly grown big and cold again. Icka was a speck of dust hidden in the Milky Way;

we'd never find her. It was hopeless.

Outside, I listlessly took over pumping gas while beside me Jamie used my phone to call his brother. Our original plan to sneak the Benmobile back before daylight was shot, so we were at the mercy of its owner's kindness. I wasn't holding my breath.

"You fucker!" Ben's tinny voice yelled into the phone. "How could you just take my fucking car?" On speaker, he sounded like an enraged mosquito.

"Dude, I'm really sorry!" Jamie said. "It was an emergency and—"

"Why didn't you give me a heads-up, asshole?"

Jamie blinked. It was a fair enough question. "You—you said you'd never cover for me again."

"I was pissed, okay? Jesus . . . bring it back already."

"Can't."

"What? You have to. It's been reported stolen."

"Oh, shit." Jamie covered the right side of his face with his hand. "Shit shit shit."

"Dad was spying from the window," Ben went on, "when Senior Number One dropped me off after our date. He asked why the car was missing. I had *no* clue what to tell him."

A squad car was cruising toward the gas station. I felt like I couldn't breathe. Jamie backed away from me, pale. I could no longer catch all Ben's words, though I still caught the gist of it.

"Thanks to you . . . Gina . . . I fell . . . playing basketball!"

Ben chortled. " . . . thinks I'm . . . and abused. Thanks a lot!"

I wish it would pass us, just pass us and go, Jamie whispered.

The squad car passed. I inhaled fresh air but couldn't seem to get enough of it.

"Where are you anyway, you little shit? No, wait, don't tell me. You finally got yourself so deep in it I can't cover for you. Free advice? Beg for solitary."

Jamie closed the phone and turned to me, his face an ashy gray. "We have to ditch this car, we have to *get it off the street.*"

"Right. Okay." I bobbed my head, numb. Without a car, we were even less likely to find Icka. Hopeless.

I felt my body sinking, my knees dragged down to the cold concrete as if commanded by the gravity of Jupiter.

And blink: Suddenly I was no longer outside the gas station. There was an orange light and I was back in the dark bedroom. The musty mattress. Silent panic. The shadow hands breathing over me, stealing my air. My heart raced and skipped wildly. Then my breath stopped. My heart stopped.

"Joy."

I could dimly hear Jamie's voice.

"Joy? What are you seeing?"

The gas-station light seemed very far away, a soft fuzzy red sun, as if I were glimpsing it from inside a long tunnel.

At the same time, I felt myself—my other, Icka self—being hoisted and carried. I was breathing again, but slow and shallow. I could no longer see. I was bumped and bounced down stairs, many stairs, then pushed against a cold metal door into the outside air. Where was I? *I wish you'd open your eyes, Jess,* I begged. *I wish you'd show me where you are.* For a moment my vision fluttered open and I caught sight of dirty pavement, brownstones, and brick apartment buildings, a faded green store sign whose remaining letters read: P**E ST**** GRO****. Then the eyes closed, and I was shoved into a narrow space that smelled like gasoline and mold and crackers, and from then on I saw and heard and felt nothing. I wished nothing. I was nothing.

I'd found oblivion.

"Hel-*lo.*" Parker's voice was quiet and groggy but clipped, halfway between asleep and pissed off.

"It's me," I said quickly. "Sorry if I woke *you* this time, but I need your help, fast."

"Oh my god, are you actually sick?" She sounded more awake now. "Tell me what you need me to do."

"I'm not sick, but you were right that something's going on with me. I can't explain it all right now, but—"

"I cannot believe you!" she cut in. "You're still being all secretive and weird!"

"I can't help that right now." I thought of how our last conversation had ended and felt sad. But my sadness was like a tiny water drop. It sizzled on the flame of my terror over Jess's being . . . what? Hurt? Worse than hurt? "I know I owe you an explanation," I said. "But it'll have to wait.

This is urgent. Just please go to your computer and type what I tell you."

To my own ears, I sounded every bit as bossy and commanding as she often did—maybe more so. Incredibly, Parker did what I asked her to.

Through Google Maps, we narrowed down P**E ST**** GRO**** to Pike Street Grocery in Seattle's Capitol Hill neighborhood. I repeated the address to Jamie, who found it on our map.

"Wait, you're not actually in Seattle, are you?"

"Tell you later, gotta go!"

"Joy. Wait." She lowered her voice. "If you're in some kind of trouble—I mean, I feel like I should tell my mom about this call."

"Can you please just trust me for tonight and I'll explain tomorrow?"

"But I'm worried about you. This feels too big for me."

I sighed. "Well, okay, do what you have to do. I'll do what I have to do."

She hesitated. "You said I don't know you that well. The more I think about it, you're right. Or at least, you're not acting like yourself lately. You seem so much . . . tougher."

I shut my eyes, part of me wishing I could give her back the old, agreeable Joy she no doubt missed, but it was impossible. I opened my eyes. "This is the real me."

Up ahead I saw the green awning, the sign: P**E ST**** GRO****. Jamie slowed the car. "I'll explain everything tomorrow," I repeated. "If you want to hear it."

Parker exhaled a sigh that was more like a dragon's fire breath. "The real you is kind of a pain in the ass," she said. "But . . . I think I'm going to like her."

"Really?"

"Yes. A lot. But you better call me tomorrow, first thing!"

Every possible inch of parking space was full, so we parked in front of a driveway and hoped its owners were too asleep to notice.

As we stepped out of the car, Jamie took a sharp intake of breath. "This is bad, really bad."

"What is it?"

"Guilt, mostly. Strong guilt, with fear mixed in. It's already hitting me," he added. "I don't know how long I can last here."

Guilt. I bit my lip. What was so bad even a drug dealer would feel guilty after doing it? "All right, where's it coming from?"

He pointed to the left, across from the store. That side of the street was a mix of seven- or eight-story apartments and brownstone houses.

I Listened but caught nothing in particular. "I can't Hear them from this far away," I said. "Which place is it?"

He hesitated. "Joy, I don't think it's safe for us—for me—to go any farther. Something bad just went down here. It's obvious. We'd be getting ourselves right in the middle of whatever it is."

"I'm already in the middle of it," I said. "If you're not coming with me, fine, I understand. But I have to keep going. Even if I have to walk up to every door of every house *and* apartment on this street."

He took a deep breath. "In that case," he said, "it's the second house on the left." I looked where he was gesturing. The lights were on. "Good luck," he added.

I opened my mouth but said nothing. Was he really going to make me go alone?

"I'm sorry. I'm really sorry. It's just too much." He shook his head. "Shit, I knew it was going to hurt when I had to let you down." He turned away from me, apologetic Whispers echoed in my mind: *Wish I was more like you. Wish I was strong.*

Strong? No one had ever described me as strong before. My teeth were chattering. I missed him already. But no one else could do this for me, and later might be too late. I walked up and rang the bell.

No answer.

I rang a second time. Nothing. What would I do if they didn't answer? Kick down the door? Camp out here and wait for Dad to reach Seattle? Pester the cops with a vague, anonymous psychic tip?

On the other hand, I hadn't actually *heard* the doorbell. Maybe it didn't work. I'd just rapped on the door when I felt Jamie's presence. Heard his wishes near me again: *I hope I can be strong.*

He was behind me. I tipped my head back to rest on his

shoulder, breathed in the warm scent of his skin. "You're back! But you said—"

"It's not safe." He smoothed my hair. "And I couldn't live with it if you got hurt when I could have stopped it. If things get ugly, maybe I can protect you. I've never used it for anything good before."

Heavy footsteps at the door. My hands and feet felt freezing, bloodless.

It dawned on me what he was saying. "You mean if a Wave knocks you down—"

"I'll just let it take over," he said. "Let it turn me into . . . what you saw this afternoon. Just stay out of my way, and if I tell you to run—"

I shook my head. "No . . ."

But I had little time to argue or even accept before we heard the popping of locks, like a gun being cocked, and then the metal door slid open.

20

I Heard a frantic Whisper, *I hope it's not the cops out there,* and then a milk-white hulk of a dude appeared in the doorway, thick arms crossed over a gray leather duster. His relief on seeing we weren't police faded fast, and he glowered at Jamie's drug slogan T-shirt. "It's three A.M., kidlets." *I wish whoever sent these clowns had told them to show up during business hours!* He started to close the door.

"Wait!" I held up my hand. "We're not here to buy from you, I'm looking for my sister! She's missing."

He stopped, blinked as if hit by bright sunlight.

"Blond, small build?" I added hurriedly. "Seventeen?"

"Huh, I'm trying to think. . . ." The dude scratched at

his sparse, carrot-colored chin hair. He looked only a few years older than Icka, with a skinny rat face that clashed absurdly with his slouching bulk. *Seventeen,* he Whispered. *I wish she'd told me she was a fuckin' minor! Man, I just want to erase this whole goddamn night. . . .*

Next to me Jamie gritted his teeth. The guy's crawling fear was clearly starting to rub off.

"Sorry, babe, can't help ya." The drug dealer was breathing hard. "Too bad I didn't see her . . . she sounds hot." His lewd chuckle sounded weak, halfhearted. He mopped sweat off his scrubby mustache.

I stared at his dirty nails. His three-dollar Hot Topic skull ring. Was this one of the shadow hands groping my sister when she was too weak to move?

Next thing I knew, Jamie's fist swung like lightning into the drug dealer's pitted cheek, landing with a solid thud.

The guy rocked backward, groaning curses, but like a grizzly bear pegged with a BB gun, he wasn't really hurt. Just pissed off.

"I'm going to kick your skinny ass." And he lunged himself at Jamie.

Without thinking, I darted past them inside.

"The fuck d'you think *you're* going?" the dude snarled. But he was too busy fighting the raw power of his own emotions to stop me running up the stairs.

An acrid stench hit my nostrils before I'd even stepped into the dimly lit living room. Except for the glowing fireplace in the far corner, and the man standing silently in front of it, all was as I remembered it through Icka's eyes. A small, squarish room with drawn blinds, windowsills caked with ash and dotted with still-smoking incense cones. On my left, the stained gray futon mattress. On my right, a hallway with at least three closed doors. I almost tripped on a laptop carelessly laid open on the skuzzy tan carpet.

The man kneeling over the flame was scrawny and long-haired, dressed in a black T-shirt and sagging-in-the-butt plaid pj bottoms. *I wish Keith hadn't made up that Oblivion shit,* he Whispered. *Let's just hope we don't both rot in prison for it.* Hurriedly his tiny hands scooped up bits of . . . something . . . from beside him on the floor and fed it to the fire. The something was soft, pale, and furry looking, like a small animal. A sleeping kitten.

Then my perspective gelled, and I realized I was staring at a pile of human hair.

Long, dreaded, white blond. *Her* hair.

On the ashes below rested dozens of reddish charred blobs, each the size of a tooth. Beads, they were beads. The crimson beads from Icka's Guatemalan wallet. He must have already burned that.

God, I hope we don't get caught, he Whispered. *Wish that dumb bastard hadn't lied to get laid.* "'Scuse me!" The little guy finally saw me. "What the fuck are you doing here?" His fussy, nasal voice squeaked with anxiety. *Is it too much to ask that Keith could go three hours without letting a random chick into our place?*

We stared at each other. I couldn't speak. My brain had

locked itself. Time shifted, opened up. The stench of burning hair grew more and more pungent, like a photo coming into ever-sharper focus. I'd been lurking here for hours. Centuries.

"You're a friend of Keith's?" The little guy peered at me through Coke-bottle lenses, his unlined face far younger than I'd guessed. "You have a name?" *Whoever she is, I hope she's too stoned to catch on to what I'm doing here.*

We heard groans and shoving from the stairwell.

"Hey, what's that?" The little guy jumped to his feet. "The hell's goin' on down there?" He'd dropped his ratty blond handful; the strands disappeared, blending into the carpet.

Her hair. I had to stop him from burning her hair.

I don't know why it mattered so much to me. Hair is just dead cells, we learned that in science. You can't make a whole new person from dead cells. Holding a piece of hair is sort of like holding on to the past.

My hand snaked out and snatched a dry, matted clump from the pile.

I want to start fresh, be a whole new person, Icka had wished in my dream.

I want to erase this whole goddamn night.

They were trying to erase her, destroy all traces of her. I couldn't let them. My fist closed in a tight grip around my lock of hair. I was never going to let it go. I was going to have to be buried with a piece of my sister's gross hair that I'd always made fun of.

"Ray!" Keith barked. "*Help* me here. I need backup."

"Oh, Jesus." The little guy's bird eyes jerked toward the front door. "This isn't fucking happening," he muttered, then yelled back, "All right, I'm coming!" and scurried past me.

I couldn't see what help the little guy would be in a fight between massive Keith and a Wave-powered Jamie.

Then I realized he wasn't heading toward the stairs but had disappeared behind one of the doors in the hallway. A bedroom, I guessed. Quickly, I followed, Listening. *I just want to wake up and have this all be a dream,* he whispered. Me too, I thought. *That chick better stay the fuck out of my way. Hope this scares her off. I don't want have to shoot anyone.*

Shoot anyone? Was he . . . oh my god oh my god. He was getting a GUN?

I heard the shriek of breaking glass, several thumps, and then a low, animal sound of pain. Jamie!

"Call off your pit bull, bitch." Keith was in my face suddenly, his sweaty hand on my throat, his sour-cream-and-onion-chips breath my only air supply. "You have no right." His voice cracked, and I saw his ferrety face was raw and red as a hunk of steak. A mix of threat and pleading in his voice. "Get out of here! Before you both end up dead."

"Dead," I repeated dumbly, and gripped the lock of Icka's hair tight.

Behind Keith I saw Jamie writhing on the floor. Bits of green glass surrounded him. As he staggered to stand, new angry cuts on his forehead trailed blood down his eyebrows.

I want you to run for it, he Whispered. *I hope you can still find your sister, alone.*

"Jamie, no." My voice came out pinched, ragged. "Icka's . . . she's . . . she can't be . . ." Dead.

Jamie opened his mouth and a howl of grief escaped him. My grief. *I wish you'd go,* he Whispered, *don't stay and see me rip his throat out.* The focused fury in his eyes told me he was past the point of controlling it. The Waves had taken over. Jamie headed straight for Keith, stalking him across the room.

"Oh, Jesus." Keith's hand fell from my neck, and he backed away, toward the door. "Don't let this berserker kill me. What's he run on—meth, PCP? Ray!" he bawled. *"Ray."*

The door to the other room burst open, and the little guy stood holding a shotgun. Trained on me.

My vision tunneled. The gun. The gun. The gun. It was all I could see. I'd never seen someone aim a real gun. My mind raced from the past—we were outside ten minutes ago, I was at my birthday party last night—to the future. My parents' lives ruined, Jamie dead or in prison for life. I might meet Icka again. What would I tell her? I should have stood by you, against this horrible world. We might have had more of a chance.

I Heard Jamie Whisper, *Wish you would run and let me cover you.*

Run. God, I wanted to. Maybe they wouldn't shoot me, they'd be too busy fighting Jamie. Jamie. He was standing with me against the world. I couldn't leave him behind.

"You think I won't do it?" Ray said. "Oh, I'll do it!" His Adam's apple bobbed as he swallowed. Owl eyes wide in their frames. Feathered hair sticking up in all directions like he'd rubbed his tiny head with a balloon. *I hope I really have the guts,* he Whispered. "Shit, where's the safety on this thing?"

These guys had no idea what they were doing. He could shoot us by *accident.*

Jamie grimaced at me. Sweat pooled in the divot between his nose and upper lip. *I wish,* he Whispered. *I had. Control.* His face twisted, eyebrows dipping, as several expressions crossed it in turn: anger, fear, suspicion, guilt, grief. I knew it came from all of us. *Wish. I could learn. To ride this Wave. . . .*

He blew a long line of air out his mouth. Then, with three running steps that seemed faster than human, he spun and kicked Ray's hands. Ray screamed. The gun hit the floor barrel first, and my heart almost stopped. But it didn't go off.

I dove for the gun. No one tried to stop me.

Jamie had collapsed in a dizzy heap on the ground. *Gotta get. Back on.*

Ray was cowering against the wall. Keith hovered by the front door. Both of them Whispering frantically, praying to stay alive.

What was I supposed to do now? My old way of decision-making was useless. Let's see: What Would Mom Do If

She Was Holding the Gun of the Drug Dealer Who She Suspected Killed Her Sister? Mom would look for the best in everyone. Against all odds, she'd assume that Keith and Ray were decent people. But wasn't it too late for that? I'd seen what people really were inside: evil. Seen what Mom was: a liar.

Channel Dad. He'd know how to be cool and logical, assess the pieces, assign priorities. Gun in hand, sister's hair on floor, scary dealers lurking, friend catching his breath before his next murderous rampage . . . that was priority one. Jamie rode a Wave for five seconds, but it left him weak. Now he needed a lifeline, and he wasn't going to get it from these guys. I forced myself to slow my breathing. Calm. Composed. In control. Then I pivoted to face Jamie so the Waves coming out of my chest would hit him directly. "Ride this," I said. He leaned toward me, as if drinking in my energy. Slowly, still dazed, he stood. Ray and Keith watched in fear.

The gun felt heavy and cold in my hands, powerful. They were going to do this to *us*. Maybe they'd done it to Icka. . . . I imagined pulling the trigger, exploding Keith's head. But as I Listened to them begging for their lives, I knew it just wasn't in me.

Instead I waved the gun at them. "What happened to my sister?" I didn't recognize my own voice. "No one gets out of here, not till I find out the truth."

Keith looked sadly at Ray. Neither of them spoke. Then, as I Listened, all the Whispers in the room grew staticky and began to change. It was the strangest sensation, as if someone had switched channels in my mind.

Keith: *I wish I hadn't been online that day and tried to impress a girl.*

Ray: *If I'd known she was going to take everything all at once . . .*

Tears ran down my face. The gun felt heavier. "She overdosed?"

"I don't know what you're talking about," Ray said primly.

Keith looked at the carpet. *I wish I hadn't lied.* "We had something special together."

"Special?" I spat the word. "You lied to an underage girl that you could solve all her problems with drugs!"

"It wasn't like that!" he roared. "We had a connection."

Ray cringed. *I hope the cops don't connect her to us when she comes to.*

Comes to? "Wait, she's alive?" A lump formed in my throat. "She's still alive?"

Ray finally broke down. "We don't know, all right?" He shrugged helplessly. "She OD'd, or had a reaction or something. At first it was just a bad trip. She went all delusional, kept talking about her special powers."

"She was kind of crazy," Keith added, fondly, "but hot, even when she shaved her head." His long face fell. "Then she started choking."

"Where is she? What did you do to her?" I realized I was waving the gun at Keith when he whimpered and

263

shrank back instead of answering.

Ray spoke up in his fussy voice. "We took her to Harborview Medical. Half an hour ago."

"The hospital?" I remembered bouncing down the stairs, hitting the metal door on the way out, passing out in the small gasoline-and-moldy-crackers space. They hadn't driven her into a lake or thrown her body off a cliff. "Jessica's alive and in the hospital?"

"Who's Jessica?" Keith said, jerking his head back in confusion. "We dropped *Allison* off at the ER."

"I checked her in with a fake phone number," Ray said, sighing. "Said she was my sister."

"She lied about her name?" Keith looked disgusted. "But she was going to be my girlfriend."

I turned to Jamie. "Are they lying?"

He shook his head.

"Take us there," I said.

21

We stepped into the clean, crisp air outside just in time to see a yellow ABC tow truck pull away, dragging behind it Ben's Land Rover.

"Goddamn it!" Now it was my turn to lose it. We were so damn close. Now how were we going to get to the hospital? "The fucking car's gone, and we're out of money."

Jamie squinted after the car and shrugged. "At least we're not getting arrested for stealing it." They were the first words he'd spoken since riding the Wave. He banged on Ray and Keith's door. "Cab money," he demanded when Keith answered, looking none too pleased to see Jamie's face again. "Our car got towed. Either the police give us a ride to Harborview, or you fork over."

Keith fished a twenty from his pocket, shoved it in our direction, and slammed the door.

Just a couple blocks down, an orange cab stopped for us. I called Dad from its backseat to tell him I knew where Icka was . . . but that I didn't know what would be waiting for us there.

"You found her!" A quavering sigh—it sounded suspiciously like a sob—rose from his throat. "I'm half an hour out." His voice was still choked up. "I'll make it in twenty minutes."

Calling Aunt Jane wasn't as simple. I'd expected just to give her a (much overdue) update on the situation and promise to call later. She shocked me by saying she and Mom were on the way to Seattle.

"Didn't you get any of our messages?" Aunt Jane said. "Here, you need to talk to your mother—"

I hung up quickly. The thought of facing Mom stressed me out almost as much as the sight of a gun had. Funny how, of all the things that drove me batty about Icka in the old days, her seemingly gleeful contempt for our mother ranked number one. Now I knew differently; there was no joy in hating Mom, only a tender ache, and some bluster to cover the loneliness.

Our cab pulled into Harborview's ER parking lot. We paid its driver the drug money, and he let us out in front of the sliding automatic doors.

The waiting room was nearly empty, a blessing for Jamie and me. He parked himself on the couch looking drained, like he'd run a marathon, while I ran up to the front desk.

"Do you have a patient named Allison Monroe?" Icka's booze-buying alter ego.

The receptionist narrowed her eyes at me. "Are you a relative?"

"I'm her sister. Just tell me if she's alive . . . please!"

A nurse led me into a cubiclelike room with sea green walls. Its single occupant was still, waxen, her head like the plumage of a neurotic bird, stray locks hanging here and there from a pale, fuzzy scalp. She was bristling with wires: hooked up to a heart monitor, a blood-pressure monitor. An IV stuck out of her arm. Then I noticed the steady rhythm of her heartbeat on the monitor. Alive, she was alive, I told myself, that's what mattered. Icka opened her eyes and looked off into space, blinking over and over. Someone, probably a nurse, had washed her face clean of mascara, yet smudges of kohl eyeliner still clung to her lids. I couldn't stop staring at her shorn head.

"Is this your sister?" the nurse said.

Tears came to my eyes. "Yes!"

Icka shivered and hugged herself, then, as if sensing me for the first time, peered up at me with round blue eyes. "Joy?"

"I'm here." I stepped forward, wanting to hug her but unable to remember the last time I'd done such a thing. It might freak her out. It might freak *me* out. "Is she going to be okay?" I asked the nurse. "What's the IV for?"

"Your sister's lucky to be alive," she said sternly. "Considering the volume of drugs she took, I'm surprised she's conscious."

"Are you real?" Icka asked me.

"I'm real," I said, my voice choking up. "I'm really here, I've been searching for you all night. I don't know what I would have—I'm so relieved I finally found you!"

"Me too," she said softly.

I listened as, in a blur, the nurse explained to me that Icka's vital signs were good, and that she'd been brought in by "Good Samaritans." Apparently, I'd need to fill out forms with her correct information. Real name and date of birth, a working phone number, insurance provider if I had it. "And we can't release her to a minor, of course," she added, "so you'll have to have a parent come get her."

I assured her that our parents were on the way, and she left the room, promising to return in two minutes with the forms.

"I can Hear you," Icka said. Her eyes filled with tears. "I can still Hear. It didn't work. I'm the same. Everything's just . . . the same."

Gingerly I eased onto the side of the bed, careful not to joggle any of her equipment. "Jessica, nothing's the same," I told her. "I just crossed a state line in a stolen car looking for you."

Her eyebrows went up. "Serious?"

268

"Yes. And I started Hearing more, like you. Like you said."

"I'm sorry." She picked at the thin white sheet. "I never wanted it to happen to you. But I thought if I warned you, it would be easier. . . ."

"I know, but you couldn't stop this from being hard for me," I said. "No one could, not even Mom."

Icka froze. "Is *she* here?"

"No. Well, not yet."

"Great." She settled back on her thin pillows. "Mommy Stepford's on her way, the last person I want to see when I'm completely powerless. Or, really, anytime."

I hesitated. This was the part where I normally defended Mom. "Has she really been lying to us," I said, "about everything?"

"Her cookies have real chocolate chips," Icka said. "Otherwise—hey." She broke into a tearful grin. "I told you that old story was true. The only thing I can't figure out is why it finally worked this time, and not all the times I *tried* to make it work, when we were kids."

"Um. I think maybe it's because I was identifying with you strongly at the time."

"What do you mean, identifying with me?"

"I . . . wished away my Hearing."

"No way!"

"This afternoon. I think that's how I first got connected to you."

"Wow." It took her a moment to take that in. "You

know, I Heard you calling to me," she said quietly, "when I was at Keith and Ray's. I was lying on the futon, staring at the ceiling, out of my mind, and there you were. Whispering to me. Sometimes I could even see what you were seeing, or wishing for. I was so glad, even though I figured you were just another hallucination."

Spontaneously I reached out and grabbed her hand. "Don't ever disappear again, okay?"

She blinked, looked at my hand like she didn't know what it was, then squeezed it back. "I didn't want to be dead, dummy," she said. "I just wanted to get rid of my Hearing. Aunt Jane said it was the key. To freeing myself."

"Yeah, but she didn't tell you to take all the drugs in the world."

Icka looked down at her blood pressure monitor, which was tightening around her right bicep. "Drugs always kill my Hearing while I'm high," she said, shrugging. "He said there was a drug that could cure me forever. I wanted to believe it so bad. . . . Then I thought, if I just took enough stuff all at once, maybe the effect would last." She took her hand back. "I don't even know why I'm still alive."

"Because you're strong," I said. "You're the toughest person I know."

She shook her head, her shorn head. "You just want me to be tough," she said. "That's, like, your image of me. But you don't know how weak I am really. I'm pathetic." She whispered the word. "The truth is, I *didn't* want to stop you from Hearing the badness. For years now I've wished you could Hear things the way I do. Because I wanted you to suffer, just like me. So at least you'd be where I was." Her red-rimmed eyes leaked tears. *I hope you can forgive me.*

"Aw, Jessica . . . this isn't your fault. I grew up and changed, but not because you wished it. You don't have that kind of power. We haven't even been that close, since . . . since we were kids." Since I shut her out of my life. I wish I hadn't done that.

"I don't really blame you for dumping me." She must have Heard me Whisper. "It was like, there was no chance for me, but there *was* a chance for you . . . you could make yourself blend in, you could have *friends.*"

"Yeah, well, about those friends . . . they weren't the greatest."

"Major understatement."

"You could have broken it to me in a nicer way, or let me figure it out myself."

She shrugged. "I was never good at holding back my feelings."

"Major understatement!" I rolled my eyes. "Wait . . ." I'd remembered something. "Have you been blocking your Whispers from me, when we're at home? "

"I didn't know if I could trust you." She sounded embarrassed. "I wanted to, but I was afraid you'd tell Mom everything I was trying to hide. If it's any consolation, blocking you was giving me killer headaches too."

271

"I probably *would* have told Mom everything," I admitted. "I really was a little too close to her. But from now on, I promise not to pass on anything you tell me unless you say it's okay. We need to be able to share information."

"Huh." Icka's eyes widened. "Are we going to be able to *keep* from sharing, as long as we have this connection open?"

"I don't know." I hadn't even thought about that.

"We should ask Aunt Jane if Hope and Faith had the ability to link for the rest of their lives."

"Speaking of Aunt Jane," I said, "did you know she has a *boyfriend*?"

"Shrimpy Stuart's great," she said. "He makes a kick-ass tofu scramble."

I laughed, and my elbow accidentally knocked against her IV drip. I looked at the IV in my sister's arm.

"You're wishing for me to be okay," she said. "I don't know how to give you that."

"You don't have to know everything right now, Jess," I said. "We can figure it all out later, together."

Her lips twisted up into a weird expression. A smile. "Jess," she said softly, as if to herself. Then her eyes closed.

"Jessica? Nurse!" I yelled, and pushed the call button madly.

But the nurse who dashed in informed me that Icka's vitals were fine. "She's unconscious from exhaustion," she explained. "I think she was just waiting up for you."

Dad was filling out paperwork on the waiting-room couch when I came out. "I saw you two talking in there," he said shyly. "Figured I'd get out of the way."

"She just fell asleep," I said.

He held up his hand. "We'll let her rest a while. I can wait till your Mom gets here."

I hugged him tight. Then I hugged Jamie. "Have you two met?"

"*Oh* yes," Dad said. "This is the boy who convinced my younger daughter to go tearing off into the night after my older daughter. Every father's dream."

"It's a good thing he did too," I said.

"I would not argue against that point." His eyebrows sagged. "I'm just sorry it had to come to that." *I wish I could have stopped all this from happening. If I hadn't been so focused on myself, on my work. . . .*

"Actually, Dad?" I said. "We could really use your advice. As an attorney."

Reluctantly, Jamie explained about the car.

"As far as I see it," Dad said, "you're not in any legal trouble. There are no charges against you, no witnesses who saw you drive it. I don't see how it's your fault if some jackal whisked your brother's car to Seattle and got it impounded . . . while you were busy studying for a history test at our house." He winked.

"I appreciate the thought, sir," Jamie said, smiling a

little. "But the thing is, I can't lie to my father. I really just . . . *can't*."

"What an incredibly principled young man," Dad said to me. "I approve."

I bit the inside of my lip to keep from laughing. Jamie pretended to cough.

Dad, in classic Dad fashion, didn't seem to notice. Earnestly he turned to Jamie. "Well, then, I guess the only thing to do is for me to tell your family the truth. That their son generously reached out to help both my daughters, risking his own freedom."

Jamie and I stole a glance at each other. Dad would never know all the things that we'd both risked in getting here.

"I'll of course pay to spring the car out," Dad went on.

"Thank you for that too," Jamie said, sighing. "But no matter what you say or do, this is probably going to get me kicked out of my house permanently."

"Kicked out?" Dad's head pulled back in surprise. "You don't mean your parents would literally throw you out on the street?"

Jamie crossed his arms, clearly defensive of them. "They just don't know how to handle . . . some stuff about me."

"Well," Dad said slowly, "I'll have to talk to my wife, but I think we may be converting our home office into a guest suite." Huh? We were? "We just might have room this winter," he went on, ignoring my dropped jaw, "for a guest who does chores. Down the road," he added, "when you're sixteen, if things *still* don't improve back home,

I'd be willing to help you get declared an emancipated minor."

Jamie leaned forward. "What does that mean, exactly?"

"It's a lot like being an adult a couple years early," Dad explained. "It means you can live independently of your parents: hold a job, pay your bills, rent an apartment. It means you're not subject to most of the legal restrictions other kids are."

Jamie not subject to normal restrictions. That, I thought, sounded right.

"On the other hand." Dad looked Jamie in the eye. "An emancipated minor can be tried as an adult. That means you can't go borrowing cars anymore. You'll need to start learning new ways to deal with problems."

Jamie looked at me and slowly nodded. "That's the plan."

As Dad turned back to his plastic clipboard, a rumpled carload of twenty-somethings in club clothes bounded through the front doors. Three girls and an ashen-faced, bleary-eyed guy.

Please God, don't let this be permanent!

Hope they can just pump his stomach and get it out.

As their anxious Whispers flooded my mind, I spun to face Jamie. He was already on his feet. "Getting a drink from the vending machines," he said through clenched teeth.

I leaped up too. "Good idea, I'll walk with you!"

Dad, still bent over his forms, didn't even look up as we slipped into the hallway.

In the relative quiet, my heels tapped the linoleum in

sync to the softer clomp of Jamie's worn black work boots. Without a word, he took my hand. I knew he could feel me relaxing with every step we took away from the ER. For once, my Waves were doing him a favor.

A drinking fountain droned beside a glowing red Coke machine at the end of the hall, across from the restrooms.

"I don't actually even like soda," I confessed.

"Convenient, since we're broke." He smiled. "I just remembered this was a quiet spot, from when I stopped in the restroom to clean up."

"Clean up . . . ? Oh. God." His forehead. The cuts. Without thinking, I leaned in and swept my hands over his hair, searching for the damage Keith's broken bottle had done. The chestnut brown locks felt soft between my fingers, and Jamie sighed, closed his eyes.

"They're not deep," he muttered.

I felt a warm shiver at the top of my scalp as I breathed in the spicy, woodsy scent of his shampoo. Then I saw the blood, dried in the cuts near his hairline. "Deep enough they could leave scars." A memento of the night he'd risked his life and his freedom for my sister. . . . No, I realized. For *me*. He'd helped me follow my feelings. Made me see that I could. Should. "Jamie? I never got a chance to say this—"

"You're welcome." His cider gold eyes were open again, gazing right into mine.

I blinked. Of course he could sense my gratitude. I wondered, what else could he sense? That being so close to him made me feel dizzy?

Closer, I want you even closer.

I thought about the way he'd squeezed my hand in the car after I spilled my whole life to him. The way he'd wished for me to be happy when he knew I wasn't. The way he'd found the courage to stay with me back at Keith and Ray's. I felt a rush of hunger, and then his warm hands were holding my face, drawing me toward him, his mouth on mine, warm and soft and addictive. I wrapped my arms around him, happy shivers trailing down my back as we kissed, knowing he was feeling the same bliss. And for a minute the whole hospital—the whole Whispering world—was silent.

Icka was still dozing, Dad and Jamie still going over the emancipation process, when Mom showed up.

For once Aunt Jane, who trailed her, looked sophisticated and put together compared to my mother. At least Aunt Jane's hair looked clean, while Mom's hung to her shoulders in greasy, honey blond ringlets. Her gray linen trousers and lacy cotton shirt were wrinkled as tissue paper. Her eyes swollen from crying, features wavering through an array of tics and grimaces. I'd never seen a human being look so stressed.

"Joy! Honey." She raised eager eyebrows at me, hoping I'd hug her, but I stayed seated with my arms folded across my chest.

Dad didn't rise to comfort her either, but in a gentle tone he said, "Jessica's going to be all right, Kel."

"I want to see her," Mom declared, defiant tears slipping down her cheeks. "I need to see her now."

I thought about how Dad redirected his thoughts so we wouldn't Hear them and feel bad. As Mom shambled toward the front desk, I focused on mentally redecorating the waiting room in cooler colors, *not* on wishing she'd go away. As angry as I was, I couldn't bring myself to hurt Mom's feelings in her current state.

After a few moments Dad sighed and stood, and I followed him.

The four of us piled into the small hospital room and stood around my sister in a horseshoe. I watched my mother take in the sight of her daughter hooked up to machines.

Icka groaned and tossed in her sleep. The same thing was happening to her that had happened to me at every slumber party I'd ever been to. The sheer volume of Whispers around her made it impossible not to wake up. She looked around the room and swallowed. Then she spoke. "Um . . . who the hell *are* all you people?"

Mom stared.

"And who am *I*? How did I get here?"

Mom made a sound like a whimper.

Icka grinned. "All right, all right. Just kidding."

This was actually Dad's brand of humor, and I half expected him to say, "Good one, pumpkin," and bump fists with her. Instead he bent down and hugged her tight.

Aunt Jane was next, petting Icka's buzzed scalp as she held her.

My stomach was getting that nervous burny feeling. Icka had made it clear Mom was the last person she wanted to see, and I truly couldn't blame her, but Mom looked so shaken up. . . . I couldn't help but feel sorry for her—even if I was still mad at her for lying. And I just couldn't deal with the thought of Icka snubbing Mom when she was like this. *Jessica*, I Whispered, *I wish you'd be nice to Mom just this one time. I'll never ask it again.*

The moment I'd thought the words, the hospital room disappeared.

And, blink: I was little again. Standing in a misty forest under a giant oak tree beside Icka and a grinning Aunt Jane, all three of us hacking with little knives at a brown spongy fungus growing from the oak's trunk. Behind us in the mist paced a gray wolf. Then I was back in the hospital room, and Aunt Jane was standing back up after hugging Icka. That scene was what Icka had wished for us, how she'd wanted us to be raised. But it wasn't what had happened.

Then, blink: Dad in his courtroom suit, taking long strides on his treadmill with a four-year-old Jess by his side. Jess was running, panting, to keep up. Her knuckles accidentally brushed the side of his leg, and he recoiled as if from a bug.

In the hospital room I saw Dad gently cover Icka's hand with both of his.

Blink: an even younger Jess, short legs swinging from a green plastic chair in a different hospital room. Across from her, Mom sat up smiling in bed, cradling a bundle

279

wrapped in blankets. Carefully Dad leaned over and picked up the bundle—a small red-faced baby—and walked over to Jess with it. Her eyes widened, and then she opened her arms—

"What have you done to your hair?" Mom's broken voice said, pinning me back to this tiny hospital room.

"Holy shit!" Icka patted her head as if searching. "You think the nurse stole it? She looked shady."

To my surprise, Mom laughed. Well, technically, it was more like a laugh-*cry*. "Jessica. Stefani." She managed to say as tears streamed down her face and into her hair. "I. Have been so. Scared for you! How could you . . . so many—*so* many things could have happened to you! Seeing you alive, I could just . . . I could just kill you!"

You would not think that such a declaration would lead to a hug, but that's what happened. Mom lunged at Icka, who actually opened her arms in time. They stayed there for a long time, both of them crying.

I stared, confused and even a bit left out. I thought I'd understood their relationship, but I'd obviously missed something key.

Dad looked at Aunt Jane questioningly.

She shrugged. *Wish I understood it myself.*

He smiled. *I just hope it lasts.* Then he took *my* hand in both of his and said, simply, "Thank you."

And then everyone in the room was saying it.

"Thank you, Joy."

"Thank you."

Icka met my eyes suddenly, making me wonder what sort of images and memories *I'd* been sending *her* over the past few hours since our mental link opened up. That day of playing hooky at Cannon Beach? Kissing Ben? Waving the gun at Keith and Ray? It seemed incredible that just days ago I'd been showered with birthday roses. Life had seemed pretty good then, other than the problem of my evil sister, Icka. I'd had cool friends, the perfect mom, and a rep for being the sweetest girl in the world. Now it was clear that whole list had been an illusion. My sister had been trying to show me this for years, had grown frustrated and started to shout, to scream, but the louder she yelled, the less I heard her. A giant crater loomed where my old identity had been, and I had no idea what to fill it with. Still, looking around this hospital room, I had hope, for all of us. I had more strength and power than I'd ever imagined. I had Jamie. I had Parker, a new kind of friendship, a peer. And I had this connection I'd finally won back, the warm blue eyes winking at me over Mom's tearful embrace.

I hoped it would be enough.

acknowledgments

I'd like to thank:

My agent, Jim McCarthy; my editors, Jill Santopolo and Kristin Daly; production editor Jon Howard; and publicist Laura Kaplan for their talent, enthusiasm, and sheer awesomeness.

The fabulous critique partners: Jeanne Barker, Barrie Bartlett, Suzanne Brahm, Jean Bullard, Billee Escott, Sam Hranac, Dorothy Crane Imm, Peter Kahle, Ruth Maxwell, Lyn MacFarlane, Jim Pravitz, Kevin Scott, Ingrid Scott, Sheri Short, and Anita Mohan.

My friends Regina Carr and Jesse Robbins. You changed my life when you dared me to drive up to Seattle, live at your house, and write books.

Peter, Ranna, Dean, and Ellie Kitanidis, for truly being there for me over the years. Your faith and support has made all the difference.

Robert. You give me courage, keep me sane, make me laugh, and inspire me to keep growing as a person.